Published 2024 by Vinci Books

DARK TROJAN

AN ADAM DRAKE NOVEL

SCOTT MATTHEWS

ONE

Adam Drake's summons to meet with the Joint Terrorism Task Force was expected, but not welcomed. The last time he'd met with JTTF, they had ignored his warning, and a cabinet member had barely survived an assassination attempt.

The official reason for his summons was a personal prerelease review of the FBI's final internal report on that matter, but Drake suspected there was more to it than that. The FBI's field office had been embarrassed by its ineptitude in dealing with the terrorist threat. He didn't think it was about to reward him with a medal for his actions.

Drake decided early on this fall morning that his drive to the FBI offices, which were located near the Portland International Airport, was likely to be the highlight of the day. But whenever he had a reason to get out of the office and drive his old Porsche, that day turned into pure pleasure. The sky was blue, the leaves were changing color, it was Friday, and the college football season was underway. He wasn't about to let a government summons spoil a day like today.

He passed through security, signed the visitors' register,

and was escorted to an empty conference room on the third floor. It smelled strongly of newly-laid carpet. A twelve-foot-long, cherry wood conference table dominated the space, with four black leather chairs on the far side and a single matching chair on the near side. A picture of the president hung on the wall next to a standing U.S. flag and a photograph of the twin towers before they collapsed. He remembered thinking at his last meeting with the JTTF that this photo was an ironic reminder of a war the current administration refused to acknowledge.

He also saw a pitcher of ice water and glasses on a black serving tray in the middle of the table. Coffee would have been nice, he thought, but he didn't think they intended for him to feel welcome. He sat in the single chair, crossed his legs, and waited. Ten minutes later, he heard the door open behind him. He stayed seated as three men and one woman entered the room and took their seats on the other side of the table. He knew three of them, especially the woman.

"Thank you for coming, Mr. Drake," Bruce Burton, the head of the Portland JTTF, said as he opened their meeting. "I believe you know Elizabeth Strobel from DHS and Robert Jorgenson with the FBI. I don't believe you know Richard Richter, though. He's from the Civil Rights Division of the Department of Justice."

Ignoring the men Drake immediately turned to Strobel. "Hello, Liz. Nice to see you again." He enjoyed the annoyed look on the faces of the three men when he addressed her as Liz.

She smiled at him. "Hello, Adam."

Burton cleared his throat. "Our investigation of your actions in June of this year is now formally closed," he said. "We have decided that criminal charges are not warranted." He cleared his throat. "We explained to the local Muslim community that your actions in killing the young men on your farm were justified. They're not satisfied with our conclusion, of course, but they were told it's not in their best interests to pursue the matter. They don't know everything, of course, but we believe they know what their men were involved in."

"You mean they knew their boys were *jihadis*?" Drake asked. "But they don't know they were trained assassins along with the others and sent to kill me? That's a distinction without much of a difference, isn't it?"

Robert Jorgenson answered his questions. "The FBI never proved they were trained as assassins. That was what you claimed. The most we could prove is they trespassed on your property and that you claimed you killed them in self-defense. You're lucky they didn't persuade your old boss, the district attorney, to indict you."

"Jorgenson," Drake said calmly, "your IQ hasn't gone up much since the last time we met, has it. Do you honestly think it was unreasonable for me to believe that three men who surrounded my house in the dead of night and were armed with AK 47s weren't about to use unlawful deadly physical force against me? Is that the way Harvard Law taught you to reason?"

The younger FBI agent pushed his chair back and started to stand, but sank back down after a curt order from Burton.

"Okay," said Burton, "let's wrap this up. We're prepared to provide you a full copy of our investigation report. If you'll sign a non-disclosure agreement. It's better if the public doesn't think there's an open season on Muslims here in Portland."

Unbelievable! I lawfully defend myself against three terrorists and I'm the bad guy.

Drake looked at Liz Strobel. "Were you aware of this BS?"

"They took it to the Attorney General," she said. "This is his idea. DHS didn't have anything to do with it."

Drake turned to Burton. "So there won't be criminal charges, but if I get sued by the ACLU for 'profiling' these guys as terrorists because they were Muslims, I can't defend myself with the truth? Is that what you're telling me?"

At this point, Richter, the civil rights attorney, cleared his throat and opened the file on the table before him. With his strawberry blond hair and his round, wire frame glasses, he reminded Drake of a slimmed-down Elton John. "The AG doesn't want to appear to be supporting vigilante action against citizens who are perceived to be terrorists. That's the government's responsibility."

Drake shook his head. "You're wrong, Richter. It's everyone's responsibility. The underwear bomber and the shoe bomber were stopped by citizens, not by the government." He pushed his chair back. "Keep your report. I'm not signing a non-disclosure agreement."

"Wait a minute, Mr. Drake," Richter shot back. "You might want to reconsider that decision. The Civil Rights Division of the Department of Justice has made it a top priority to investigate and prosecute bias crimes and incidents of discrimination against Muslims. Your violent assault with a dangerous weapon that resulted in the death of a total of seven Muslim men constitutes such an incident. I have the authority to initiate an investigation of your disregard of these men's civil rights.

Drake stood up without a word and strode out, resisting the urge to slam the door behind him. This was the second time his government had threatened to throw him under the bus. As he walked down the hall, he vowed it would be the last time.

TWO

Liz Strobel caught up with Drake in the parking lot.

"Adam, wait up! We need to talk."

He stopped and turned to face her. "Not much to talk about, Liz. Richter made the government's position pretty clear."

"Richter doesn't speak for the entire government."

"But the AG does, at least regarding law enforcement."

"It won't come to that. Will you follow me back to our new office? We're just around the corner on northeast Alderwood. I have something for you."

As angry as he was with the FBI and its gutless decision, he knew it wasn't her fault. The FBI and the DOJ were as politically correct as every other branch of the government was these days, and they had their own share of problems with the local Muslim community. They had falsely arrested a young Muslim lawyer in Portland in connection with the train bombing in Spain in 2004, and it had cost them dearly.

He looked at his watch. "I need to get back to my office, Liz."

"Please, Adam. This won't take long. It's important."

He agreed with a nod and watched her walk to a white Chrysler 300. She was a beautiful woman, he had to admit, even if she was collaborating with the enemy at the moment.

The Department of Homeland Security's new office was modest in size, a single-story, red brick building obviously (he thought as soon as he saw it) not designed to impress anyone. It was government-office-functional and hummed inside with the quiet energy of people working hard at their jobs.

She led him to a small office with a view of the vacant lot next door. "They let me use this when I'm visiting from Washington," she said as she put her light gray wool jacket on a hanger and hung it on the back of the door. "How's your arm? Is it healing well?"

"It's coming along. Thanks for asking." A block of C4 charge had exploded in a resort home in central Oregon where he thought a man they were chasing was hiding. The exterior wall had blown outward and he'd been buried under the debris. When they dug him out, he had a broken left arm, a severe concussion, and multiple abrasions and contusions. She had volunteered to drive him home when he'd been released from the hospital.

He sat in the chair in front of the red oak desk and waited for her to sit down.

A black hard-side attaché was sitting on the left side of the desk top. Before she sat down, she spun the wheels of the combination lock on the attaché and took out two files.

"This is a copy of the FBI report," she said as she leaned over the desk to hand it to him. "They made an extraordinary attempt to portray you as a loose cannon—a guy who still thinks he's in the army and believes that every Muslim is a terrorist. You'll see there's no mention of their colossal failure to act on your credible information about an imminent terrorist threat."

Drake had to smile at this. "The chewing out your boss gave them when he was almost assassinated didn't get through to them, did it?"

"No, it didn't. They agree with the president that these are just violent criminal acts of individuals that should be prosecuted accordingly. That's why your direct way of dealing with things makes them so mad. There's no one left for a trial when you're finished."

Drake slapped the file down on the desk. "Screw them! This is the second time I've been threatened for doing my duty. I'm through playing their game."

When he was in Afghanistan, he and his sniper partner had been threatened with court martial when a tribal leader accused them of torturing a villager. The villager was a Taliban commander the tribal leader had been hiding. Drake and his partner had never entered the village as alleged. They had killed the Talib with a sniper round from a half mile away. Both he and his partner had left the army when the chain of command had not supported the after-action report they had submitted.

Now Strobel sat down in her chair and studied him. "Does that mean you're not going to keep the promise you made to the Secretary? I'm talking about the agreement that you would help him from time to time, as an outside troubleshooter, if he let you go after the man responsible for the assassination attempt that almost killed your in-laws, as well as the Secretary himself. You got your man. Now he needs your help."

"That's not fair. If the government doesn't have my back, why should I defend their back? Why should I continue?"

"Now you aren't being fair," she said. "We had your back when we collected the bodies of those terrorists from your farm and didn't get the police involved. We had your back when we picked up the tab for the friends you called in to help you. And we covered for you with the imams. We had an agreement. We expect you to keep it."

It was his turn to study her. She was both his liaison with the Department of Homeland Security and the executive assistant to the DHS director. Her reputation as a tough-as-nails administrator was well-known. It was also clearly warranted. And, he reminded himself, he *had* agreed to act as a troubleshooter for the director if there were delicate matters that needed to be handled by someone on the outside.

"Okay, what's in the other file?" he asked.

"Information on a company in San Francisco he wants you to visit. The CEO and his board have agreed to pay your expenses and your hourly fee. They're finishing a government defense grant and are worried about how much they have to disclose to the SEC about some recent cyber attacks." She paused until he nodded. "They're expecting you next Monday."

Drake picked up the second file and stood up to leave.

"Have a nice flight," she said.

He forced a smile. "Tell the Secretary thanks for the business."

THREE

Back in his office, Drake stood at the window and stared down at the boats bobbing below in the Willamette River marina. He'd only returned to his law practice two weeks ago, and now, barely recuperated from his injuries, he was being asked to keep a promise he'd made while his blood was still hot after he stopped the assassination of Strobel's boss.

One of these days he was going to learn to keep his mouth shut.

The Secretary's first request was for him to visit a company in San Francisco next Monday. That meant he had to put out all the fires represented by the stack of files on his desk before he left for the weekend. He turned from the window and walked to the half-wall of his loft and called down to his secretary.

"Margo, would you help me triage this stack of files?"

Drake's law office had once been a rare-book store with a separate apartment one floor above. Its owner had died shortly before Drake had left the D.A.'s office and bought both the bookstore and the apartment. He had remodeled the main floor of the bookstore to include a reception area, a conference room, and a work area for his secretary. The loft that had been used for files, records, and office supplies had been converted into his office. Floor-to-ceiling bookshelves on two walls of the loft had been added, the window enlarged to span the length of the exterior wall.

Margo Benning, his secretary, had worked with him in the DA's office. When he'd left, he'd asked her to come with him. Now he waited at the top of the stairs as she walked up with a cup of coffee in one hand and a file in the other. The look on her face did not bode well for a quick review of the work he needed to do.

"There's nothing to triage," she said. "They're *all* dying from lack of attention. You haven't been around much this last month...chasing after terrorists."

Margo was a slender black woman with short, kinky, gray hair framing a round face that usually wore a friendly smile. When the smile disappeared, he had learned, he needed to measure his words and tread lightly.

"Those terrorists are dead, Margo. I need to get through these files now. I have to fly to San Francisco on Sunday to see a new client. The company is paying expenses and our full fee, so put a smile on your face. I just wanted to know which files I should work on first."

For the next twenty minutes, he took notes as she reminded him of deadlines and clients he needed to talk to. When she finished, a little bit of her old smile had returned; the lingering headache from his concussion seemed a little worse.

Headache or not, he worked on the stack of files until seven in the evening before heading home for the weekend. He'd finished three motions Margo would file Monday morning and written all the letters, and made all of the calls she'd insisted he attend to before leaving for San Francisco.

After locking his office, he walked out the back door on the loft level to the adjoining parking structure. His metallic gray, 1997 Porsche 993, a hobby of his for the last five years, waited for him in his reserved space.

It was only since his wife of three years had died a year ago that he'd started hating the drive home. Before Kay died from an aggressive breast cancer, she had taught school and was usually home before he was. Looking forward to seeing her each night had made the forty-minute drive to their farm in the heart of the Oregon wine country tolerable. Now Lancer, his German shepherd, was the only one at home to greet him.

Buying the farm and its old abandoned vineyard had been Kay's idea. She'd fallen in love with the romantic idea of growing grapes and making wine. While she had worked to make the old stone farmhouse into a comfortable home, he had spent weekends pulling out diseased grape vines to prepare the forty-acre vineyard for a future replanting. Before she died, he had promised her he would replant their vineyard.

Now he usually spent Friday nights alone. He ate whatever he found in his refrigerator and then settled in his favorite chair to read a good thriller with a glass of bourbon in his hand and Lancer at his feet.

Tonight, however, he intended to end the week by stopping at the Ponzi Wine Bar in Dundee to buy a bottle of his favorite wine, Ponzi Tavola Pinot Noir. He also picked up a beef tenderloin the local butcher was holding for him. He'd be eating out in San Francisco, so a home-cooked meal tonight sounded good. He might even share a little of the tenderloin with Lancer.

Drake stopped at the wine bar and waved to Brett, the

owner, who was behind the bar helping his manager serve a three-deep, Friday-night crowd. Without a word, Brett reached behind the bar and handed over the bottle of Tavola Pinot Noir.

"It's on your tab. Enjoy."

FOUR

After his five-mile run the next morning, Drake stopped on the porch, dripping sweat onto the gray sandstone pavers, and tapped the screen of the sports watch on his wrist. He saw that he was only ten seconds off his personal record, even though he'd taken time off from his regular exercise routine while he recovered from his injuries. But now he was close to reaching the post-recovery level of fitness he'd set for himself, and he was pleased. There was still a little weakness in the left arm he'd broken, but otherwise he felt as strong as before.

As he wiped his face with the bottom of his sweatshirt and headed inside to fix breakfast, he saw that he had a visitor coming up his gravel driveway from the county road below. The white Harley Davidson Sportster was familiar; it belonged to the pastor of his church. He hadn't been to church since Kay died, but he liked Pastor Steve and appreciated the friendship they had developed during her fight with cancer.

"I thought I'd stop by and see how your recovery is coming

along," Pastor Steve said as he got off his bike at the bottom of the turnaround and pulled off his helmet.

"How did you hear about my injuries?" Drake asked.

"I have friends in high places," the pastor laughed. "Invite me in for a cup of coffee and I'll reveal my source."

While Drake loaded the coffeemaker, his guest hung his black leather jacket over the back of a chair and sat at the kitchen table.

"When I was playing basketball in college, I broke my forearm," the pastor said. "Took a charge and got knocked on my keister. It was two months before I convinced the team doctor my radius was healed and I'd regained my strength. So how are you doing?"

"I'm almost there. The ulna is healed and the strength is probably ninety percent," Drake said. "So how did you know I'd been injured?"

"As much as I'd like you to believe I have a private line to heaven, your father-in-law asked me to check in on you. I got to know your in-laws when I visited Kay in the hospital. I like to get out and ride on Saturdays as much as possible before the weather gets bad. This ride through the wine country is one of my favorites."

"I'd think you'd be working on your sermon for tomorrow," Drake said as he poured them each a cup of freshly-brewed coffee and sat down across the table.

Pastor Steve nodded his thanks and took a sip of coffee. "I usually finish my sermon by Friday and use Saturday to run through it in my head. I can do that while I'm riding. The senator said you were hurt when a house at Sunriver blew up. You mind me asking if this involved the same people you were hunting the last time we talked?"

Drake held his cup of coffee in both hands and thought of

their last conversation as he sipped his coffee. He had visited Pastor Steve to pick his brain about homegrown terrorists...and whether they were likely to martyr themselves.

"I was after the man who blew up the senator's house in Portland," he said. "He was spotted in Mexico and wound up here in Oregon. Trying to blow up a dam in the mountains."

Pastor Steve stretched his long legs out and sat back in his chair. "The senator mentioned that you might be helping the government from time to time. He also said your mother-in-law was furious about it. Does that mean this will put you in harm's way again?"

Drake didn't want to give a complete answer that would make his mother-in-law worry. "I joined the army after 9/11," he said briefly. "I guess I'm still just a soldier at heart."

And will be until the day I die. One blink, and I see a nine-year-old girl who ran to our forward operating base when her father was beheaded by the Taliban. She wanted protection, but the next day when the village leader came for her, we had to let her go. The whole village was forced to stone her and then leave her headless little body beside the road where we would find her. The rage I felt then still burns white hot and sears my soul. So, yes, if I'm asked to help fight that enemy, I will gladly put myself in harm's way.

Pastor Steve straightened up in his chair when he saw the look on Drake's face. "Adam, I didn't mean to pry. I only wanted to know if I should pray for your safety."

At that, Drake smiled. "Tell my mother-in-law she doesn't need to worry. I'm on my way to San Francisco to help a company there. No terrorists involved that I know of."

His pastor looked across the table for a long moment, and nodded. "All right then, I'll be on my way. Come see me some Sunday."

Drake walked him out to his Harley and watched him ride off. He knew his father-in-law probably did call him, but it would be his mother-in-law who put her husband up to it. The senator would have just called him directly and asked how he was doing.

FIVE

R. David Klein III stood on the deck of his lakeshore mansion 565 miles southeast of Portland and admired the clarity of the aquamarine water of North Lake Tahoe. His sixty-five-foot, solar-powered catamaran was moored at his dock in Crystal Bay. Everything he'd sacrificed during the last ten years was represented by his mansion and his yacht, and he was not about to lose either of them.

He turned and walked back into the great room, where his college roommate, Robert Parker, was fixing his third dirty Martini.

"Go easy on those," Klein said. "He'll be here soon. If this guy's as good as Congressman Sanchez says he is, we need him. This is business, Bob, not a party."

"I have a good reason to be drinking and so do you," Parker said, "so lighten up. In six months or less, we might be explaining to Congress why a half-billion-dollar green stimulus package didn't do much to stimulate our companies."

Parker's solar company, Ra Solar, Inc., named after the

Egyptian god of the sun, had developed a home solar recharging station for electric cars. Klein's company, Apollo Motor Company, named after the Greco-Roman sun god, manufactured electric cars. The companies, which had been the subjects of their master's theses at Stanford, were designed to complement and support each other. The public, however, didn't seem to be ready for such an advancement in engineering.

One drunken night they had come up with plan to save their companies: create widespread electrical blackouts so people would want to live off the power grid and rely on solar energy. Klein had had an epiphany that evening, standing on his deck and looking down the shoreline at a neighboring estate that was owned by a well-known genius, the CEO of Energy Integrated Solutions, Inc.

EIS had landed a government grant to develop IT security software for America's smart grid project and its major electric utilities. Smart grid was a plan to computerize the electrical utility network to provide both better efficiency and better security for America's energy infrastructure. Klein and Parker had tried to hack the EIS system without success, and then Klein had had another idea.

"What if we could slip someone into EIS and plant a virus in the security software Bradford's developing?" he wondered aloud. "Like Israel did with Iran. If it worked for Israel, why couldn't it work for us? All we need is a virus like the worm and someone to infiltrate EIS."

That was when Parker had suggested they reach out to the congressman who had helped them get their green energy stimulus grant. Alexander Arturo Sanchez, congressman from San Francisco's twelfth district, always had a hand out for generous campaign contributions. From what they had learned, Sanchez didn't particularly care if the money he received was earned legally or not. Rumors had been circulating for years, in fact, that he had ties to the drug cartels and other connections that might prove to be useful.

The man Congressman Sanchez had suggested to help them was the man they were waiting for at Klein's Lake Tahoe mansion.

"Were you able to find out anything more about this fixer?" Parker asked as he sat down in a blood-red leather arm chair.

"Not much," Klein said. "His name is Ryan Walkur. He's on the board of directors of the Pacific First Security Investment Bank of California, the same board Sanchez was on before he ran for Congress. Walkur has a big place in Pacific Heights, but he's not there much. He travels a lot. He's supposed to be a financial wizard. If he runs in the same circles Sanchez does, he's got to be wealthy."

"Sanchez thinks we're wealthy, too, or he did, so that doesn't mean much. Why does Sanchez think this guy can help us?"

"He wouldn't come right out and tell me, but he suggested Walkur's connected. We'll see. If this doesn't work out, there'll always be another government frontier to cash in on." Klein raised an imaginary glass to toast the future.

"That's not why I started my company," Parker said. "To get rich. I believe in solar energy. You're the one that wants to show your old man you can make more money than he can."

"Don't go there, Bobby," Klein warned. "I don't need you to psychoanalyze me. You know I don't give a damn what my father thinks of me—if he thinks of me at all. The only thing he thinks about is finding his next wife. Someone to tell him what a big man he is because he was a big football star at Oklahoma and played in the NFL."

"Then why go nuts every time he opens a new Cadillac dealership somewhere?"

"Because he's a bastard. There are plenty of men who deserve to be successful. But they never will be because they couldn't run over people with a football in their hands. Make me a martini, Bobby. I have time for just one before our guest arrives."

SIX

Ryan Walkur parked his Mercedes under the porte-cochere and had his finger on the brass doorbell to the right of the massive, carved mahogany door when it was opened by a tall, heavy-set man in his late thirties.

"Mr. Walkur," David Klein said, "come in."

As Walkur stepped in and shook hands with his host, he was surprised at the strength in the large man's fleshy hand. He followed Klein through the foyer and into the great room, where he saw another man standing at the bar to the right of a stone fireplace.

Klein made the introductions. "This is Robert Parker, the CEO of Ra Solar. Care for a drink?"

"Single malt, drop of water, would be fine," Walkur said. "Is that your boat down there?" he asked as he walked to the floor-to-ceiling picture window overlooking the lake. He knew the answer, of course, but he wanted to get a read on the man.

"It's a solar-powered catamaran," Klein answered. "Biggest boat on the lake. We could take a cruise later, if you'd like."

"I can't stay that long. Congressman Sanchez tells me both

of your companies are in trouble," Walkur began as he took a seat in one of the leather arm chairs near the fireplace.

"How much did Sanchez tell you?" Parker asked.

"Not much. So I did my own research. You, Mr. Parker, couldn't turn your company around with less than a quarter of a billion dollars. There's no market for your solar-powered home charging stations for electric cars." He smiled and turned to Klein and added, "Just as there's no market for Mr. Klein's electric cars. Despite your president's lofty goal of putting a million electric cars on the roads, no one will be buying that many electric cars. And no one is going to be foolish enough to loan you that kind of money."

"Then why are you here?" Klein asked.

"Because Congressman Sanchez also hinted that you might have something other than capital investment in mind."

"Assuming we did have something else in mind," Parker said, "how do we know we could trust you to discuss it?"

"I'll give you two reasons," Walkur said in a level voice, "and then I want you to stop wasting my time. First, I think you both suspect Congressman Sanchez has connections to the drug cartels. He does, and it's because I helped him establish those connections, which net him far more money than the paltry sums you have given him. "Second, I know the government would be happy to arrest you, Mr. Parker, on environmental terrorism charges if they knew about the logging equipment you blew up in the Northwest. You've always been an activist, but some of it wasn't always legal, was it?"

As the partners looked at each other, Walkur came to the point. "Now, if I'm willing to offer my services to you and admit that I work with the drug cartels and a dirty politician, why do you think you can't trust me to consider whatever it is you have in mind?"

Klein turned to Parker. "Is he telling the truth about your tree-hugging days?"

Walkur saw by Parker's steely glare there was a lot Klein did not know about his quiet, nerdy friend.

An hour later, after listening to their rambling and sophomoric plan to crash the U.S. electric energy grid, Walkur drove back to the airport in Reno with their pledge of $10 million for his assistance. As he drove, a plan began forming in his mind. He remembered learning from an old client of his that their plan had been considered and discussed. Hezbollah and its sponsor, Iran, wanted to destabilize America in the very way Klein and Parker were suggesting. Walkur's new plan. If they were willing to stand up as front men for a terrorist strike of this magnitude, why not help them in every way possible?

SEVEN

As soon as he was settled back in the study of his Pacific Avenue residence in San Francisco, Walkur sent an encrypted email to his contact in the Brotherhood. With its blessing, he knew he could quickly line up the players he would need to carry out his plan.

The two solar geniuses had told him how they'd tried to gain access to Energy Integrated Solutions' IT system the same way hackers all over the world were attacking companies. But the hackers' phishing attack hadn't worked. Sophisticated companies, especially ones doing research for the government, were too security conscious for amateur cyber attacks like those of the sun gods (so to speak) to be successful.

But Walkur's other plan—to buy or borrow a copy of Stuxnet, the malicious worm program that had caused Iran's centrifuges to fail—might work. Walkur was confident he could find someone with access to the infamous malware who could be bribed or blackmailed into getting him a copy. Once he had the virus, it could be tweaked to disable transformers or other critical utility company systems to cause a blackout that would leave fifty million people or more in the dark for at least six months. The dollar loss to the U.S. economy would be incalculable.

All he would need would be one upper level manager at EIS to have an unfortunate heart attack. The vacancy could then be filled by someone capable of inserting the worm into the EIS security software, which would be distributed to utility companies all over the country.

While he waited to hear back from the Brotherhood, Walkur walked to the window and looked up and down the tree-lined street below. His modest residence, a restored 1915 Beaux-Arts beauty in Pacific Heights, was valued at a cool $7 million. It thus gave him the proper cachet in the City's banking community to easily handle his financial dealings. Although the residence didn't have all the amenities his old mansion in Asuncion, Paraguay, had, it was quite comfortable.

Nevertheless, he deeply missed sitting in the shade of the covered terrace next to his swimming pool with its two magnificent waterfalls and sipping iced *yerba mate* tea. Asuncion was where the Alliance had been created with the plundered Nazi loot his grandfather, Rainier Walkur, had helped Martin Bormann smuggle out of Europe. Rainier Walkur's bloodline had directed the organization's growth since then, and now he, Ryan, was its leader. His mission was to create a worldwide fascist movement.

As soon as he heard his computer signal that an email had been received, and he returned to his desk to read it.

Proceed with your plan. Contact our friend in Tijuana. We believe he has the skills you will need. We will reimburse your out-of-pocket expenses, and pay the management fee you have requested.

So the game was on. He hadn't expected the Brotherhood to provide the Hezbollah commander in Tijuana for the operation, but he was pleased they had. Saleem (Sal) Canaan was an American Muslim who had grown up in San Diego and been recruited for *jihad* at his family's mosque. Hezbollah had arranged for him to receive a scholarship to attend San Diego State University and obtain a master's degree in computer science.

Walkur retrieved the number for the young Hezbollah commander from his computer and called him.

"Mr. Canaan," he said, "our mutual friends have recommended you for a project I'm planning. I'd like to send my jet for you so we can talk. I know about the services you provided a client of mine last month in Oregon."

"I heard his plane crashed," Canaan replied. "How do I know this isn't payback for his bad luck?"

"Because my client was the one who paid for his bad luck."

Canaan was silent for a minute. "So what services are you interested in?"

"The skills you developed in college. Not your more deadly ones."

"When do you want to meet?"

"Tomorrow."

"That soon. Okay, have your jet pick me up at Brown Field tomorrow morning, nine o'clock."

Brown Field was a general aviation airport located a mile and a half north of the U.S./Mexico border in the Otay Mesa community of San Diego. Otay Mesa was infamous for the number of tunnels dug under the border by the drug cartels. Walkur knew Hezbollah had provided the engineering skills to build the tunnels in exchange for access to the cartels' smuggling routes in the U.S. Given the work Hezbollah was doing in the area, therefore, Canaan's use of Brown Field didn't surprise him.

EIGHT

At ten o'clock the next morning, Sal Canaan was ushered into Walkur's second floor study.

"Do you come to San Francisco often, Mr. Canaan?"

"San Francisco's not really my type of city."

"Do you think you could work here?"

"Doing what?"

"Using your computer skills working for a company that I'll arrange," Walkur told him.

Canaan was interested. "For how long? I have responsibilities in San Diego."

"It's your leadership that recommended you, so I'm sure arrangements can be made. Plan on being here for a month or so."

"So who was your client in Oregon?"

"I think you know the answer to that. I was asked to coordinate the efforts of Hezbollah and the Tijuana cartel and assist the man you took orders from."

Canaan stood and walked around Walkur's desk to the side bar and helped himself to a cup of coffee from a stainless coffee carafe. As he filled his cup, he said over his shoulder, "If the Brotherhood was your client, why did you have their man killed?"

Walkur swiveled his chair and looked over steepled fingers at his young guest. "Do you think I had something to do with his jet exploding? He failed to detonate the nuclear device you helped him smuggle across the border. Perhaps you had his plane brought down."

Canaan gave a brief nod. "Perhaps," he said. "But someone called a certain cartel boss and told him the man who assassinated their former leader could be found in Oregon. The call that tipped the cartel off came from Asuncion, Paraguay."

Walkur waited a minute before asking his next question. "Does his unfortunate death create a problem for you?"

"Not at all. I would have killed him myself, if I had been told to do so. I just wonder if that's the way men who help you are rewarded."

"Failure in our line of work is often rewarded that way. The man you speak of had failed too many times. Your concern should be not to follow his example." Walkur paused again. "If the possibility of failing frightens you, Mr. Canaan, I can ask your leadership to send someone else."

Canaan's eyes narrowed and his lips tightened as he returned to his seat with his cup of coffee and looked across the desk. "I think I can handle it. Why don't you tell me what you need?"

"Providence, or Allah as you would say, has presented us with an opportunity to create chaos in this country. I have been asked to help two young fools who want to crash America's electrical power grid. What I want you to do is be the person who helps make that happen for them."

"And how am I supposed to do that?'

"A company here in San Francisco is developing security

software for the utility companies that form the electrical power grid. One of the company's managers will have an accident. You will take his place. Once you're inside this company, you will infect their new software with a worm that will bring down the entire American electrical power grid."

Canaan considered this for a minute. "Do you have such a worm?"

"I will by the time you need it."

"How will you get me hired by this company?"

"One of the men I mentioned is a neighbor of the CEO of this company. You will be referred as an IT security consultant. I'll put together a resume for you with a new name and legend. He won't be able to pass up the opportunity to replace their recently deceased manager so quickly. I have a condo in Mission Bay that my bank just repossessed. You can use it. And you can drive a new BMW the bank owns. You'll receive ten thousand dollars a month to cover your expenses."

Canaan nodded. "One last question: Who will handle the accident this manager is going to have?"

"You will. There are things you can learn from this man before he dies that will assist you when you take his place."

NINE

Nick Kawasaki walked out the front door of the Hunter's Point office building of Energy Integrated Solutions, Inc., to his new black Subaru WRX STI in the parking lot. He stood beside the car for a moment, thinking about the modifications he wanted to add to it that would make it the fastest street racer in the city. At twenty-nine years of age, he wasn't the youngest of the program managers at EIS, just the best, and he deserved to be driving the car he'd been dreaming of owning for years.

As he took the key fob out of the pocket of his jeans to open the door, he felt his muscles lock. Pain invaded every inch of his body, and he felt himself falling. While he was aware of what was happening, he had no control over his body. Then he felt himself being lowered to the ground. As he felt his body pulsating, he tried to scream, but no words would come out.

Then he felt a needle stick in his neck. And then nothing at all.

When he regained consciousness, he was on his back, tied down on a single bed in a cheap motel room. He knew it was a cheap motel because it smelled of urine and mold. There was duct tape over his mouth and he was naked.

He sensed, then managed to turn his head to see the man sitting on a chair next to the bed and looking at him. Of mixed race, he thought, perhaps Middle Eastern or Italian. The man's dark brown eyes were studying him dispassionately, just like a doctor had once looked at him before operating on his pelvis that had been fractured in a motorcycle accident.

"Mr. Kawasaki," the man finally said, "I have several questions I want you to answer. How quickly you answer them will determine whether you live to drive that nice new car. You were tasered in the parking lot. You'll be fine...if you cooperate. The drug you were given incapacitated you, but it will have no lasting effects." The man paused, then held up another syringe. "This syringe, however, contains potassium chloride, the drug used in state-sanctioned executions."

Kawasaki's eyes widened and he began thrashing his head from side to side and trying to yell through the duct tape for help.

"Relax," Sal Canaan said. "No one could hear you even if your mouth wasn't taped." He smiled. "I rented the rooms on either side, and, besides, it's early. The people who stay in this motel are still out trying to score drugs for the night." There was a narrow smile. "If you cooperate, you can join them shortly."

He stood up and leaned over his victim. "But allow me to continue. When a man is executed, he's given three drugs. First, he's injected with sodium thiopental. It's an anesthetic that causes unconsciousness. Then he's given pancuronium bromide, which causes paralysis of all his muscles, including his diaphragm. That causes him to begin to suffocate. But he's unconscious by now, so he doesn't experience the agony of suffocation. The last drug he's administered is potassium chloride, which, of course, causes cardiac arrest and death. Are you with me so far, Mr. Kawasaki?"

Kawasaki was frozen in fear, unable to process what he was hearing.

Canaan nodded and sat down again. "I believe I have your attention, Nick—may I call you Nick?—so I'll continue. I confess that I neglected to obtain the first two drugs that are normally used for an execution. I only have the potassium chloride here in this syringe. So listen closely, Nick. There is no medical dispute, I'm told, that if the person is not unconscious, an injection of potassium chloride causes excruciating pain. It feels like your veins have been set on fire. What I intend to do is give you less than a lethal dose each time you refuse to answer my question. That way, I can make you wish you were dead for as long as I choose. Nod your head if I have made my intentions clear."

What choice did he have? Kawasaki nodded his head.

Two hours later, he had described the work he was doing at EIS, the security procedures that were in place, and everything he knew about Bill Bradford, the CEO of the company.

Canaan leaned closer. "You've been very cooperative, Nick. However, for this information to be useful to me, you must die. Sorry." He plunged the hypodermic needle into the throbbing jugular vein in Nick Kawasaki's neck.

During the four minutes he sat watching the death throes of the former EIS manager with a satisfied smile on his face, he thought about the interview for his new job. He needed to prepare for it.

TEN

Drake took the 10:15 a.m. Alaska Airlines flight out of Portland International Airport to San Francisco and arrived at 12:18 p.m. An hour later, he had checked into the San Francisco Marriott Marquis, his favorite hotel, and was sitting at a table in the 4th Street Bar and Grill. The grilled buffalo chicken sandwich and pint of Anchor Steam beer he had ordered were good, but the beat down he was watching on the nearest flat screen TV that the 49ers were putting on the Buffalo Bills was even better.

He'd played football at Oregon and still followed his old team, but he didn't have a favorite NFL team. The spoiled antics of some professional players, guys who were paid a fortune to play a game he would have played for free, disgusted him. He had to admit, however, that watching a game in a sports bar in a town that loved its NFL team was fun.

When he'd polished off the last of his sandwich and most of the fries, he paid his bill and took the elevator to his corner room on the twenty-fifth floor. The CEO of EIS had asked him to call when he arrived.

Margo, his ever-efficient secretary, had put together a file on the company and its founder that he'd reviewed on the flight. William Bradford, age 61, had graduated from the University of California at Berkeley with post-graduate degrees in electrical engineering and computer sciences. He'd worked for Lockheed Martin in the engineering and business services division that had developed state-of-the-art technical innovations for the nation's utility companies. After becoming the head of the division, and developing a reputation as the leading engineer in his field, he had left Lockheed Martin and started Energy Integrated Solutions, Inc. The company was located in the South Bay area, where many of the hot new tech firms were settling. Bradford lived across the Golden Gate Bridge on Belvedere's Corinthian Island.

Drake picked up the phone and dialed. "Mr. Bradford, this is Adam Drake. You asked me to call you when I arrived."

"Are you at the airport?" Bradford asked.

"No. I'm staying at the Marriott Marquis. Would you like to set a time for us to meet tomorrow?"

"I think we'd better meet sooner than that. I've just been grilled by the police about one of my managers. His body was found in his car this morning. They think he might have been murdered."

"Why do they think that?" Drake asked.

"Because he had marks on his neck they think could have been caused by a taser. Look, I'm at my office now, but I'll be finished here in another hour or two. Are you available for dinner tonight?"

"Sure. I don't have plans for tonight. Where would you like to meet, Mr. Bradford?"

"Let's eat at my place. That'll give us the privacy we need. I'll call you when I get to the Marquis, say, four o'clock? And call me Bill."

"All right, Bill, if you'll call me Adam. See you at four."

Drake walked to the window and looked down at a ferry leaving the terminal. Bradford seemed like a competent guy, he thought, and from what he'd learned, he ran a tight ship. But with the work EIS was doing for the government, and the security clearances his managers were required to have, a messy murder investigation was the last thing Bradford needed right now.

With two hours to kill before Bradford picked him up, Drake changed into his sexy gym attire, a T-shirt and a pair of black shorts, and headed for the fitness center and spa. He put in thirty minutes on the treadmill, warming up at eight and a half miles an hour, then increasing his speed to ten miles an hour and finishing the last ten minutes at eleven miles an hour. Having worked up a good sweat, he moved on to his free weight workout to continue building up the strength in his left arm. He figured he was at ninety percent strength in his injured arm and maybe a month away from a full hundred percent.

After a shower back in his room, he put on a pair of black lightweight wool trousers and a black merino wool crew neck sweater and slipped his feet into soft black calfskin loafers. With half an hour yet before Bradford arrived, he turned on the TV and searched the channels for news about the dead EIS manager. There were reports of several murders and a jumper off the Golden Gate Bridge, but only one short mention in a police log of a tech manager. San Francisco wasn't like Chicago, where there were too many murders to report each day, but Drake thought the manager's death would have received some attention if the police thought it was suspicious.

If there was any news about the manager, he thought, it was more likely that someone would be blogging about it, so he opened his Dell Ultrabook computer, sat down in the armchair near the window and waited for the Wi-Fi connection. A quick search of the local blogs didn't turn up anything, although one blog featured photos taken that day that showed police investigating a black Subaru WRX, which appeared to be cordoned off with yellow crime scene tape.

The Subaru WRX was the type of car Drake could see a young tech manager in San Francisco driving. It was a favorite of the street racing crowd, and a great little car for squiring beautiful young women around the city, too. Drake wondered if that was the type of manager Bradford had hired.

Before he had a chance to check more of his favorite news sites and see what was going on in the rest of the world, Bradford called to say he was parked near the valet stand in a white Audi A8. Drake grabbed his gray cashmere blazer and left the room.

ELEVEN

Bill Bradford was sitting in his car and looking at his cell phone when Drake tapped on the passenger side window.

"Sorry," Bradford said after he'd unlocked the door and Drake got in, "I was reading a text message from the detective on my manager's case. It looks like he had a heart attack and the taser marks might not be related." He shook his head. "They're not sure what happened."

The two men shook hands as Drake asked, "How old was he?"

"Nick was one of my younger managers. Too young to have a heart attack," Bradford said, shaking his head as he drove away from the hotel.

They turned onto Market Street from Fourth Street, and then turned again on El Camino Real, Highway 101, and headed north toward the Golden Gate Bridge. Bradford drove confidently through the Sunday afternoon traffic.

"I haven't ridden in an A8 before," Drake said. "Nice car."

"It's comfortable and fast," Bradford said. "Four liter twin-turbo engine, eight-speed Tiptronic transmission and all-wheel drive. It's an engineer's dream and a mechanic's nightmare. You like cars?" He glanced at Drake.

"I have a Porsche 993 that I drive daily. It's not as sophisticated a machine as this, but it's fast and fun to drive."

"Have you rented a car to drive while you're here?"

"No, not yet," Drake said.

"Then drive my Audi TTS coupe while you're here," Bradford offered. "You can drive it back tonight, save me a trip back into the City."

Drake liked his new client more each minute. Bradford was successful and had the toys his success had earned him, but he also enjoyed them like a little boy. And he was generous with them, not like some wealthy men Drake knew who bought expensive things and hid them away to be enjoyed privately.

The drive across the Golden Gate Bridge provided a spectacular view of the bay, with a hundred or more sailboats skimming across its silver surface. Then it was on to the Redwood Highway and the Tiburon Boulevard until they reached the Belvedere Cove and Corinthian Island.

Bradford's waterfront home, he said, had been built for a well-known yacht racer. He parked the car next to a black Audi TTS coupe in the garage, then led Drake to the kitchen door.

"My passion," he said as he walked Drake through the kitchen and dining area to the floor-to-ceiling windows that looked out over the bay, "is club racing in my sailboat. I spend as much time on the water as my work allows."

Drake looked down at the water. A sleek, white, forty-foot Beneteau sailboat was moored next to the floating deck that extended from the lower level of the three-story house.

"We'll go sailing if we have time," Bradford said. "Hey, would you like a drink? Help yourself while I get out a couple steaks for dinner."

Drake poured two fingers of Knob Creek bourbon from a bottle sitting on a drinks tray and watched Bradford pulling things out of his refrigerator. It was obvious that the man was comfortable in the kitchen. "Is your wife joining us for dinner?" he asked. The file his secretary had put together didn't mention a wife.

Bradford chuckled. "Are you wondering if I'm married or if I have a *partner*?"

"Neither," Drake said with a smile. "This is a big house for one man."

"Yeah. My wife's visiting her mother in Denver. If she were here, I would have taken you to dinner in the City. I don't discuss business over dinner when she's home."

Bradford used a dry rub on two New York strip steaks and poured some Grey Goose vodka over ice in a shot glass. Drink in hand, he led Drake to two leather barrel chairs facing each other across a square, glass-topped, coffee table.

"I imagine you have a few questions for me while the steaks are seasoning, Bradford said.

"I do. For starters, why did you reach out to my father-in-law, Senator Hazelton? Surely you have your own people who can handle things."

Bradford set his glass on the table and studied Drake for a moment. "My industry is highly competitive. Its young princes, the tech stars, are loyal as long as you pay them more than your competitors are willing to pay them. If word got out that I was having more than the average security problem, not only would my shareholders panic, but, well, my rivals would start picking off my best people.

"Any idea why you're having more trouble than normal?" Drake asked.

"I think a lot of companies in America are experiencing the same thing. The number of security holes in software used to control refineries, factories, and utilities critical to our infrastructure are being probed every hour of every day by our enemies. The more holes they find that haven't been patched, the bolder and broader the attacks get. That's why my company was awarded the contract to develop security software for electric utilities. A power-grid cyber attack has the capability of keeping millions of people in the dark for months."

Drake nodded. "But you're not part of the infrastructure. Why is your company being attacked?"

Bradford got up and motioned for Drake to follow him back to the kitchen. "That's what I hope you can help me find out, Adam. My hunch is that someone would like to take us out of the picture. Maybe a competitor. Or someone doesn't want our power grid to be protected and as safe as it can be. I don't really know. That's what I'd like you to find out."

Drake sat on a stool at the black granite-topped kitchen island while Bradford open a bottle of cabernet to breathe for dinner. "Could someone infect your new software with one of these cyber attacks?" he asked. "Is that what someone's hoping to do?"

Bradford put the two steaks on a plate. "Possibly. But they have to get through our security measures first. We have as good a system as there is, but no system is impenetrable. It's easier to get someone within our system to infect the software," he explained. "Plant a virus in a thumb drive or a laptop that has access to our system, and when that device accesses our system, the damage is done. Okay, bring the wine and a couple glasses and let's go out on the deck and grill these."

Drake did as he was told and followed his host out to the covered deck, where Bradford had a built-in gas grill. The sun had gone down and the City on the Bay glimmered across the water.

Drake gave the view an appreciative look, then turned back

to Bradford. "How do you prevent someone with access to your system planting a virus?"

"I'll introduce you to my cyber security expert tomorrow if you like. Basically, you make sure devices that have access to your system never leave the building. Smart phones that can check email from the office aren't allowed. Telecommuting isn't allowed. Our employees can't work from home. You monitor login logs, things like that." Bradford turned the steaks over. "Rare or medium rare on your steak?"

When both steaks were medium rare, the two men returned to the kitchen, where Bradford fixed a quick salad and steamed some asparagus as the steaks rested.

Before they sat to eat at the dining table near the windows, Drake asked if he thought any of his employees were behind the cyber attacks.

"I know my people," Bradford said. "They're not doing this. Someone's targeting us, and we don't have a clue who it is. I need to stop these attacks, Adam. Or find a way around telling the government about them and risk losing my research grant."

When Drake left that night, driving Bradford's Audi TTS back to the Marriott Marquis, he realized he might need more than his legal skills to solve this client's problem.

TWELVE

It was nine o'clock Monday morning when Drake pulled into a guest parking space in front of the EIS building in Hunter's Point. Once a naval shipyard just north of Candlestick Park, the area had been redeveloped to create an urban campus for offices and research companies.

EIS occupied the entire third floor of the new building. When Drake told the receptionist Mr. Bradford was expecting him, he was escorted to a corner office with a view of the bay. Two walls were tastefully decorated with framed photographs of racing yachts. The other two walls were lightly tinted windows, one of which looked out to the bay, and the other overlooked the open-design workspace where employees were clustered in four main groups.

As Drake walked in, Bradford was sitting behind a large glass-topped desk talking on the phone. "Come on in," he said, covering the phone with his hand. "I'll be finished in a minute."

Drake studied the photographs of the yachts and saw that several of them featured Bradford standing at the helm of his yacht as it sliced through heavy seas, throwing white spray over the front half of the boat.

Bradford ended the call and stood up to greet Drake. "That was the detective again," he said. "He's waiting for the autopsy report, which, around here, could take a week before he gets it. Unless there's evidence of foul play, he's going to write this off as a heart attack and close his file."

"Has he found out what your manager was doing before he died?"

"Our surveillance cameras show him leaving here at eight-thirty Saturday night," Bradford replied. "Nick liked to work late when it was quiet. With our flex-hour system, he could choose the hours he worked. They don't know where he went after he left here. He was found in his car in a parking garage down in the wharf district."

Something seemed to be bothering Bradford. He suddenly turned and looked out at his employees working in their cubicles.

"Something wrong?" Drake asked.

"I had a call this morning from a neighbor. Asking if I had anyone in mind to replace Nick. He has someone he thought I should interview."

"Is that helpful?"

"It might be. It just seems wrong to be thinking about hiring someone to take Nick's place the day after he dies." Bradford walked to the door of his office and waved at Drake to follow. "Let me show you around. Then I'll introduce you to our security analyst. He'll tell you about the problem we're having."

Drake walked beside Bradford down a perimeter hallway to the office of the company's IT security analyst.

With two raps on the door, Bradford walked in. "John," he said, "I want you to meet Adam Drake. He's the attorney I hired to look at our SEC reporting requirement about these cyber attacks. Brief him on what you do and what we've learned. I've scheduled a meeting with Richard—Adam, that's our corporate counsel—at ten thirty, so you have an hour."

Drake sat in the only chair in front of the desk and looked between two flat-screen monitors at the IT Security Analyst on the other side. John Lewiston looked to be in his late thirties. His hair was short and his pewter Oakley eyeglasses sat on top of his head. Drake looked around for a minute and noticed that Lewiston was a cyclist who kept his Trek mountain bike in his office.

"How much has Bill told you?" the IT manager asked.

"Just a general description of the cyber attacks," Drake said, looking between the monitors again. "Why don't you tell me when they started and what, if any, damage they've caused."

"Our managers began noticing spear-phishing about three months ago. Do you know what spear phishing is?"

"It's where hackers send emails to targeted individuals with attachments or links that release malware or a virus into your computer system," Drake answered. "I thought that was fairly common."

"It is. Our employees are trained to be careful. We don't allow employees to sync mobile devices to both home and our computers. Mobile devices, like company laptops, PDA's, and smart phones, can't be used for personal use. We have a very complete IT security plan, I can assure you, Mr. Drake."

Drake wasn't surprised that Lewiston thought so highly of the company's security plan, which he had developed and supervised, but he was surprised that such a common hacking problem was so troubling to the company. "If these cyber attacks are common and you have them under control," he said, "then what's the problem?"

Lewiston smiled. "We're fairly small for a software company. Only seventy- five employees. Every one of them has reported receiving tainted emails on a regular basis that use personal information no one should have access to. But our security plan has protected us so far. The problem is that none of this makes any sense."

"I don't understand," Drake said.

"Look, we develop software to protect companies. We're good at what we do, so you wouldn't expect us to be a target, right? That's why Bill thinks one of our competitors is behind this. By forcing us to report the spear phishing as a serious risk to the company on the SEC Form 10-K, we invite DHS and the FBI to come trooping in. This gives the competitor an argument that if we can't protect our own company, our software can't protect anyone else."

This made sense. Drake nodded. "Any idea which competitor might be doing this?"

Lewiston stood up and took a file from the back bar behind his desk. Then he reached across his desk and handed it to Drake. "There were twenty two companies that applied for the Defense Advanced Research Projects Agency (DARPA). We got the award, so there are twenty-one possible competitors." He sat down again and typed something on a keyboard.

Drake opened the file and looked at the summary page. The twenty-one companies with names he didn't recognize were located all over the country. With each company listed on the summary page was a brief profile and a list of company officers.

"Did you identify a suspect?" Drake asked.

"I checked financials to see if any of them were in trouble," Lewiston said. "And I looked online for comments that might explain a motive. I even checked Twitter and Facebook and LinkedIn. I didn't find anything that raised a red flag."

"Have you hired anyone recently who might have a connection to any of these companies?"

Lewiston shrugged. "Human Resources should have run background checks, so I didn't. You could ask them."

"I will," Drake said as he got up to leave. "Which way to HR?"

"It's the office to the left of the elevator. But you'll need to get clearance from Richard Bryce, our attorney, before they let you see anything. He's big on employee privacy rights. A real ACLU fan."

Drake left the office. He was looking forward to meeting Bryce. His years as a prosecutor in the district attorney's office in Portland had instilled in him a perverse fondness for irritating defense attorneys and ACLU fanatics.

THIRTEEN

Rein Walkur was waiting for Saleem Canaan in the study of his Pacific Avenue mansion. His plan was working out nicely, and now it was time to show his Hezbollah soldier a little appreciation. While he didn't know how the EIS manager had been killed, his source in the police department had reported that the death was being treated as a heart attack. Walkur didn't involve himself in the violent end of his business enterprise, but he was interested in knowing how the heart attack had been caused. If new techniques had been developed, he needed to know about them.

One of his six bodyguards knocked on the door and informed him that his guest had arrived. Walkur followed the bodyguard down the curving staircase to the dining area on the second floor and stopped next to the table.

"Saleem," he said when the young man entered, "please join me for lunch. I ordered some of my favorite San Francisco foods for us."

The table was already set with the mansion's china and silverware and loaded with a large silver bowl of Crab Louie salad, a heaping platter of crab cakes, a tureen of clam chowder, and bread board with sourdough bread.

"I try to eat as much of the wonderful seafood here as I can when I visit," Walkur said. "How have you been?" he asked.

"I've been shopping for a wardrobe to go along with the condo and car you provided me," Canaan said as he pulled out a chair and joined his host. "So I've been busy."

Walkur smiled and handed him a plate with a healthy serving of Crab Louie salad piled on it. "Was that before or after you took care of the man you're to replace?"

Canaan tore off a chunk of sourdough bread and buttered it. When he finished chewing his first bite, he said matter-of-factly, "I shopped first so I could savor my evening."

"Try the crab cakes," Walkur suggested. "My chef makes them with sour cream and horseradish. Tell me how you killed the man."

"I executed him in the state-prescribed manner," Canaan replied calmly. "He suffered a heart attack caused by the sodium chloride I gave him, without the rest of the usual cocktail."

"Very painful way to die, I would assume. Does the sodium chloride remain in his system?" Walkur ladled some clam chowder into his bowl.

"It's something I've used before in Mexico," Canaan replied, digging into the crab salad, "so when it's discovered, they'll think it's cartel and drug related. Don't worry. It can't be traced to me."

"Make sure it isn't," Walkur said after he'd swallowed a spoonful of chowder. "I don't want the police questioning you and screwing up your chances for a job with EIS. Your new identity and background have been prepared by my people, and the CEO's neighbor has made the referral he was told to make. You shouldn't have any trouble getting the job. Study the file I have for you and call them tomorrow. Ask to see Mr. Bradford. He's expecting you."

Continuing to eat while a servant poured coffee for both of them, Canaan asked when they would have the worm virus they were going to use.

"One of the businesses the Alliance operates is an online gambling site," Walkur replied. "Very lucrative. And very useful when someone needs to be persuaded to do something for us. We've been keeping an eye on a man who works for the Pentagon's Cyber Command. He worked on the Flame cyber weapon America used on Iran. He's providing us a copy of the virus in exchange for writing off a rather large gambling debt. We'll modify it here to suit our needs, so I should have it on a thumb drive for you later this week. After the blackout, the subsequent investigation will discover a large deposit in his bank account." He smiled. "We'll make sure that it will be traced to one of the men who will be blamed for all of this. The government likes to label acts of terrorism 'homegrown,' so we'll perpetuate the myth."

Canaan nodded his approval. "What if I'm not on the team working on the software for the utilities? I won't have the password I'll need to access that program."

"The man you killed worked on that team, so you should be the one to replace him. If you aren't, we'll figure something out. Perhaps someone else will have to suffer an unfortunate and untimely death."

At this point, Walkur checked his watch and rose to excuse himself. "I have a call coming in from South America I need to take in my study. Finish your meal and pick up the file I mentioned from my assistant when you leave. Good luck, Mr. Canaan. Call me when you are successfully employed at EIS."

FOURTEEN

Drake returned to the CEO's office after his meeting with the security analyst. Bradford hadn't mentioned that he thought one of his competitors might be behind the cyber attacks. If there was evidence of that, investigating EIS employees wasn't necessary.

Bradford was working at his desk when Drake knocked on his door. "Bill," he said as he walked in, "your security analyst said you thought one of your competitors might be behind the cyber attacks. Why didn't you mention that to me?"

"Close the door and have a seat," Bradford directed. He picked up a file from a stack on his desk. "This is the investigation Lewiston did after I mentioned, in an off-hand way, that maybe it's a competitor trying to make us look bad. He wasted a lot of time on this and didn't find anything. I know most of these guys. This isn't the game they play. You're welcome to review it if you think it's important."

Drake took the file. It was a duplicate of the file Lewiston had shown him. "Bill," he said, "why am I here? As far as I can tell, none of this spear phishing has been successful. You don't suspect a competitor is engaged in corporate espionage or sabotage. Why not just report on the 10-K that you have determined there's no material impact on your company or its financial results? That's what most companies are doing."

Bradford stood up and walked to the window, where he stood looking out at a sailboat coming into the marina nearby. After a minute, he turned to Drake.

"Your father-in-law, Senator Hazelton, and I are friends. Our two senators here in California have a different take on security issues. When I've needed help in Washington, he's helped me. He told me that if there was something involving the work I was doing that didn't feel right to give him a call. This doesn't feel right, so I gave him a call."

He walked back to his desk, but did not sit down. "I can't put my finger on it exactly," he continued, "but these attempts are clumsy. The skill we usually see from hackers, whether it's the Chinese or criminal hackers trying to steal intellectual property, is missing. They aren't probing my key people who have access to the things they might be after. They're probing *everyone*. It's like someone hired a novice hacker who didn't know what he was looking for.

"My company attorney, Richard Bryce, deals with compliance matters," Bradford glanced at the window, then faced Drake again. "He thinks we should report the phishing just to be safe. Google has stepped forward and reported Chinese raids on its system, and so have several others, like Intel and Adobe. But those attacks breached their systems. This is something else. I'd like to know what it is.

"Adam, I was told that you were successful helping that defense contractor in Portland last month when his secretary was murdered and it turned out to be more than just a homicide. My gut tells me this is more than just one clumsy hacker. The software we've developed to protect America's energy grid will prevent blackouts that could cripple the nation. I need to be sure this isn't something like you dealt with in Oregon. Does that answer your question?"

"Yes, it does," Drake said. "If you've discussed your situation with the senator, then you know I operate. Alone. If I need help, I'll bring in someone and put it on your tab. If this involves something big, we'll discuss it with the senator and let him decide how to proceed. Is that acceptable?"

"It's what I was hoping to hear. Let's go meet my attorney, and then we'll go to lunch." Bradford patted Drake on the shoulder and led him out of the office.

Richard A. Bryce, as Drake saw on the diploma hanging on the wall of the attorney's office, was a graduate of Berkeley Law, housed in Boalt Hall on the UC campus across the bay. He was tall and thin and looked like an attorney in his starched white shirt and blue silk tie with thin red stripes. When he removed his reading glasses and stood up to greet them, Drake estimated his height at six foot five or six.

When Bradford introduced the two men to each other, Bryce said, "Bill told me he wanted you to look over our compliance matter. Is that something you do, Mr. Drake?"

"I'm a former prosecutor, Mr. Bryce. I've handled a number of financial fraud cases that involved SEC filings. I'm familiar with compliance requirements."

"What will you be doing here?" Bryce asked as he sat back down and left the other two men standing.

"I'd like to start my review by taking a look at the personnel files of your employees. John Lewiston said I needed you to clear it with HR."

Bryce looked sharply at Bradford. "Bill, is that really necessary?"

The CEO spoke. "If Drake feels it is, then it is. I expect you to cooperate in this review, Richard."

"Is there anything else you think you need, Mr. Drake?"

"I would also like to see the log-in reports on all your systems. And a list of employees with access to those systems."

"I suppose you want employee passwords for their social media as well?" Bryce asked with a smile.

Drake was amused at the attorney's attempt to embarrass him in front of Bradford. California had recently passed two bills into law that protected the privacy of college students' and employees' social media accounts. He smiled and said, "I hope you have already prohibited your employees from using the social media while they're working, Mr. Bryce. While there's a right to maintain control of personal information, your recently passed laws have exceptions for investigations. You know I can request content relevant to my investigation. Even the ACLU conceded an employer that right."

Bryce bristled at this back-handed swipe at his pet cause, but before he could begin a rebuttal, Bradford looked at his watch and intervened.

"Richard, we need to be going. I'm taking Drake to lunch. You're welcome to join us."

"I'm meeting someone at my club, Bill. I'm sure you two will get along fine without me." Bryce picked up a handy file and opened it.

Bradford walked Drake to the elevator. When the elevator arrived and they were alone inside, he turned to him with a smile on his face. "Adam," he said, "you seem to have enjoyed that. Is it his law school or the ACLU you don't care for? I saw you looking at his diploma."

Drake returned the smile. "It must be an old habit. When two dogs meet, they sniff out their competition. I needed a whiff of his scent."

"Bryce is a good attorney," Bradford said. "He's a little stiff, but he's doing a good job. Now let's take a walk." They stepped out into the sunny fall afternoon. "There's an oyster bar down by my yacht club with the best fish and chips in San Francisco. You probably thought we were headed for a power lunch somewhere, but I try to get down there as often as I can. Hope you don't mind."

Drake said he didn't mind. They walked across the parking lot where the EIS manager had been abducted two nights before. He was eager to get started with his investigation, but it could wait until he had tried the best fish and chips in San Francisco.

FIFTEEN

As they walked back from the oyster bar on the pier near the yacht club, Bradford told Drake that his first task that afternoon would be to interview a man to replace his dead manager.

"I have a place at Lake Tahoe," he explained, "and a neighbor there is the CEO of a solar company here in the City. He's the one who called this morning and suggested I see this guy."

"That's quick," Drake said. "Do you usually see applicants the same day they call?"

"This will be a first," Bradford admitted. "I need someone to join our utilities software team as soon as possible. I'm hoping to field test the software next week if we can complete our testing here. I'll let HR know you want to see all the personnel files, and let's plan on meeting tomorrow morning." They entered his building and headed toward the elevator.

"Where do you want me to work when I'm here?" Drake asked.

"Use the conference room next to my office. I'll have the personnel files brought there."

With Drake on his way to the conference room, Bradford went to the reception desk to meet his one o'clock appointment.

The young man sitting in the reception area stood up as soon as Bradford reached the desk. He looked to be in his early thirties, five foot ten or so, with black hair worn long in back. Bradford thought he looked like a young Antonio Banderas.

"Mr. Capelli," he said, reaching out for a handshake, "I'm William Bradford, CEO of Energy Integrated Solutions. Come. We'll talk in my office."

When they arrived, Saleem Canaan, aka Anthony Capelli, said "Thank you for agreeing to see me, Mr. Bradford. I'd like to come work for you."

"I'm curious, Mr. Capelli. How did you know that I might be hiring?"

The younger man smiled. "Please call me Anthony. Mr. Capelli was my father. I've been working for Ra Solar in its residential solar-powered charging stations division. Bobby Parker, the CEO there, is cutting the staff back until the next round of federal funding comes through for electric cars and charging stations. I didn't want to wait around on unemployment until that happens, so I asked Mr. Parker if he'd help me find a position and he called his friend, Mr. David Klein, who I believe is a neighbor of yours. He suggested that I come see you."

"I see," Bradford said, looking up from the man's resume. Masters degree in computer science and engineering from the University of California San Diego, father had been an electrical engineer, and his mother was a pianist. "Does your mother live around here?" he asked.

"No, sir. Both of my parents are dead."

"Brothers or sisters?" Bradford asked, looking for anyone to help, if needed, when they did a background check on this guy.

"Sorry, I'm an only child. Mom's career as a pianist didn't allow for a big family."

"I don't imagine it would." Bradford kept digging. "Where did she perform?"

"My mother was Spanish, Mr. Bradford, and my father was Italian. They immigrated here before I was born. My mother played in an orchestra and night clubs, that sort of thing, in Florida. When they died, I finished high school and came to California. I didn't care for Florida."

"Well," Bradford said, "I'll show you around then give your resume to HR. They'll want you to fill out an application, and then we'll get together and make a decision. If I decide to hire you, are you available immediately?"

"I can start tomorrow if you need me."

"Excellent. Let's walk this way, and I'll show you what we're working on."

And as they passed, the conference room where Drake was reviewing personnel files, Anthony Capelli, aka Saleem Canaan, just happened to glance into the room. He stopped dead.

Bradford turned back to see why had Capelli had stopped.

"Sorry," the younger man said. "I thought that was someone I knew. Is he one of your employees?"

"No." Bradford signaled for him to start moving again. "He's an attorney I hired for a special project."

SALEEM CANAAN KNEW he had almost blown his cover when he recognized the man in the conference room.

A month ago in Oregon he had tried to kill Drake twice;

once when he had arranged a traffic accident Drake had managed to avoid and again when he had detonated an IED at a polo match Drake was attending. His failure to kill him had resulted in a failed attack on a mountain dam that would have killed thousands of people by flooding the valley below. It had also meant the death of the leader of the mission for the Brotherhood.

As he followed the CEO of this company he hoped to work for around to meet the team managers and was then left in HR to fill out his employment application, he silently debated whether he should eliminate the risk Drake presented to him or report to Walkur and let him decide how they should proceed. Either way, one thing was clear: Adam Drake had to be taken out of the game if they were to succeed.

By the time he was finished in Human Resources and was seated in his BMW, he decided that this time he would let someone else decide how to deal with Drake.

"We have a problem," Canaan said without any preamble when he called Walkur. "Remember the man last month we had trouble with in Oregon? I just saw him at EIS."

SIXTEEN

Drake finished reviewing the personnel files. When he stood up to stretch and look down into the EIS parking lot, he spotted a metallic gray BMW M3 pulling out of its parking space. The files had showed him that none of the employees had a connection to EIS's competitors, and as far as he could tell, HR had vetted each of them pretty thoroughly.

The file that Lewiston, the security analyst, had sent to the conference room for him to review hadn't added anything to the puzzle. Traffic analysis of the malicious emails was not successful because the hacker was using software that routed traffic to at least three servers manned by anonymous volunteers around the world, who sent the emails on to their destinations. This shotgun approach the hackers were using—spearing all of the EIS employees instead of targeting just a small group—also didn't allow Lewiston to reverse social engineer anything about the goal or identity of the hacker.

Back when he was in the district attorney's office, Drake had worked with IT investigators who knew more about this kind of investigation than he ever would. That was the kind of help he needed, but they were no longer available to him. Well, he told himself, he knew where he might find help now.

His former Delta Force partner, Mike Casey, was the president of and major shareholder in Puget Sound Security, one of the biggest security firms on the west coast. The company ran risk and threat assessments for large hi-tech firms, provided personal security protection for VIP's, and occasional hostage recovery missions when a case involved one of its clients or their families. One of Casey's star employees was a world-class white hat hacker, the kind that hacked IT structures of companies to locate their vulnerabilities.

Drake pulled his phone out of his pocket and called his friend at his office in Seattle.

"How's the wounded warrior doing?" Casey asked when he answered.

"Still having a few headaches, otherwise I'm fine. I'm in San Francisco on that thing I promised to do for my father-in-law. I think I need some help."

"You need a bodyguard to protect you from young men asking you for a date?"

"Are you volunteering? I know how much you love this place."

"I liked it better in the 'Don't ask, don't tell' days when it wasn't in your face. What kind of help do you need?"

"The CEO of Energy Integrated Solutions, thinks something strange is going on," Drake said. "His company's been having cyber attacks over the last three months that don't make any sense to him. No breaches of any system, and his security analyst hasn't been able to trace the hacker. I thought this might be something Kevin could look into."

"He's just finished an assessment for a client," Casey said. "He's probably got some time. Do you want him to work with their security analyst or do his own thing?"

"I'll let the CEO know he's helping me, but have him work alone. Will he need anything from me?"

Casey laughed. "If Kevin needs anything, I'm sure he can find it on his own. This is the kid that hacked through Microsoft's security shield when he was fourteen. How long are you going to be down there?"

"Maybe a week or so. Why?"

"I'm speaking at a conference in Las Vegas next week," Casey said. "I could reroute through San Francisco on the way home and you could buy me dinner."

"You're on. I'm staying at the Marriott Marquis. Let me know when you're arriving. I'll pick you up at the airport."

"See you next week, and watch your six," Casey laughed as he hung up.

Drake shook his head at his friend's lingering homophobia. Casey had grown up on a ranch in Montana. *Brokeback Mountain* wouldn't have fared well in the local theaters when he lived there.

There wasn't anything else that Drake could accomplish at EIS that day, so he told Bradford he was leaving. He drove the borrowed Audi TTS back to the Marriott. Monday night football in the 4th Street Grill at the hotel would satisfy his entertainment and nutritional needs that night. It would also eliminate the need to drive in a city he wasn't familiar with when he'd been drinking.

With a couple of hours to kill before kickoff, he decided to drive across the Golden Gate Bridge and see if the TTS was as good a car as it was reported to be. Its engine was smaller than the one in his Porsche 993, with only two liters of displacement, but with 265 turbocharged horsepower, it was almost as powerful. With zero to 60 speed in 4.9 seconds and Quattro all-wheel drive, the car was a rocket on rails.

Drake was having fun using the paddle shifters behind the

steering wheel as he ran the direct shift six-speed gearbox through its paces. So much fun that he didn't notice the metallic gray BMW M3 following three cars behind.

As he drove north on Highway 101, the Redwood Highway, past Sausalito and Marin City before he detoured onto Highway 1, the coast route, he let his mind slip into neutral and just enjoyed the drive. Driving with some old, familiar rock and roll playing in a car like the TTS, which was meant to be driven fast, was one of his favorite things to do.

When he reached Stinson Beach, he turned around and headed back to the City. The afternoon sun was in his eyes when he made a U-turn. This prevented him from getting a good look at the driver of the metallic gray BMW M3 that drove past him. The M3 seemed to be popular in San Francisco, he thought. He also thought it would probably give the TTS a good run for the money. A shame it was continuing on north, he thought a minute later. He and the driver of the M3 could have had some fun on the road back to the City.

SEVENTEEN

Saleem Canaan turned his BMW M3 around and followed the black Audi TTS coupe back to the Marriott Marquis in the City, where he watched Drake hand his car keys to the parking valet, walk to the corner of Fourth Street and Mission and then enter the 4th Street Bar and Grill.

When he was sure Drake wasn't coming back out, he drove toward his condo in the Mission District. Keying his cell phone in its cradle, he called Rein Walkur for instructions.

"I followed Drake on a drive to the coast and back to the Marriott Marquis, where he might be staying," he told Walkur. "He's in the hotel's 4th Street Bar and Grill on Fourth and Mission. What would you like me to do?"

"We can't take a chance that he saw you at EIS this afternoon," Walkur said. "Go to your condo for the night. I'll send someone down to the Marriott and find out if he's staying there. Call me tomorrow and we'll decide what needs to be done."

Canaan knew how he would handle this. San Francisco didn't have as many drive-by shootings as they had in the East Bay, but a little gang violence might work. Or they could knife him in an elevator. That had worked for him in San Diego, when an FBI agent had gotten a little too close to one of their operations. His choice, however, would be a sodium chloride induced heart attack like he had administered to the EIS manager. Two heart attacks would be a little suspicious, but he thought Drake deserved a painful death for interfering in Oregon and now turning up here.

For tonight, though, he would have to be satisfied with Walkur's promise that Drake would be dealt with. He'd have to find another way to satisfy his blood lust. He had an evening to kill. Two favorite possibilities came to mind. He could pick up a prostitute no one would miss tomorrow, or he could watch mixed martial arts on TV, with a little hashish to relax with until an order of takeout Chinese could be delivered to his condo. He decided it was better to play it safe and chose a night of mixed martial arts and food.

When he was eight, the mosque where his Lebanese father had worshipped offered classes in Pencak Silat, a traditional Muslim martial art developed in Indonesia and taught in mosques and Islamic centers in America. Even as a boy, he had excelled in the art, and when he was in high school, after being identified as a future *jihadi* warrior, he had traveled to Iran each summer and trained in Hezbollah's hand-to-hand combat training center. He loved both the sense of power his martial skill gave him and the opportunity his secret life provided to use it. Tonight, he would have to vicariously enjoy watching the cage fighters doing what he knew he could do better.

AFTER A DINNER of Crab Louie and two glasses of Russian River pinot noir, which didn't do anything to mask the headache that had lingered all day, Drake left the 4th Street Bar and Grill at halftime and took the elevator in the hotel up to his room. The lobby was bustling with business arrivals checking in for a week in the City.

He stepped into an elevator that was nearly full, then had to move further to the back when two men squeezed in just as the door was closing. Both men were taller than him and from his view behind them and the way they stood, he guessed they were probably ex-military. Both men wore dark suits that made their short blond hair look even blonder.

Drake smiled as he kept his eyes looking straight ahead. No one ever spoke or even smiled at the person standing only inches away. This was an elevator custom that always amused him, especially here in one of the friendliest countries in the world. The first sound he heard, in fact, was the elevator signaling its first stop on the seventh floor.

A small woman nudged him in the back and made her way toward the opening door. When people shuffled to let her out, Drake noticed the bulge of a weapon under the right arm of the tall blond at one o'clock in front of him. It automatically registered in his mind that the man was left handed and probably was a resident of California. It was, he knew, almost impossible to obtain a concealed carry permit in San Francisco. Non-residents couldn't even apply for one and permits from other states were not recognized. So either the man was on-duty law enforcement and a Californian with a concealed carry permit or he was carrying illegally. Drake wondered which it was.

The numbers above the elevator went up until they reached the twenty-fifth floor. The two blond men were now flanking Drake. The elevator stopped, the door opened, and he stepped out alone. As he walked down the hallway to his corner room, he felt the muscles in his shoulders relax. He knew he had experienced a subliminal response to the potential threat of the two men in the elevator. It was an unconscious alarm system that had served him well in the past, and it was one he trusted. Tonight, it was probably the sight of the tell-tale bulge under the man's arm that had set it off.

As Drake focused on inserting his card in the key card door lock, he failed to notice one of the blond men opening the door from the stairway at the other end of the hall. After watching him enter his room, the man stepped back into the stairway and sent a text message that they had found where the attorney was staying before returning to his partner waiting on the floor above.

EIGHTEEN

Before returning to the EIS office the next morning, Drake received a call from Kevin McRoberts, Mike Casey's young, white-hat hacker.

"Mr. Drake," McRoberts began, "Mr. Casey told me to call you and report my finding about the spear phishing at Energy Integrated Solutions. I hope I'm not calling too early. I worked on this all night, and I thought you'd want to know what I found right away."

Drake had just finished the omelet, toast, and coffee that room service had delivered at seven o'clock. "Not too early, Kevin. Fire away. Mike's told me a lot about you."

"Not all of it's true, Mr. Drake. A lot of things get blamed on me that I didn't do. I haven't done any of the black hat stuff since I started working for Mr. Casey. A lot of guys—"

"Kevin," Drake interrupted, "what did you find out?"

"Nothing. I didn't find anything. The security at EIS is top notch with very few vulnerabilities. The two I found, most people wouldn't, and they weren't serious ones. I didn't find any links to employees' mobile devices that could be exploited to access the EIS system. I hacked into all the competitors that were in the file they gave you. I couldn't find any connections to any of the EIS employees. All of the companies are doing well with plenty of business of their own. The spear phishing wasn't traceable. They were onion routed encrypted emails from all over."

"What's onion routing?"

"It's where they route traffic through at least three servers around the world. They used TOR software. That's free, open source software that hackers use. Volunteers run servers so the users' hacking can't be traced."

"If this hacker was that clever, why wasn't he successful?" Drake asked.

McRoberts paused to take a sip of an energy drink before continuing. "Using TOR software and onion routing is basic stuff, Mr. Drake. This guy was sending emails to everyone, just shot-gunning it. He wasn't world class, by any means. He just wasn't good enough to get what he wanted from EIS."

"Kevin, this is your field, not mine, so I'm relying on your expertise. In your opinion, does this spear phishing at EIS constitute a material risk to the company's business, operations, or financial results?"

"No way, Mr. Drake. There were no breaches of the system and no impact I can see. Other than being a nuisance."

"All right, Kevin, thank you. Send the bill for your time directly to EIS. Mr. Bradford's expecting it."

Drake refilled his coffee cup and walked to the window. The San Francisco Bay was covered in a low blanket of bright white fog that he hoped would burn off in time for a trail run through the Presidio. Advice that the spear phishing incidents didn't need to be reported to the SEC on the company's 10-K report would please the security analyst, counter the advice of corporate counsel, and leave Bradford without an explanation to explain his hunch that something wasn't right. But that's what he was able to determine. It was all he had been asked to do.

When he arrived at EIS, he was told that Bradford was on a conference call, so he detoured to the security analyst to tell him what he'd be advising Bradford when he saw him. Lewiston was at his desk, staring at one of his monitors.

"Got a minute, John?" Drake asked after he knocked on the door and was waved in. "I wanted to give you a heads up before I meet with Bradford. I'm advising him that, based on what I could find, there's no need to report the incidents you've been having to the SEC. Your security is top notch and your employees are being very careful, as you've trained them to be."

Lewiston looked up. "I suppose you're responsible for the guy who's been poking around our system," he said.

"I had to be sure," Drake said. "Mr. Bradford wanted a second opinion on the SEC reporting, but I'm not an IT expert. I can handle the legal end of things, but I needed an outside opinion. So I used a security firm that does threat assessments for a lot of high-tech firms."

Lewiston motioned for him to close the door. "Your guy's very good. In case I ever need someone to run a threat assessment, would you be willing to give me his name?"

"I don't see why not. Call me when you need it." Drake leaned over the desk and shook hands with Lewiston.

By the time he got back to Bradford's office, the CEO was off the phone writing in an open file on his desk.

"Come in, Adam. Did you get all the files you wanted to see?"

"Yes, thank you. I also had someone assess your security and try to trace the cyber attacks. He also checked out your DARPA competitors. Your security is very good, Bill. I think you know that the cyber attacks weren't traceable, as Lewiston told you, and we couldn't find anything that linked your competitors to any of this. In my opinion, there's no need to report these incidents to the SEC."

"My attorney won't like hearing that," Bradford said, "but I agree with you. I still can't shake the feeling there's something going on, though. I've learned to trust my instincts about such things, but there doesn't seem to be much more I can do. You think of anything?"

The CEO sat back in his chair and stroked his chin with one hand as he waited for an answer. The tightly pressed lips and slightly squinted eyes told Drake that Bradford wasn't finished worrying about whatever it was that was bothering him.

"Bill," he said, "I can't think of anything else. I'm going to be here for another day or so. I have a friend coming in from Las Vegas tomorrow night to meet me for dinner. If I think of anything else, I'll let you know."

"If you have the afternoon free tomorrow," Bradford said, "would you like to go sailing? I try to go sailing mid-week to avoid the weekend crowd. I'll bring the wine and some snacks, and we can leave from the marina here, say, one o'clock. You'll enjoy it," he promised.

"I'd like that. See you then." Drake left to return to his hotel and change clothes for an afternoon run.

NINETEEN

The five and a half mile run Drake had discovered on the Internet was called the Presidio Extreme. It began in the parking lot of the Sports Basement, a favorite athletic and outdoor equipment store near the Golden Gate Bridge.

He parked the borrowed Audi TTS and cut through the parking lot at a slow jog to warm up. Then he set off along the route he had memorized until he reached the Ecology Trail. Picking up his pace, he ran up the hills past Inspiration Point and then continued until he came to the sandy trail along the Lobos Dunes. By then, he was sweating lightly. Another mile and a half on the Coast Trail and then down the hill at Chrissy Field until he saw the sign of the Sports Basement in the distance. He finished the run with a sprint back to his car.

As he slowed to a walk in the parking lot, Drake savored the sensations that lingered from one of the best runs he'd had in a while. Judging by the number of customers he saw carrying merchandise to their cars, the Sports Basement was having a good sales day.

A white Subaru Outback was parked next to his Audi and a

woman was struggling to lift a new mountain bike onto a roof rack. An eight- or nine-year-old boy was trying to help her. "Need a hand with that?" Drake asked as he approached them. He unlocked the Audi with his key fob to show he was parked next to her.

The young Latina wearing a red 49ers pullover jacket and skinny jeans smiled cautiously. "Thank you," she said. "I can't lift it high enough. I should have brought my husband."

Drake took the bike from the woman as she moved to the rear of her car to give himself more room to lift. "Is this bike for you?" he asked the boy.

"It's my birthday today. I'm eight," was the proud answer.

With the bike's front tire fitted snuggly in the front loader on the rack, Drake stepped around the boy to lock in the back wheel. In his peripheral vision, he noticed a black Ford Explorer pull out of the next row to his left and move slowly toward them.

"There," he said as he reached to shake the hand of the birthday boy, "that'll keep it safe..."

The passenger in the Explorer had a blue bandana over his lower face and was pointing a Tec-9 semi-automatic pistol out the open window.

In an instant, as the shooter began firing, Drake pulled the boy down to the ground reached for his mother. The first bullets hit the woman in her right side and back. She staggered to her left, shielding her son from the shooter. As the SUV drove by, more rounds found their mark in her back and knocked her forward into Drake's arms.

As he lowered her to the ground, he also grabbed the boy's shoulder and kept him down until he heard the Explorer accelerate out of the parking lot. When he checked the woman for a pulse, he knew the sobbing boy beside him would never see his mother watching him ride his new bike.

He stood up and waved at two men looking at them over the roof of a nearby Camry. "Call 911! This woman's been shot!"

Then he turned to the boy and moved in front of him so he couldn't see his mother. "What's your name, son?"

"Jeremy. Is my mom dead?"

"I afraid so, Jeremy. I'm sorry," Drake lifted the boy into his arms.

One of the store's security guards ran up. He was talking on his two-way radio. "Ambulance and police are on the way," he said to Drake. "Is she...?"

Drake nodded and walked to the other side of the white Subaru. "Her purse is in the front seat. See if there's a number to call her husband."

He stood quietly, the boy's head resting on his shoulder, as a crowd formed and then parted as the first of the police cruisers made its way to them. He waited while they checked to see if the woman was indeed dead and then took control of the crime scene.

An unmarked police car drove up behind the two cruisers, and a detective and his partner got out. After a brief conversation with one of the officers, the detective approached Drake.

"I'm Detective Cabrillo. Is this your son?"

"No. I was just helping the boy's mother with his bike. His name is Jeremy. My name is Adam Drake. The Audi's mine."

"John," Detective Cabrillo said to his partner, "why don't you take Jeremy to our car while I speak with Mr. Drake."

Jeremy didn't want to be handed off.

"It's okay, Jeremy," Drake said. "I'll stay here until your dad comes."

When they were alone, the questioning began.

"What happened?"

Drake organized his thoughts. "I'd just finished my run

through the Presidio and was walking to my car. She was trying to get Jeremy's bike on the bike rack, but she wasn't tall enough. I offered to help. I noticed a black Ford Explorer pull out from that empty parking spot over there and drive toward us. The passenger had his window down and had a Tec-9 in his right hand. He had tats across his four fingers of his right hand and a blue bandana over his mouth. I pushed the boy down and reached for her, but the bullets hit her first. She fell against my car, which shielded me, and then fell forward in my arms. The Explorer roared off. I checked. She was dead."

"You noticed a lot in a few seconds," Cabrillo said. "What do you do?"

"I'm an attorney. Used to be a prosecutor up in Portland. I've tried a couple gang drive-by shootings. Blue bandana, tattoos on each of his four fingers, MS-13?"

"That's my guess," Cabrillo said. He pointed at the red 49ers jacket Jeremy's mother was wearing. "The Nortenos are a rival gang. Red's their color."

"She sure doesn't look like the gang members I'm used to seeing."

Cabrillo just shook his head. "You don't have to be a member," he said. "You just have to look like one. Be dressed in red. We'll know soon enough. Do you live here?"

"I'm doing some work here for Energy Integrated Solutions and staying at the Marriott Marquis." Drake handed the detective his business card. "I think that might be Jeremy's dad that just arrived. I'd like to say goodbye to the boy and go take a hot shower, if that's okay."

Sure," Cabrillo said. "Drop by tomorrow and make a statement and let me know when you're leaving the City. Thanks for staying with the boy."

Drake walked toward the police cruiser where a sad little boy was waiting for his father.

TWENTY

Rein Walkur took the news badly that MS-13 had failed to kill Adam Drake. He had agreed to pay way too much for what should have been a simple field exercise for an organization used to killing people. MS-13 was known for its brutal and indiscriminate lust for blood and its efficient methods. But maybe, Walkur thought, it was also just PR.

"Tell them they need to return the money," he shouted at his cartel contact on the other end. "Or the heads of the shooters. Unless *you* want to return the money, and the fee I paid you to arrange it."

Walkur slammed the phone down and took a deep breath. His connection to the Alliance, the creation of his grandfather after World War II that had been run by his father until he was killed, was more important than any one operation. Law enforcement's discovery of its connection to terrorism was something he could not risk.

It had been a delicate exercise in management—his specialty—to keep his client organizations working together for a common purpose. The *jihadis* wanted to rule the world and restore the caliphate, the old Muslim empire. The drug cartels wanted to profit from America's insatiable appetite for drugs. They also wanted to kill each other and, too often, to kill their golden goose when citizens grew tired of all the violence and tried to run them off.

His purpose, however, was to create lawlessness in the world that begged for a return of order that only a strong nationalist government like the one his forefathers had created in Germany in the first half of the 20th century. For that, he needed the efforts of both the *jihadis* and the cartels.

He did have something good to consider, he reminded himself. His plant at EIS was making progress and in position to infect the new security software. The cyber analyst in the Pentagon's Cyber Command he was blackmailing was also in place to steal a copy of the Stuxnet virus that had shut down the centrifuges in Iran. As soon as his own team modified the worm and his man planted it within the EIS software, his job was finished. Then he could return to South America and the safety of his fortress there.

But, first, he had to make sure his plans had not been compromised.

Walkur got up from his desk and poured himself a large snifter of Camus cognac. France was a miserable country, but they still made the best cognac. From the window in his study, he looked out over the San Francisco skyline to the east. The attorney he had failed to kill might, or might not, be the attorney Canaan had warned him about, but now he could not allow said attorney to become suspicious of Canaan or their operation. He needed to find another way to eliminate the risk.

Hardly even seeing the lights of the City, he ran through the catalog of his options. It was too soon for another accident. Heart attacks, car accidents, and drive-by shootings that connected Drake in any way to EIS would only lead to a more thorough investigation. A simple assassination would have the same result. Walkur needed something more subtle, something that would lead the authorities in a different direction.

A deadly encounter with a gay prostitute was an option...if there was anything that suggested the attorney was homosexual. But from what his men had observed at the Marriott, where Drake had ignored the obvious flirtation of a male prostitute at the bar, that wasn't an option. According to what Saleem reported, Drake liked to drive fast cars, but they missed their chance with that yesterday. The man ate alone, slept alone, and did his running alone.

Walkur considered the possibility of a female prostitute. Perhaps Drake would welcome companionship; a woman who could lower his defenses, among other things, until she could permanently cool his passion.

He called Canaan. "Are you alone," he asked.

"Why do you think I wouldn't be?" the younger man returned.

"Please, Saleem," Walkur sighed, "do you think I'm not aware of your pastimes? I'm calling because of them. Have you used our escort service since you've been here?"

"Why do you ask? Did someone make a complaint?"

"Answer my question!"

"The answer is no," Canaan said. "I can find my women without your services."

"Excellent. I want you to meet a woman and point Drake out to her. She may look like a high-class hooker to you, but she's very good at what she does. Pick her up tomorrow at noon at the terminal where you arrived last week and take her to lunch before you return to work. How is work going, by the way?"

"Don't worry," Canaan said. "When you deliver the worm,

there won't be a problem. I'm on the team, they have accepted me, and I have the access to the system you need."

Walkur stayed at the window gazing out across the Bay. The woman he was about to call had worked for him before. If there was one woman in the world he could trust to seduce a target and fulfill a contract, it was the Brazilian beauty who lived just an hour's flight away.

TWENTY-ONE

Drake reported to the office of Detective Cabrillo the next morning to give his statement regarding the drive-by murder of Jeremy's mother. He learned that she was a college graduate, that she and her husband had never been arrested, and neither of them had any known connections to street gangs in San Francisco.

"The only connection to violence I can find," the detective said, "is to you and that company you're working for."

"What's that supposed to mean" Drake asked.

Cabrillo put his digital recorder in his pocket. "That manager we found dead in his car Sunday morning worked at Energy Integrated Solutions. You're working for the same company."

"I thought he had a heart attack."

"We did, too, at first," Cabrillo said. "The medical examiner wants to run some more tests. He hasn't been able to link the marks on his neck to the cause of death, but he's suspicious. I talked to the detective handling it because you and the vic both work or worked for the same company."

"So you think EIS somehow connects his death and the drive-by?" Drake asked. "That's pretty thin, Detective."

Cabrillo grinned. "You were a prosecutor, Mr. Drake. You've probably seen cases that turned on thinner threads than this. Relax. It was just an observation. It only holds together if you were the real target MS-13 was gunning for. You weren't... were you?"

Drake thought of other close calls he'd survived in the last several months before he answered. "No one knew I'd be in that parking lot yesterday, so it's unlikely. You have any leads on the shooter?"

"I asked the Gang Task Force to see if any of their CI's know anything. I'm not hopeful. MS-13 has a reputation for hacking up snitches." Cabrillo signaled that the meeting was over by standing up and walking toward the door of the conference room. "You have a nice day, Mr. Drake. And thanks for coming in."

The detective's unlikely suggestion that EIS was the link between two murders in three days had been made without any knowledge of the problems Bradford's company was having. Drake's intuition was beginning to flash a warning light on his mind's dashboard as he left the police station. He'd told Cabrillo that no one knew he'd be in the Sports Basement parking lot, but he'd had no reason to be watching for someone following him. It was possible, then, but why?

Drake drove back to his hotel looking for signs of surveillance and wondering if he had missed something at EIS. Hacking and cyber attacks for the purpose of industrial espionage were more common than most people knew, but they usually didn't involve this kind of violence. He had read that nations like Israel, that were entrenched in cyber warfare with their enemies, received as many as a thousand cyber attacks a minute. He'd heard that one Israeli electric company had reported receiving 20,000 attempts in one day.

But even if EIS was involved in some cyber war that went beyond someone trying to steal intellectual property the company had developed, Drake asked himself, why would someone come after him?

He had planned on going home after meeting his friend, Mike Casey for dinner, but now he was beginning to think he might have to stay around a little longer.

He used the Audi's Bluetooth smart phone connectivity to call his client. "Are we still on for sailing this afternoon?"

"We are," Bradford said. "One o'clock at the marina."

"Good, because I think we need to rethink your situation."

Drake drove toward Fisherman's Wharf, where he intended to order a hot seafood platter at Capurro's. He'd let his subconscious mind work on the EIS puzzle while his conscious mind focused on crab cakes, Monterrey calamari, and beer battered jumbo shrimp.

SALEEM CANAAN PARKED his BMW in front of the Signature Aviation Support terminal and waited for Walkur's hooker. He didn't know what she could do to Drake that he couldn't, but it that's what Walkur wanted, so be it. He didn't mind taking the woman to lunch and getting to know her. It would save him a call to the escort service later.

He saw four men walk out of the private aviation terminal and hand their luggage to a limousine driver, and then turn, one by one, and look back into the terminal. A tall goddess of a woman was just leaving the reception area. Canaan was amazed that the buffoons were allowing her to pull her own rolling suitcase.

He was even more amazed when she walked past her gawking admirers and continued on toward him. *Dios mio,* he thought, could this be the woman he was sent to meet? He casually got out of the car and walked around it to meet her face to face.

She stood still, waiting for him like he was a bell boy dispatched to carry her bags.

"Are you Mr. Walkur's boy?" she asked.

He ignored the insult and took her suitcase. "Only if you're his *piriguete*."

She flashed him a tight smile and said, "Not one that you can afford, *morano*."

After her suitcase was stowed in the trunk and they were leaving the terminal, the Brazilian model, who had introduced herself as Adriana Hermann, said coldly, "Walkur needs to be more careful with the passwords he gives us. You may be used to being called boy and pig, but I do not let anyone call me a whore. I do many things for money, but not that."

"Isn't that what he wants you to do with the attorney?" Canaan asked.

"He wants me to kill him. How I choose to do that is my business."

TWENTY-TWO

Drake parked next to Bradford's Audi A8 and saw his white racing yacht waiting for him at the end of the dock. Judging from the yacht club pennant snapping on the club's flag pole, a steady wind out of the north was blowing up some white caps in the Bay off Hunter's Point.

It was warm, at least seventy degrees, and Drake left his windbreaker in the car. A yellow Oregon sweatshirt and a pair of jeans should be enough for the afternoon. He waved to Bradford and started down the dock.

"Permission to come aboard?" he asked brightly when he reached the yacht.

"Cast off the bow line and join me," Bradford replied. "It's a great day for sailing."

Drake slipped the dock line off the forward cleat and stepped into the rear cockpit and joined his host.

"Have you sailed the San Francisco Bay before?" Bradford asked.

Drake shook his head. "This will be my first time."

"Then we'll sail the Bay and give you the grand tour." He turned north and set his sails.

They had passed the central wharf area of San Francisco and sailed under the Bay Bridge before either man spoke. The view of the City from the water and the immense size of one of the longest bridge spans in the world was enough to silence both of them.

"I never get tired of the view out here," Bradford said. "It's the main reason I kept my business here, despite the taxes I get to pay for the pleasure. There's beer and Pepsi in the cooler if you're thirsty."

Drake opened the cooler on the floor and pulled out a bottle of Anchor Steam.

"What did you mean when you said we need to rethink my situation?" Bradford asked.

Drake opened the beer and took a pull. "I was involved in a drive-by shooting yesterday. The detective I met with this morning thinks I might have been the target."

"I read about the young mother who was killed. I didn't know you were involved. Why does the detective think you might have been the target?"

Drake steadied himself with a hand on the chrome handrail at the rear of the yacht. "Because the medical examiner is conducting tests to determine if your manager they found last weekend was murdered. He doesn't think it's a coincidence that we're both connected to your company."

Bradford reached for the electric winch controls and let some air out of the main and Genoa sails to slow the yacht down. "That doesn't make any sense," he said. "Nick Kawasaki was dead before you arrived. What possible connection could there be?"

"What was Kawasaki working on?" Drake asked as he sat down across from Bradford. The sails were flapping as they slowed and then stopped in the middle of the Bay between Treasure Island and Angel Island.

"The Defense Advanced Research Project for the Department of Defense," Bradford said. "We're developing security software to protect the country's electric grid from a virus like the one that devastated power plants in Iran. Nick was in charge of the team that was doing the final testing of the software."

"Do you think the DARPA project is the reason for the cyber attacks?"

Bradford pointed to the cooler. "Pass me a beer and tell me why you'd ask that."

Sitting in the middle of the San Francisco bay on a warm fall afternoon with a bottle of beer in his hand made it hard to think about dark conspiracies, but that's where Drake's mind was going.

"The Secretary of Homeland Security asked me to see you," Drake said, "I suspect that's because you told Senator Hazelton, my father-in-law, you didn't know how much you needed to report about the cyber attacks on your 10-K to the SEC. They're good friends, and both of them are involved in matters of national security. Since you're working on something that involves national security, it crossed my mind that Kawasaki's death, if it turns out that he was murdered, could be related to the DARPA project."

"But how would that involve you?" Bradford asked. "Even if he was murdered, which I hope to God he wasn't, you don't have anything to do with the software we've developed."

"I don't know yet. I was a prosecutor in Oregon. Maybe someone thinks I'm here because of his death. He dies on Saturday. I show up the next day. Who knew I was coming?"

"Just me," Bradford said as a power boat flashed by and its wake rocked the yacht. "Senator Hazelton called me last week to say you might be able to come down. I didn't mention it to anyone."

Drake watched as the sails were trimmed and they began to sail north toward another island. The possibility that he would investigate the death of Bradford's manager seemed like a pretty puny reason to send gang bangers to kill him, he thought. Unless there was a lot more going on than he was able to see right now. Kawasaki's death didn't seem to have slowed the project in any way. So why would anyone care that he was here?

"Show me the big picture," he said to Bradford. "I don't know a lot about the electrical grid, but I know it's an important part of our infrastructure. What's at stake here?"

Bradford smiled. It was a question the government didn't want the public worrying about. "Imagine a blackout that lasted all across the country and went on for months, maybe as many as six months," he began. "You saw what happened in the wake of Hurricane Sandy in 2012. With a catastrophic failure of the electrical grid not just around New York but all over the U.S., the loss would be unimaginable. No electricity means no lights, no heat, no water, no phones or Internet, no functioning gas stations, no banking services or money transfers. Grocery stores have enough food to last three days on average, so people will start to starve and then turn on those who have food. You'd have roving mobs looting and rioting. Gas supplies will be quickly used up and people wouldn't be able to go anywhere, wouldn't be able to escape the mobs even if they wanted to." Bradford paused to give Drake a minute to consider all this, then he went on.

"How many people do you know who have a week's supply of nonperishable food and water for their families, let alone two or three months' supply? If they did, would they be able to defend that supply when their neighbors thought they had to steal it or their children would die?

"Adam, our electrical grid is old. The average substation transformer is forty-two years old. That's two years older than the designed lifespan of a substation transformer. When transformers fail, we can't replace them quickly enough. They're huge. They have to be moved on flatbed rail cars Most of them aren't even manufactured here in the U.S. Our grid hasn't ever been modernized." Bradford shook his head. "It's mechanical equipment operating a digital world. I'm working on just one part of the system. And it might not even be the most important part. The whole system has to be made more resilient and more digital. The big picture is that a failure of the electrical grid and the infrastructure it supports is the Department of Homeland Security's biggest fear. It would destroy our country."

Doomsday lecture completed, Bradford sailed around Angel Island and without a word steered his yacht toward Hunter's Point across the Bay. Drake sat across the cockpit and looked at the city skyline set against the bright blue sky to the west. He didn't see how any of the dots connected, but he was beginning to understand what was at stake if they did connect.

TWENTY-THREE

Adriana Hermann watched Bradford's white racing yacht glide into a slip at the Hunter's Point Marina just as Walkur's boy had said it would. The attorney she was waiting for would be jumping off the yacht and going to his car, which was parked two rows over from her rented Mercedes E350 convertible. She had been waiting patiently, studying the file on the man from Oregon and thinking of how she would kill him.

There wasn't much in the file about her target. He'd played football in college as a linebacker, been in the army, and been a criminal prosecutor in Oregon. Recently widowed and apparently fit, she read. Observed working out in the fitness center at the Marriott Marquis where he was staying and running one of the trails in the Presidio the day before.

She watched as the two men prepared to leave the older man's yacht. The younger man looked to be a little over six foot tall and with good shoulders. He was wearing a sweatshirt, so she couldn't tell if he had six pack abs, but it wouldn't surprise her if he did. Well, she would soon find out. And it would be a pleasure to toy with him when he was paralyzed and couldn't use his strength to resist her.

At the end of the dock, the two men shook hands. The older man turned and walked toward the Hunter's Point Yacht Club and the younger man walked to the black Audi. He was careful, she saw, as he casually searched his surroundings.

She laid the file she'd been reading against the steering wheel and kept her eyes down as he got closer to his car. With the sunglasses hiding her eyes, she knew he couldn't see her watching him. But he could sense that he was being watched. She'd been taught that the human brain had evolved a gaze detection system that rang an inner alarm when someone was staring directly at them. She kept from turning her body and followed his movements with her peripheral vision.

This one would be a challenge, she told herself. If Walkur's information was correct, he had killed or been involved in the killing of seven terrorists in Portland, Oregon. Then, less than a month later, he had prevented an attempt to blow up a dam and killed another handful of terrorists at the same time. She wasn't planning on eliminating him by playing a game he was good at. There were more elegant ways. Beauty would have her beast, and when he was at her mercy, she would kill him in a most indelicate way.

Adriana Hermann was a German Brazilian, or *teuto-brasileiro*, and proud of it. Her ancestors had immigrated to Brazil in 1850 and settled in Vitória, the capital of Espirito Santo, the southernmost state of Brazil. Her father was a banker who had been active in the failed Nazi Party movement in Brazil before World War II. Through his connections, she had been recruited by the Alliance after she killed a man in self defense who had raped her. The Alliance had financed her modeling career and when she approached the age when runway models moved on to other careers, trained her to be its honeypot assassin. It had been an easy and satisfying career move, using sex to get men in bed so she could kill them in their sleep. And it paid well.

She waited until her target passed her car before she lowered his file and started her own car. When he reached the end of the parking lot and turned onto the street that led out of Hunter's Point, she followed him, expecting him to return to the Marriott Marquis where she had reserved a room. Instead, he turned left onto Third Street and drove south.

When he took the freeway entrance to Highway 101, she panicked for a moment when she realized he might be heading to the airport. Walkur's boy hadn't said Drake had checked out of the Marriott, but it was a possibility she had to consider. If he was leaving, did Walkur want her to follow him or would the contract be canceled? She decided to wait until she knew if he was leaving.

The black Audi stayed on the freeway until it took the exit to the San Francisco Airport, where it suddenly turned onto ramp to the Domestic Parking Garage. Adriana slapped the steering wheel with her hand and continued to circle the terminals with the rest of the traffic. None of the cars between her car and the attorney's had followed him into Domestic Parking, and she would have been right behind him when he stopped to collect his parking stub. She couldn't afford to be recognized yet. She had to break off surveillance.

But the good news was that she knew the Domestic Parking Garage was short-term parking only. It was unlikely that he would be parking there if he was leaving San Francisco. She made a quick call to the mansion that Walkur used when he was in the City and told his head of security to find out if her target had checked out of the Marriott Marquis. She had her answer before she completed one more lap around the terminals. According to the Marriott's computer system, which the

Alliance had hacked into when the attorney became a concern, Drake was still registered there.

Adriana Hermann drove out of the San Francisco Airport terminal area and got back on Highway 101. Her plan was to return to the Marriott to prepare for the night. The big orange sun was setting to the west and she had work to do.

TWENTY-FOUR

Drake waited for Mike Casey's Southwest Airline flight from Las Vegas to arrive in Terminal 1, and it arrived right on time. His friend was easy to spot, with his red hair towering above the heads of the other passengers. When Casey spotted Drake's face in the crowd, he smiled and walked over.

"How was Vegas?" Drake asked they turned and followed the herd to the baggage claim area.

"Profitable but boring," Casey said. "Eighty seven companies offering executive protection services to maybe thirty potential clients, and three days of speakers with nothing new to say. Every time some poor head of security said his company might be looking for a new security service, it turned into a shark feeding frenzy around him."

Drake chuckled and nodded. "Sounds like lawyers at a business conference," he said. "Did you get a room at the Marriott?"

"Yep. And I'm ready to do the town. How's your thing coming along?"

"I'll tell you over dinner. If you're still hungry."

Casey laughed. "Peanuts and pretzels just made me thirsty. Of course I'm hungry. Especially since you're paying."

They continued their friendly banter and small talk until Casey's luggage came riding along on the carousel. Within minutes after that, they were fastening their seatbelts in Drake's car.

"Did you rent this?" Casey asked as Drake drove to the exit of the parking garage.

"My client loaned it to me. He's into Audis and racing his forty-foot yacht when he's not developing software for the government." Drake paid at the booth and continued, "I thought you might like prime rib for dinner. That all right with you?"

"Excellent choice, says your ever-faithful gourmand. Are you back on your feed after that stint you did in the hospital last month?"

"Almost there, Mike. A few headaches still. I've recovered about ninety percent strength in my left arm. But I'm running again, and I'm getting faster. If my reflexes were as good as they used to be, before...well, I might have saved that woman Tuesday."

Casey turned in his seat to face Drake. "I thought this was just a consulting gig for this company."

"I did, too, but now I'm not so sure." He spent the rest of the ride to the hotel detailing his last four days in San Francisco. Casey wanted to check in at the Marriott, and Drake needed to change his clothes. The House of Prime Rib, the landmark restaurant at the foot of Nob Hill where he had reservations, didn't require a suit and tie, but he was still wearing the lightning yellow Oregon sweatshirt he'd worn sailing that afternoon. There was no need, he told himself, to blind the other dinner patrons with Nike's latest fashion statement.

An hour later, he handed his key to the parking valet at the restaurant and they ordered a round of drinks before dinner, Maker's Mark for Drake, Jack Daniels for Casey, Drake watched Casey studying his menu. No one he knew enjoyed eating as much his tall, thin friend.

"You look good, Mike," he said. "When we were slogging around the Middle East, did you ever think you'd wind up being the CEO of Puget Sound Security?"

Casey looked over the top of his menu. "I thought I'd be running the family ranch in Montana. Raising prime beef and selling it to places like this. If my folks hadn't decided to sell the ranch when mom got sick, you know, that's where I'd be right now. Did you ever think you'd be chasing bad guys again?"

Drake shook his head. "When we left the army, I wanted to be a prosecutor and put them in jail, not chase them like I've been doing lately," he said. "It's funny, we're both doing something closer to what we were trained to do in the army than what we were trained to do in college."

Their drinks arrived and Drake proposed a toast, "Here's to higher education and student loans."

When a red-vested waiter arrived to take their orders, Casey fulfilled Drake's expectations by ordering the extra-generous, thick-cut prime rib with all the trimmings. Drake ordered a smaller cut and a bottle of Chalone pinot noir.

"Mike, you help companies deal with cyber crime, right?" he asked after the waiter left. "So tell me...how aggressive are these cyber criminals?"

"How do you mean, *aggressive*? Their attacks can be very bold and relentless. Or extremely subtle. Are you asking if we also have to protect our clients from the more common types of theft, like burglary or robbery?"

"Yeah, I guess," Drake said. "If the detective is right and there's a connection between the ESI manager's death and the drive-by shooting in the parking lot, what does that accomplish when what they're after can be stolen without killing anyone?"

"It wouldn't accomplish anything that I can see," Casey said. "Which is probably why I haven't run into it before. Maybe the manager's death and the mother's death aren't connected," he offered. "Maybe the gang bangers were shooting at you because you're tall and good looking and you were standing with a woman, ergo, you're heterosexual. This is San Francisco, after all."

"Thanks, Mike," Drake laughed. "You're a big help."

By the time Casey had finished eating the slab of prime rib that been carved for him at their table and polished off an English trifle for desert, it was almost ten o'clock. Tables around them were being cleared for the night.

"That, my friend, was a treat," Casey said. "Thank you. I might not need breakfast tomorrow."

"I'll believe that when I see it," Drake shot back. "What time does your flight leave?" He slipped the credit card receipt in his wallet and thanked the waiter for their meal with a generous tip.

"Not until nine thirty in the morning," Casey said as they maneuvered around tables on their way out of the restaurant.

"I thought I'd run another of the Presidio trails," Drake said. "Come with me. It's a good way to work off that dinner. I'll also show you where the mother was killed. See if it reads like a drive-by shooting to you."

"If I run with you," Casey said as he threw his arm around Drake's shoulders, "I might need breakfast. Throw that in and I'll gladly allow you to chase me through the Presidio."

While they waited for the parking valet to bring Drake's car around, challenges were exchanged and bets made on their friendly jog the next morning.

TWENTY-FIVE

Adriana Hermann was waiting in her executive suite for a call from the lobby. After returning from the airport, she'd had nothing to do until one of the spotters confirmed that her target was alone in his room.

Her little black dress lay on the bed for now. She was naked, just as she would be when the man was paralyzed and wondering why there were stainless steel surgical tools on the nightstand. After she showered to make sure there were no signs of the little procedure she always performed on her victims, she would still need to leave his room without frightening people. So the tight little dress had to look as good coming out as it did when she went into his room.

To pass the time until the call came, she had showered, put on makeup for the night, and played solitaire on her iPad. Then, sitting patiently just in her black panties and bra, she checked email messages from her friends in Los Angeles and watched an episode of *Criminal Minds*. It amused her that so many people actually thought that profilers might understand how her mind worked. When she had killed the man who had raped her, her first kill, she hadn't been angry or revengeful, and she didn't have a daddy problem that made her do it, either. The man hadn't waited to give her the same pleasure he was having. That wasn't fair. Besides that, he had bad breath.

She didn't expect tonight's target to have bad breath. She hadn't seen him smoke, and he appeared to have good hygiene. The only bad odor she thought she would encounter would be his fear when he realized he was paralyzed and couldn't breathe. It was always in those first couple minutes, when she stood over men and looked down into their unblinking eyes, that she wished she could read their minds. Did they appreciate that they had been chosen to die at the hands of a beautiful naked woman? Did they know what a select group of men they were about to join? Men who were deemed by her employers to be so dangerous that only a beautiful woman could get close enough to kill them.

And that was what would make tonight special. The attorney was supposed to be good. She would know soon enough if that were true.

In her black leather clutch was a tiny Austrian-made spy gun with the poison dart attachment. She had already loaded the curare-tipped dart that would paralyze Drake within a minute and stop his breathing within four minutes. The clutch also held a black pen that had been modified to pick the hotel's electronic keycard locks. To exploit the vulnerability in the lock, all she had to do was push the pen into the DC port on the underside of the lock and it instantly opened. When she picked the lock to his door and stepped in, she would act like she'd had too much to drink. When she started to undress, a moment's hesitation on his part was all the time she needed to fire the dart gun. It had worked before, and she was confident it would work again. Men were such little boys when confronted by a naked woman.

The leather clutch also held latex gloves and her surgical tools. After she hung a *Do Not Disturb* sign on the door, she would have all the time she needed to clean up, return to her own room for a change of clothes, and leave the hotel before dawn. There would be nothing that could be traced to her, except the male body parts left on the night stand. These were the signature of the world's deadliest woman.

The call came at ten thirty. The attorney had returned to the hotel and was in his room on the twenty-fifth floor.

She walked to the bed and slid into her little black dress, slipped into her five-inch, black stiletto heels, and stopped one last time at the mirror in the bathroom to check her hair and lipstick. Her blue eyes searched her reflection for any flaw in her appearance and found none. She was ready.

TWENTY-SIX

Mike Casey threw his blue, hardshell, rolling Pullman on the end of the bed and sat down next to it. He'd had so much fun with Drake at dinner that he'd forgotten to call Megan, his wife, and let her know he was fine and would be home tomorrow, just as soon as he'd won his bet on the Presidio run. He checked his watch and saw that it wasn't past Megan's bedtime, so he decided to call before turning in.

"Hi, Megs," he said when she answered. "I didn't wake you, did I?"

"You know I can't sleep when you're gone. I'm working my way through Season One of *Downton Abbey* that I rented to keep me company. Are you and Drake back already? I thought you'd be out on the town."

"No. Drake's starting to show his age. I thought I'd get him to bed early."

"Be nice to him," she laughed. "You're older than he is. Maybe you're the one who needs to get to bed early after a week in Vegas. Go ride the trolley to the Buena Vista and have an Irish coffee. You've always wanted to do that."

"And if I don't, I suppose I won't hear the last of it. You're a hard woman, Mrs. Casey, forcing me to go out on a night when the moon is full in a place as strange as San Francisco."

"I am a hard woman," she laughed again, "and don't you forget it. Tell Adam hi for me. And be home before five. The children are going to surprise you and cook dinner."

Casey smiled at the thought of his two young children cooking dinner. He knew he would probably be feasting on mac 'n' cheese and garlic bread tomorrow night. That was the kids' all-time favorite meal.

But she's right, he thought. Ten-thirty is too early for two thirty-something studs to be in bed. "Drake'll just have to suck it up and deal with it," he muttered. "Besides, if he did need the rest and stayed up too late, he'd be that much easier to beat tomorrow at the Presidio. He retrieved his wrinkle-free sports coat from the closet and left the room with it draped over his shoulder. He knew Drake's room was on the twenty-fifth floor, but he didn't know the room number.

"Hope you're not in bed, buddy," he said when Drake answered his call. "Megan's making me take you out for a proper cup of Irish coffee. You up for that?"

"Is this about our run tomorrow? Some devious plan to make sure you win our bet?"

Casey laughed. "I'm sure I won't need a devious plan to win. You're forgetting I ran cross country in college. What's your room number?"

"I'm in 2535, last room at the end of the hall. Are you on your way now?" Drake asked.

"Just getting in the elevator. I'll be there in five."

Casey had the elevator all to himself for the ride up six floors. When the door opened again on 25, he saw that rooms 2501 to 2535 were down a hallway that angled off to the right and that rooms 2536 to 2571 were down a hallway to the left. He started down the long hallway, thinking about where the closest trolley car station was that would take them to the Buena Vista. Megan was right. He and Drake were too young to be in bed this early. Drake did have an excuse, though. He'd almost been killed in that explosion just a month ago.

Then he noticed a woman kneeling in front of her door at the far end of the hallway and fiddling with the key card lock. He hoped she wasn't drunk, because the last thing he wanted to do tonight was be accused of coming on to a vulnerable woman when he stopped and asked if she needed help.

As he got closer to her, however, he was surprised to see that she was trying to get in Drake's room. It was the last room on the right side of the hallway and that was the door she was trying to open.

"May I help you, Miss?" Casey said, possibly louder than necessary, as he approached. He noticed her small purse lying open on the floor beside her and that she was about to push a black pen up into the bottom of the key card lock on Drake's door. That's when he knew then she wasn't drunk and didn't need his help. She was using an electronic lock picking device to break into Drake's room.

As Casey reached for his cell phone to call security, the woman grabbed her purse and took out a tiny revolver with a funny attachment on the barrel. She kept the gun in her right hand pointed at his chest while she picked up the purse with her left hand.

"There's no need for that," Casey said as held his cell phone out to show her it wasn't a gun. "I'll just move against the wall and you can leave."

Casey saw that she was five foot ten in her stiletto heels and beautiful. She circled around him. He turned slowly, trying to get his cell phone pointed to get a clear shot of her face, when she shot him in the stomach and ran down the hallway.

As he fell back against the door of room 2535, he tried to call for help, but no sound came out of his mouth.

TWENTY-SEVEN

Drake, who was sitting at the work desk in his room, reading an email from his secretary, heard something crash against the door. If that's Mike, he thought, he needs some help with his hotel etiquette. That crash was loud enough to wake people up.

"That you, Mike?" he asked as he looked out through the peephole. When no one answered and he couldn't see anyone at his door, he cracked the door. His friend was lying on the floor.

"Mike! Can you hear me?" Kneeling down, he felt for a carotid pulse and found it racing. Casey's eyes were unblinking and staring up. He wasn't breathing. He tilted Casey's head back, made sure his airways were clear, and immediately started CPR, thirty chest compressions followed by two rescue breaths per cycle. After two cycles, Casey still wasn't breathing.

"Come on, Mike—breathe!" It was time to get help. "Someone call 911," he shouted.

The door across from his room opened and a man in blue boxers looked out.

"Call 911," Drake said. "He's not breathing." He continued his rhythm of chest compressions and mouth-to-mouth rescue breaths. He knew that if it was a stroke, he had to keep blood flowing to Casey's brain. But his heart was beating. He just wasn't breathing. Whatever it was, all he could do was continue CPR and pray that help would arrive soon.

The man across the hall came back in jeans and a T-shirt, talking with someone on his cell phone. "They want me to stay on the line," he said to Drake, "but the EMT's are on the way."

"Tell them he's not breathing." Drake paused and dropped down for two more rescue breaths. "But there's a pulse. I think he's conscious, but non-responsive. Male, thirty-seven, no known medical problems."

While the information was being relayed to the 911 operator, two women came out of their rooms and asked if they could help.

"Call the front desk," Drake responded. "Say there's a medical emergency on the twenty-fifth floor and keep an elevator available for the EMT's."

He maintained the CPR rhythm, but his broken left arm was starting to ache, and sweat was dripping from his chin onto his friend's blue shirt.

Jeans and T-shirt stepped back into his room and came back with a hand towel and wiped Drake's forehead. "Want me to take over?" he asked.

"I'm good for now, thanks," Drake said. "They say how soon the EMT's would get here?"

"Should be about now. Would one of you two women go stand by the elevator? Direct them down here when they arrive."

Drake continued checking for any sign of consciousness and for a carotid pulse each time he leaned down for the rescue breaths. He also kept praying that help would arrive soon. Very soon.

"They're here," the man across the hall shouted, as they heard the EMT's running down the hallway.

The lead EMT, whose name tag identified him as Harris, knelt down beside Casey and did a quick assessment while Drake continued CPR.

"Let's bag him," EMT Harris said as he got out of the way to allow two of his men to begin nonresponsive resuscitation.

Drake scooted back and watched as one man put a mask over Casey's face and held it there with both hands while a second man began squeezing the ventilation mask's bag. They were all watching to see that Casey's chest started rising with each inhalation. Satisfied, Drake nodded at Harris.

Harris nodded back. "Do you know this man?" he asked.

"Yes, he's my friend. His name is Mike Casey. Lives in Seattle."

"Do you know what happened?"

"He was coming to my room to take me out for an Irish coffee. I heard a crash against my door and found him here on the floor. I have no idea what happened." As Drake continued answering questions until the EMTs' yellow gurney was pushed down the hallway. "Where are you taking him?"

"San Francisco General Hospital Medical Center," Harris said. "It's three miles away. If you're coming, take a cab, the parking's lousy."

Drake stepped back into his room, grabbed his blazer and cell phone, and watched as they prepared to lift Casey onto the gurney. When they lifted him up, a small black object fell to the floor. Drake reached down to pick the thing up and follow the gurney. He froze.

"Harris," he called out, "you need to see this."

The dart was half an inch long with black feathering on the tail end.

"Don't touch it," he told the EMT, who squatted down for a closer look. "That's what happened to Mike. He's been poisoned."

TWENTY-EIGHT

When Drake arrived at the hospital, he quickly found Casey in the emergency room. EMT Harris was standing outside the curtain of his cubicle, talking to one of San Francisco's finest. Harris raised a finger, mouthed "one minute," and spoke to the officer for another minute before he joined Drake.

"They're testing the dart to see what kind of poison it is," he said, "but they think it's probably curare. If that's what it is, your friend's a lucky man. Your CPR kept him from suffocating. Unless there's some brain damage, he should make a full recovery."

"How soon will they know?" Drake asked.

"It shouldn't take too long if it is curare. They use an artificial curare, succinylcholine, in some surgical procedures, so they're familiar with it. You have any idea why someone would want to poison him?"

As the CEO of a security firm, Drake knew, Casey had probably made a few enemies, but he didn't know that Casey was worried about anyone. And none of them could have known that he was going to make a last-minute detour to San Francisco for dinner with a friend.

"No idea," he said. "I need to call his wife. Is the doctor with him?"

"She just left to check on the lab tests. Her name is Dr. Jessica Martin. I've got to finish my report. Good luck with your friend," Harris said as he offered his hand.

"Thanks." They shook hands. "And thanks for getting there so fast. I was starting to tire a little."

He pulled the curtain aside and saw that Casey was being attended to by two nurses in blue scrubs. He was breathing with the help of a ventilator now. "How's he doing?" he asked the nurse on the right side of the bed who was monitoring the ventilator.

"And who might you be?" she said without looking up.

"Adam Drake, his friend. I gave him CPR until the paramedics arrived."

She turned and nodded to him and smiled. "Nice to meet you, Mr. Drake. I'm Lucy Johnson. I'll send Dr. Martin to find you in the waiting room when she gets back. You'll have to ask Dr. Martin about his condition."

He didn't remember the last time he'd been dismissed so smoothly.

Without knowing Casey's condition, he decided to wait to call Megan. Instead, he called Larry Green, the man who managed the L.A. office of Puget Sound Security. Green was a retired police officer with a master's degree in criminology with whom Drake had worked before. He was also one of the best street cops he'd ever met. Until they learned who had poisoned Casey, and why, Green could arrange to have someone guarding him around the clock.

"I called the number on the back of the card you gave me," he said after Green had answered his phone. "I was hoping I'd reach you at home before you went to bed, but I didn't realize how late is was. Have a minute?"

"All night if you need it," Green replied. "What's up?"

"Mike Casey's just been poisoned. I'm with him here in San Francisco. I think he needs protection until we know what happened. Can you get someone up here?"

"How do you mean poisoned?" Green asked.

"Shot with a poisoned dart. Just like in the movies. The paramedics think it's probably curare, but the hospital hasn't confirmed that yet."

"So what the hell happened? Do they know who shot him? Where was he when he was shot? Is he okay?"

"Slow down, Larry," Drake said, "I can only answer one of those questions right now. He collapsed outside the door of my hotel room tonight about ten-thirty. He wanted to go out and get an Irish coffee and was coming to get me. That's all I know."

"Wow. Okay, I'll round up a couple of my men and head your way. Can you stay with him until I get there?"

Drake saw a petite young woman enter the waiting room and walk toward him. "I need to go," he said. "I think the doctor's here. And, yes, I won't leave him until you get here."

Dr. Martin extended her hand as he stood up to greet her. "Mr. Drake," she said as she pushed her wire-frame glasses up to sit above her short blond bangs, "let's go to my office so we can talk about your friend."

She led Drake through the emergency room to her office, which was down a short hallway lined with dictating stations for doctors and alcoves where monitors allowed staff to view medical records and test results.

A framed diploma from the Leland Stanford Junior

University School of Medicine was hung above a physician's license issued by the Medical Board of California on the wall behind her desk. Next to them was a beautiful abstract watercolor painting of red, pink, and purple flowers.

Dr. Martin sat down and leaned forward, with her elbows on the desk, her fingers steepled. "How well do you know Mr. Casey?" she began.

"We served together in the army," Drake said, "and he's my best friend. I guess I know him as well as anyone besides his wife. Why?"

"He appears to be in good shape. Does he have any major medical problems that you know of?"

Drake didn't like the direction her line of questioning was taking. "None that I know of. What's this about, Doctor?"

"Mr. Casey has been poisoned with curare," she said. "He should be breathing on his own by now, but he's either reacting in a strange way because of something peculiar to him or something peculiar about the curare. I'm trying to discover which it is."

"I thought there was an antidote for curare."

"There is. We administered an acetylcholinesterase inhibitor, which should have restored muscle function despite the presence of curare. It hasn't worked." She lowered her glasses and opened the file in front of her. "I see that he lives in Seattle. Is his wife here in San Francisco?"

"She's in Seattle. Mike was in Las Vegas for a conference and detoured here to have dinner with me tonight. I wanted to know how he was doing before I called her."

Dr. Martin stood up and took a business card from the middle drawer of her desk. "Why don't you call her and let her know he's here. Tell her I'd like to talk with her. I want to make sure he doesn't have a condition you're not aware of before I send a sample of this curare out for a more complete analysis than we can do here. Tell her he's in no immediate danger, but she should plan on coming down to be with him...just in case."

Drake left the doctor's office with a growing sense of concern. What the hell is going on here?

TWENTY-NINE

It was late the next morning, and Drake was trying to sleep sitting up in a chair that wasn't designed with his comfort in mind when Larry Green found him in the room Casey had been moved to earlier.

Green stood for a moment at the foot of the bed and watched his boss breathing with the help of the ventilator. "What's the doctor saying?" he asked.

Drake stood up and stretched. "She's having the poison analyzed. There's no reason he shouldn't be breathing on his own by now, if it's really curare. Otherwise, she says he's fine. Just paralyzed."

"Just paralyzed, that's all?" Green grimaced. "Is his wife flying down?"

"She gets in at twelve-thirty. Mike's brother is coming down with her."

"You don't look so good yourself," Green said. "Why don't you go get some coffee. I'll stay with him for a while."

Drake accepted Green's offer and walked down the hall to the waiting room, where he discovered that coffee had yet to be made by the day shift just now reporting for work. When he retraced his steps and found the elevator so he could search for the cafeteria, he was met by Detective Cabrillo as the doors opened.

"I hoped I'd find you here," Cabrillo said. "We need to talk."

"I'm headed to the cafeteria," Drake said. "We can talk there." He joined Cabrillo in the elevator. "How did you know to look for me here?"

"Your hotel told me when I asked to be put through to your room. I can be very persuasive. The manager's also my cousin," Cabrillo added with a smile. "I got the call about your friend being poisoned because I was on the Kawasaki case. What happened last night?"

Drake had given him the short version of events by the time they reached the cafeteria.

"Trouble seems to follow you in my city," the detective said as he loaded his tray with a bagel and some cream cheese to go with his coffee. "You have any idea why?"

"No. Do you?"

Cabrillo waved off Drake's offer to pay for his bagel and coffee and flirted with the young cashier before taking a seat at a small table near a window. "I think it has something to do with Energy Integrated Solutions," he said.

Drake watched the detective take a bite of his bagel and waited for him to continue.

"Nick Kawasaki was executed," Cabrillo said. "He was tasered and then lethally injected with potassium chloride, the drug we use to execute criminals. The medical examiner thought the taser might have caused a heart attack, and with the taser burns on his chest, that was the easy conclusion. After you were involved with the drive-by shooting, though, I asked them to take a closer look. They found the potassium chloride, but they didn't find any trace of the two other drugs that are used in legal state executions. Without those other two drugs, Kawasaki died a horrible death."

"That doesn't mean that Mike's poisoning is connected to Energy Integrated Solutions or my consulting there," Drake said, challenging Cabrillo's reasoning. "Kawasaki was killed before I arrived."

"It's possible. But my money's on the energy company. And I didn't say it was connected to your consulting. I think it's connected to the company itself. Maybe something they're working on. Or intellectual property someone's trying to steal. Maybe it's the Chinese. They're stealing our companies blind, I hear."

Drake didn't tell Cabrillo about the cyber attacks the company had been experiencing. The reason he had been asked to pay a visit to EIS was to keep the problem out of the news. If Cabrillo launched an investigation into Kawasaki's death and started poking around, it would mean headlines in no time. But he was willing to consider the possibility that recent events were connected to the company and work it was doing for the government.

He had a question of his own. "Have you checked the closed circuit video surveillance at the hotel? Is Mike's attack recorded?"

"Yes, but it doesn't identify his attacker. It shows a woman kneeling in front of your door, then Casey walks down the hall. When he gets closer, she stands up and walks back toward the elevator. Casey backs up against the wall and then falls against your door. It looks like he tried to get a shot of her face on his cell phone, but he only got from her chin down. We never get a good look at her face on the CCV either. " Cabrillo paused. "Were you expecting a visitor?" he asked.

"No, I wasn't. And I don't like your insinuation."

"I'm not insinuating anything, Mr. Drake. We're accustomed to businessmen being visited in their rooms late at night by working women. I'm not making a judgment about your sex life. I'm trying to find the person who poisoned your friend."

"Look, Cabrillo, I don't use prostitutes, and I don't have any idea who this woman was. But you must have seen enough on the hotel's surveillance video to have some idea."

"Like I said," the detective repeated, "the video doesn't show her face. She held her purse up in front of her face on the way to the elevator, then took the stairs down. Great body. Tight black dress. She's a pro. She knew where the security cams were, and there's no video of her leaving. She could have slipped out or still be in the hotel, for all we know."

Which meant that he, Drake, was the target. The woman had been at his door. She'd had no way of knowing that Casey would show up when he did. He was the reason his friend was paralyzed and in a hospital bed upstairs.

"Detective," Drake said as he stood up, "I need to get back and see how Mike's doing. If you need to talk with me, I'll be in town until this gets resolved."

Resolved on my terms, Drake promised himself. *On my terms.*

THIRTY

Adriana Hermann was now standing at the window of her room at the Marriott Marquis, waiting for a male companion to arrive. The rising sun was beginning to put an end to a night she wanted to forget. But she knew her employer wasn't about to let that happen.

To minimize the risk of being identified, she had been ordered to wait for a man who would pose as her husband and leave the hotel with her. In her entire career, she had never needed a man to help her carry out an assignment, and she didn't think she needed one now. But she had never failed before.

Everything had gone as planned...until Mr. Helpful had shown up at the target's door. She should have been warned. No one bothered to tell her that the attorney had a friend or that they had returned to the hotel *together*. She would have waited if she'd known, waited until she was sure she wouldn't be interrupted.

But her employer didn't want to hear any excuses. He just

wanted her safely out of the hotel. And that made her nervous because the fake husband was to be the charmer who had picked her up at the airport.

She was good at reading men. It was a prerequisite for her line of work. But this young man with the looks of a Latin movie star that Rein Walkur was sending to her had the eyes of a snake, a viper that would just as soon kill her as try to kiss her. If the Alliance was concerned that her failure to kill the attorney would somehow be traced back to it, if Walkur had decided to terminate her contract permanently, her soon-to-be fake husband was the right man for the job.

Saleem Canaan, aka Anthony Capelli, knocked softly at the door of Adriana's room at seven-twenty. When he slipped into the room, the first thing he saw was her Walther PPK. It was aimed at a spot between his eyes.

"Walk to the bed and lie down on your back," she commanded.

"You don't need a gun," he smiled, "if that's what you have in mind." He obeyed her instruction.

She walked to the foot of the bed and pointed the gun between his legs. "If I wasn't ordered to leave here with you," she said, "you would die right here. I would do to you what I was going to do to the attorney."

"But that's why I'm here," he said. "Isn't it? You failed to kill him."

"He is alive because Walkur's spotter failed to tell me he returned to the hotel with a friend," she said softly. She kept the gun pointed at his groin. "You would be wise to remember that I was the one Walkur chose to kill him. Not you. Did you park your car, or do you need to call the valet to have it brought around?"

"I parked it myself," Canaan said. "Why don't you put that

gun away. We both know you're not going to use it. I'm essential to Walkur's plan, and you're not crazy enough to screw this up for him."

"You have no idea how crazy I am," she said. She walked over to the window. "Get up and get my luggage. We'll walk out of this hotel with smiles on our faces, but don't think for a moment I won't kill you if you try anything. You may be essential to Walkur's plans. But you're not essential to mine.

Keeping a smile plastered on his face, Canaan did as he was told.

Even though Adriana Hermann knew all about Saleem Canaan and his reputation as a smart operator and fanatic Islamist, she wasn't impressed. *He thinks he could take me anytime he wanted to,* she thought. *And enjoy himself. But he doesn't know how good I am and how unimportant he really is in the scheme of things.*

Walkur and the Alliance used terrorists when the opportunity presented itself, but she knew something Canaan did not. The Alliance didn't trust Muslim *jihadis* anymore now than the Germans had trusted the Arab Nazi collaborators in World War II. They were just pawns who let their hatred of the Jews make them the perfect patsies for an operation as subtle as the one Walkur was running. When the big blackout in America happened, it wouldn't be the Alliance that was ultimately blamed. It would be Canaan and the two solar CEO's it would be made to appear he was working for.

Rein Walkur was too smart to have made this man essential to his plan. He would have a backup and a backup to that backup. But he was also smart enough to remind her, by sending Canaan, that failure was not acceptable and that she would have to make it up to the Alliance. She hoped that would be by killing Canaan.

Adriana Hermann walked beside her *faux* husband down the hallway to the elevator with a smile that matched his as she cherished the thought of revenge.

THIRTY-ONE

When Drake got back to Casey's room, he found Larry Green talking with a nurse in the hallway and Dr. Martin standing at the foot of the bed and writing on the chart. He knocked lightly on the door and entered the room.

"Good morning, Dr. Martin," he said.

"I believe it will be good, Mr. Drake," she said. "The tests that we ran confirm your friend was poisoned with curare, a synthetic curare on steroids that someone developed. We've induced a coma so that he will relax and recover faster. We'll let him rest a little longer and then bring him out of the coma this afternoon and see how he's doing."

"Thank you, Dr. Martin," Drake said with a quick fist pump. "That's great news. His wife should be here by that time. You said a 'synthetic curare on steroids.' Any idea who developed the stuff?"

"It's not something that's commercially available," she said, "so I have no idea who developed it or why. I can't conceive of a purpose for enhancing the poison to prolong the paralysis."

Unless it's to make sure someone dies, Drake said to himself.

"You've been here all night," she continued, "why don't you and Mr. Green go get some rest or something to eat. We'll keep a good eye on him while you're gone."

"I think we will, thanks, Doctor."

Drake left Casey's room and motioned for Green to follow him. "I'm going to get something to eat," he said when Green joined him at the elevator. "Why don't you join me. We need to talk."

Larry Green, a former LAPD lieutenant in the Metro Division, had supervised a platoon that dealt with counter-terrorism. He'd also been a member of the division's SWAT team. When he was wounded in a raid on a Somalia safe house and later met Mike Casey at a conference on Security in an Insecure World while on medical leave, Casey had offered him a management position in Puget Sound Security. Currently in charge of the PSS branch office in Los Angeles, Green had maintained a close relationship with the Metro Division.

When they were seated in a small café a block away from the hospital and had placed an order, Drake told Green he wanted to find the woman who had poisoned their friend.

"Larry," he said, "the detective handling Mike's case found me when I left for a cup of coffee. He told me the hotel's closed circuit security video doesn't identify Mike's attacker because she kept her purse in front of her face. They believe she's a pro. I think I was her target, not Mike."

Green added cream to his coffee and said, "Why do you think you were the target?"

"Because she was trying to get into my room and because it's the second time this week I've been close to someone either killed or attacked. As Detective Cabrillo reminded me." He next told Green about the drive-by shooting and the mother who'd been killed two days earlier.

Green gave all this some thought. "I haven't heard of a

female assassin using curare," he said, "but that doesn't mean there isn't one. Does SFPD have a good description of her?"

"Cabrillo said she had a great body and was wearing a tight black dress. That's not much to go on."

"Maybe. But the security video may allow us to scan every great looking woman coming and going in the hotel and narrow it down a bit. I might even volunteer for that duty," Green said with a grin. "But tell me, why would you be her target?"

"That's what I can't figure out."

When their food arrived and they had a chance to savor their omelettes, Green continued his questioning. "Could this have anything to do with the guy who tried to blow up that dam in Oregon?" he asked. "Homeland Security kept your name out of the media when you stopped him, but maybe someone he was involved with found out it was you."

"But why me?" Drake asked. "You were there with Casey, too. And the rest of his team. Has anyone targeted you? If that's what this is about, why wait until I'm in San Francisco?"

"What are you doing in San Francisco, by the way? Could it be connected?"

Drake shook his head. "I don't see how. I met with a company that wanted a second opinion on a SEC reporting matter. I was supposed to return to Oregon today with Mike. Would you be willing to meet with Detective Cabrillo and see if he's turned up anything on Mike's attacker?"

"Sure. I'm not leaving anyway until I know Mike's out of the woods," Green promised. "I'll also check with LAPD Metro and find out if they've heard of a lady assassin who has a great body and favors curare."

When Green mentioned contacting the LAPD Metro division, Drake remembered that he, too, had someone he could reach out to, someone with the resources to conduct a worldwide search for Casey's attacker. His liaison with the Department of Homeland Security, Liz Strobel, had access to anything the other alphabet agencies of the federal government might know. Since he was in San Francisco as a favor for the Secretary of DHS; it was the least she could do to help.

THIRTY-TWO

After a quick check to see that Casey's condition hadn't changed, Drake found an empty waiting room and called the Department of Homeland Security in Washington, D.C.. .

"Liz," he said as soon as the receptionist put his call through, "do you have time to answer a few questions for me?"

"Give me a moment to finish what I'm working on," she said, "and I'm all yours."

He heard her keyboard clatter for half a minute, then she was back.

"Are you in San Francisco," she asked.

"I am, and I need to know why. What haven't you told me anything about the company the Secretary asked me to visit?" He knew that she was expecting the cold tone of his voice when she took too long to answer his question. He considered her to be a friend, but with the guilt he was feeling over the attack on his buddy, he was tired of walking through a minefield without a map.

"What's happened?" she finally asked.

"Mike Casey is in the hospital. Paralyzed. Poisoned. I suspect I was the actual target, so I need to know if it has anything to do with Energy Integrated Solutions. Why was it important for me to go to EIS?"

"Oh my God," she gasped. "Adam, I'm so sorry! Is Mike going to be okay?"

"His doctor thinks so. He was poisoned with a potent synthetic curare. They put him in an induced coma. What's going on, Liz?"

"Adam, I don't know. Let me close my door. Then I'll tell you everything I know about EIS."

As he waited for a minute, Drake thought of the last time he had seen her. He'd been released from the hospital and she had driven him home from Bend to his farm outside of Portland. The terrorist who had smuggled a nuclear demolition device into the country, and tried to blow up a dam with it, had booby-trapped the resort home he was using as his headquarters. He'd been about to enter the home when the terrorist had detonated Semtex and buried him in the rubble. Liz had stayed in Oregon until he'd been released, and then returned to Washington and her job as the special assistant to the Secretary of Homeland Security.

"You know what EIS is working on," she said when she returned, "and you know about the cyber attacks on their systems. William Bradford called your father-in-law. He was worried about an SEC requirement to report all threats that investors had a right to know about. So Senator Hazelton asked Secretary Rallings to send you to troubleshoot the matter for him so an official investigation by DHS wouldn't leak to the media and spook the company's investors. Secretary Rallings agreed. We had intel from our Intelligence and Analysis section from a source that Iran is planning to retaliate for our Stuxnet attack on their nuclear program."

"What does that have to do with EIS?" Drake asked.

"The retaliation is supposed to target America's energy grid."

"But EIS isn't on the energy grid. I don't understand."

"We don't have anything that suggests EIS is the target. The Secretary just wanted to make sure the phishing attacks at EIS aren't somehow connected to the Iranian threat. Bradford's concern about the SEC reporting was an easy way to get you in there to check it out."

"Hmmm. Does Bradford know about the Iranian threat?"

"We didn't tell him, but it's the kind of cyber attack his software is designed to defeat. He wouldn't be surprised to learn of it," Strobel said. Then she switched gears. "Who poisoned Mike? Tell me it wasn't an Iranian."

"I don't know who the woman is. The detective who's handling the case says the security video shows that Mike surprised a good-looking woman trying to get into my room. She shot him with a poison dart. Apparently you don't get a good look at her face on the video."

"Adam, if you can send me the closed circuit security video, I can get the FBI to run it through their new facial identification system. Even if the video doesn't show her face, we can identify a person from a tattoo or any other distinguishing feature. We can scan street photos from street corner CCTV cameras or the security cameras at our airports. You get me the security video from the hotel, and I'll find Mike's attacker."

"Thanks. Larry Green is running Mike's LA office. He's keeping an eye on Mike now. I'll tell him to get the video to you."

"By the way," Strobel said, "what's a good looking woman doing trying to get into your room? Were you expecting someone?"

"You sound like Detective Cabrillo," he said, his disgust

clear in his voice. "Asking if I had arranged for female companionship that night. No, I wasn't expecting anyone. And I don't pay for sex."

The uncomfortable pause that followed made him think she was either embarrassed by his admission or doubted that it was true. Either way, it was none of her business. "Look," he said, "I've got to get back. Mike's wife is arriving from Seattle, and I want to be there to reassure her he's going to be okay."

"Tell Mike I'm pulling for him," Strobel said. "And you be careful, all right?"

Drake ended the call and left the waiting room, thinking about the remote possibility of an Iranian connection to the violence swirling around his visit to San Francisco.

THIRTY-THREE

Rein Walkur was waiting impatiently for Saleem Canaan to arrive. He had summoned the young Hezbollah commander to his mansion as soon as he'd learned that the man Adriana Hermann had poisoned was, unfortunately, alive and expected to make a full recovery. If she was identified as the woman who had poisoned him, it was possible that she could be traced back to the Alliance. That was a risk Walkur could not take.

During the past ten years, Adriana Hermann had fulfilled contracts in Europe, the Americas, and the Far East for the Alliance without a single failure. In only one killing had she left evidence that could identify her, and that had been a witness who quickly went missing. But now there was a witness who had seen her face and perhaps a hotel security video that might also identify her.

Walkur knew that he would have to proceed very carefully. Adriana knew her failure made her a liability. She had in fact terminated Alliance men who had failed him in smaller ways than she just had. And she was good, very good, at analyzing situations and anticipating risks. There wouldn't be many opportunities to get close to her, and having a sniper kill her from a distance would only invite an investigation. Adriana Hermann was a celebrity model who, even though it was late in her career, was still well-known and popular. The fashion shoot she was doing in Los Angeles was proof of that.

What he needed was a plan that maximized success and minimized the risk of exposing her work for the Alliance in any way. A plan that perhaps eliminated both Adriana and her killer at the same time. A plan executed in a way that would leave no doubt as to her killer's motive or identity and still conceal her work for the Alliance.

Walkur closed his eyes, massaged his forehead, and let his mind sort though the options that came up. As the solution slowly formed, he smiled at his own brilliance. He would give some martyr a chance to reach paradise and make a real difference on the way.

When his blond bodyguard, one of the two who had spotted Drake at the Marriott, announced that Canaan had arrived, Walkur directed that he be escorted to the basement, where his two programmers had just finished modifying the malware he had purchased from the cyber analyst in the Department of Defense. "Purchased" wasn't the right word, of course; he had blackmailed the analyst with his online gambling debt that, if discovered, would have cost him his job. But Walkur preferred to think of the transaction as a purchase. He had at least *promised* to wipe out the $78,000 debt if the man handed over a copy of the Iranian malware he was analyzing.

Canaan was talking with one of the programmers when Walkur entered the basement room that housed his communications and IT system manager's control room. The mansion had been the consulate for Kuwait before Walkur was allowed to purchase and remodel it to serve as the North American headquarters for the Alliance. He was able to direct the financial holdings of his organization from this mansion when he was away from his base of operations in Asuncion, Paraguay. The Alliance maintained similar facilities in London, Munich, Vienna, Tokyo, Singapore, and Dubai.

Now Walkur beckoned Canaan and led him to the IT manager's office. When they were inside with the door closed, he told the younger man that the malware that would be used to infect the EIS software was ready.

"Your work at EIS is almost finished," he said. "The last modules are coded and added to the virus. All you need to do is use the thumb drive at your work station. Because this is a new virus no one's ever seen before, the anti-virus program they have won't detect it. The attack on the grid transformers is set for next week when the software you've run the final tests on has been shipped to all the major utilities. At that time, you are to thank EIS for allowing you to work on the project, say that working there isn't what you had hoped it would be, and terminate your employment. By the time America goes dark in the big blackout, you will have disappeared."

"I thought you wanted me to take care of the two solar guys before I disappeared," Canaan said.

"You'll have plenty of time for that," Walkur assured him. "They'll be in Lake Tahoe early next week before they attend a big solar power convention in Reno. Pay them a visit and terminate our relationship."

"You still want it to look like suicide?"

"Indeed I do. A double suicide. And be sure to leave a note I've prepared with the bodies. It says how sorry they are for the damage they caused the country. The suicide note will lead the authorities to their offices, where they will find copies of the malware virus that caused the blackout."

Walkur could see from the gleam in the young man's eyes that he was eager to get to the killings.

"But before that happens," he said, "I need your help with another matter."

"The attorney?" Canaan asked.

"No, but you're close. Adriana Hermann. I'm concerned that she will be identified. I want her silenced before that happens."

Canaan couldn't help but smile. "That will be a pleasure. We didn't hit it off."

"Although I'm sure you tried, correct? She's a very attractive woman. But she's more than you can handle, I'm afraid."

When Canaan started to protest, Walkur held up a hand. "I want you to arrange for a martyr to make a statement against the disgraceful way women these days flaunt their bodies. Then he can take Adriana with him to paradise." This time it was Walkur's turn to smile.

"You want her killed by a suicide bomber?" Canaan asked. "Isn't that taking a big chance? What if the martyr is discovered or loses his nerve? I can think of a lot of ways to get the job done with a better chance of success."

"Do it my way. You detonate by remote control so nothing's left to chance. The *jihad* gets a nice headline, and we give the authorities an easy-to-believe explanation for Adriana's death. Can you do this job?"

"How long do I have?"

"The sooner, the better. She's in Los Angeles finishing a photo shoot on the *Queen Mary*. I'll get you the details in time for you to plan something for this weekend. Can you arrange it by then?"

"That's the day after tomorrow!" Canaan exclaimed. "I'd better get going. I'll be at EIS until six or so. I'll start making arrangements as soon as I get off work. Use my email and send me as much information about her as you can by the time I get to the condo."

Walkur led Canaan out of the IT manager's office and nodded to his bodyguard to escort the younger man out. As much as Canaan wanted to claim the kill, Walkur knew he was no match for Adriana Hermann. When Canaan failed to kill her, as he surely would, based on what Walkur knew of her extraordinary skills, she would know who was responsible for the attempt and come after him. That was not something he wanted to worry about.

THIRTY-FOUR

After Larry Green left Mike Casey's hospital room to arrange for the security video from the Marriott to be sent to DHS, Drake waited beside his friend's bed and watched the steady rise and fall of his chest.

As long as he'd known Casey, from the days in Iraq when he had first teamed up with the tall, gangly sniper from Montana until now, he had never seen him unconscious or injured in any way. There had been plenty of opportunities for him to take an injury, but he always landed on his feet. He was like the solid, steady, fifth-year senior who never missed a game in his college basketball career.

Seeing him lying in a hospital bed now, on a ventilator, Drake was feeling injured himself, knowing it was because of him. He didn't understand why yet, but he thought Detective Cabrillo was probably right. He had been the target twice in the last two days. Now he had to consider the possibility that it might involve an old enemy from the Middle East.

Mike, he thought as he stared at his friend, *I need you wake up, buddy. You're good at helping me work through things. Your wife is going to figure it out that this is my fault, and I'm not going to know what to tell her. I need you to be able to think things out while I watch you eat, which happens a lot because you're always eating, and it gives me some quiet time to think. Not that I don't like it when you crack one of your dumb jokes, trying to get me loosen up, 'cause I do. I just don't always get your jokes. And I'm not being critical of you eating all the time. You burn calories at such a rate you can eat all day and never gain any weight. I'll bet your wife wishes she could eat as much as you eat. Now I'm not saying that Megan needs to watch her weight, just that we all marvel at the way you can put it away. And your kids are just like you. Lean. I started to say "lean and mean," but that's not what I meant, Your kids are great and it's an honor to be called Uncle Adam. I promise I'll get up to Seattle more often to see them...well, once my life settles down and I can get back in a routine. It's been rough since Kay died a year ago, but I know you know that. I'm not using that as an excuse. I've just been in a bit of a fog, trying to figure out what I'm doing with my life. I had it all planned out when I married Kay. Kids, life on the farm, restoring the old vineyard, my law practice.*

I wish I'd settled down sooner like you did. You've got a great wife and kids who are always waiting for you, so don't mess things up this afternoon and do something stupid like die when they bring you out of the coma. Larry Green is here to help Megan get you home, so don't worry about that. The doc hasn't told me how you'll feel when the paralysis wears off, but I'm counting on you being fine. You'll be fine, Mike. I know that. If you aren't, I'll be there to help you if you need help. Like you're always there to help me. I probably should have told you sooner that I think of you as my brother. Not just because we were in the sandbox together. You're my best fr—

"Did you say something," Green asked as he walked into Casey's room.

"Sorry," Drake said as he rubbed his eyes before he stood up and stretched. "I must have been thinking out loud."

"I spoke with the head of security at the Marriott. He's sending the security surveillance video to Liz Strobel for us."

"Thanks, Larry. Let's hope the FBI's recognition system is as good as they say it is. If we can find the woman who poisoned Mike, maybe we can figure out what's going on. Did you get ahold of Megan before she left Seattle?"

"She was at the airport when I called. I offered to pick her up when she arrives, but she said she'd take a cab. She doesn't want Mike left alone."

"Damn it," Drake said, shaking his head, "since the detective said he thought I was the target, not Mike, I haven't thought about making sure he was protected. He can identify his attacker when he wakes up. She might want to make sure he doesn't."

"I'll get someone from our LA office up here to stand guard. Any idea how long Mike's going to be here?"

"We won't know until he's brought out of his coma," Drake said. "I better let my office know I'll be here a little longer, too. I have a feeling my consulting job here isn't gonna be done until I find out who sent the lady with the poison dart."

THIRTY-FIVE

Megan Casey, accompanied by her husband's brother, Philip Casey arrived at the hospital at one o'clock. She maintained her composure out in hall as she introduced her brother-in-law to Drake and Larry Green, and then she entered the hospital room to kiss her husband's forehead and stand holding his hand as she cried. When she came out of the room, she marched past the three men to a nurse and asked to see Dr. Jessica Martin as soon as possible. She stayed at the nurses station, watching the men from a distance.

"How's she doing?" Drake asked Philip Casey.

"Scared to death. But she's keeping it together. She a nurse, so she knows how curare is used as an anesthetic. She's scared because Mike should be breathing on his own by now."

"Mike's doctor says the synthetic curare on the dart that hit him is curare on steroids," Drake said. "But she also says he'll be okay. His recovery is just taking longer that she expected."

"Let's hope she's right. What the hell happened?"

"We don't know. Mike confronted a woman apparently

trying to pick the key card lock on my door at the Marriott. He backed away, but she shot him anyway."

"So this didn't really have anything to with Mike?"

"She was probably coming for me. I don't have a clue why."

"That's good news, I suppose, for Mike. Not so much for you, though. Have you told this to Megan?"

Drake shook his head. "Not yet. I haven't had time."

"Well, she may or may not be relieved. She's pretty insistent that he leave the field work to guys like Larry and the others. They had quite a spat when he helped you with that assassin thing last month."

"Thanks for the heads up, Phil," Drake said. "Mike didn't mention it."

Drake nodded toward the nurses station. They could see that Dr. Martin had her hand on Megan's shoulder and was talking to her. Together, the two women turned and walked their way.

"Gentlemen," Dr. Martin said brightly, "let's see if Mr. Casey is ready to join us." She led them into the room.

It took under ten minutes for the first sign to show them that her patient was coming out of his coma.

"As I told Mrs. Casey," Dr. Martin explained as she closely monitored his progress, "I didn't induce a coma because I felt that his brain needed to rest due to oxygen deprivation. Mr. Drake got CPR started almost immediately. I induced the coma because the breathing tube is irritating and the coma makes it a little easier to tolerate."

When Mike Casey's eyes opened, he seemed surprised to see all the people standing around his bed.

The doctor leaned down to him. "Mr. Casey, I'm Dr. Jessica Martin," she said. "I want you to relax. You have a breathing tube down your throat, so I don't want you to talk right now. I want you to squeeze my hand. Can you do that for me?"

When Mike blinked once and tentatively squeezed her hand, Dr. Martin moved around his bed and asked him to do the same thing with his other hand. She then moved to the foot of the bed and had him push against her hand with both of his feet.

"That's good, Mr. Casey," she said. "I want you rest now for a little longer, and then we'll see if you're ready to get that breathing tube out. I know that will make you happy."

Then she turned to the others and said, "The paralysis is not as profound, but his responses are still weak. We'll see how he's doing in a couple of hours. He'll enjoy having you beside him, Mrs. Casey. You may tell him as much as you want about what happened, but he might not understand what you're telling him. Just let him know everything will be okay in time."

As Dr. Martin smiled at her patient and left the room, Megan Casey moved to her husband's side and began to reassure him that everything was going to be okay.

Drake followed the doctor and caught up with her at the nurses station. "Dr. Martin," he said as she interrupted her charting to look up at him, "does the lab analysis of the curare Mike was poisoned with explain why it's taking so long for him to recover?"

"We don't have the expertise to determine that," she said, "but I sent a sample to the toxicology lab at the California Department of Justice. I'm waiting for the results."

"Will those results tell us anything about who produced the poison?"

"I doubt it, but we might get lucky. Detective Cabrillo asked me the same thing. Check with him in a day or so. Now, if you'll excuse me, I've got to finish Mr. Casey's chart and see my other patients."

Drake returned to Casey's room.

"Megan," he said softly, "I'm so sorry."

She didn't know whether to be pleased or angry. "If I hadn't insisted that he go out for an Irish coffee with you, Adam, he wouldn't be here. So it's not your fault."

"Yes, it is. She...that woman, was trying to get into my room."

"He's squeezing my hand, Adam. I'm guessing he's wanting you to stop blaming yourself. I'm also guessing he's saying you owe him an Irish coffee." They both saw her husband's nod of agreement.

Drake smiled at his friend and put his arm around Megan's shoulders. "I figured you'd find a way to work nourishment into my obligation column," he said. "Mike, you hurry up and get out of here, and I'll take you both to the Buena Vista for all the Irish coffees you can drink."

After calling the Marriott and reserving rooms for Megan and Mike's brother and making sure Larry Green had taken care of providing protection for Casey, Drake returned to his hotel to find out what his father-in-law knew about an Iranian threat to attack America's energy grid.

THIRTY-SIX

Senator Hazelton was still in his office on the third floor of the Hart Senate Office Building when he took the call from his son-in-law.

"Senator," Drake began, "do you have a moment?"

"Certainly, Adam. How are you?"

"I'm fine, sir. How's Mom?"

"She's fine, we're both fine. When do we get to see you again?"

"Soon, I hope," Drake said. "I'm in San Francisco now. That's what I need to talk to you about. I seem to have stepped into a pile of dog doo. Two people have been killed and someone poisoned my friend, Mike Casey. It looks as if the poison was really meant for me."

"Is Mike okay?" the senator asked.

"His doctor says he should make a full recovery."

"Let me know if there's anything I can do." The senator paused, then asked, "Does this in any way involve the company I asked Secretary Rallings have you visit?"

"I think so, but I don't how. The reason I called is Liz

Strobel said there's intelligence that Iran is planning a cyber attack on our energy grid. Have you heard the same thing?"

Drake waited for the senator to answer. He knew that the Senate Select Committee on Intelligence was regularly briefed by the country's intelligence apparatus. The senator should therefore know what DHS knew. He also knew the senator would be very careful about what was said over an open phone line.

"It's possible, I suppose," he finally said. "We have openly blamed Iran for the cyber attacks on U.S. banks, which were understood to be retaliation for the cyber attacks on Iran's nuclear program. The mullahs assumed we assisted Israel with those attacks." He smoothly changed the subject. "By the way, have you seen Liz recently?"

"Not for a while. Why?"

"Next time you see her, ask her about changes at DHS. I'll keep my ears open here and let you know if I hear anything new about threats from Iran. Adam, I've got to run. I hope we get to see you soon." And with that, the senator ended the call.

Drake leaned back in his chair and stared at the screen of his cell phone that showed the call had indeed ended. He couldn't remember a conversation he'd ever had with the senator that had ended so abruptly. The brush-off he'd just received wasn't the way he was used to being treated. And why would he want to talk with Liz Strobel about changes at the Department of Homeland Security?

He was still puzzling over his call to the senator when he got back to the hospital and found Dr. Martin directing the removal of Casey's breathing tube.

The breathing tube being pulled out of Casey's throat was at least three feet long, and as soon as it was out, he was given oxygen through the soft plastic prongs placed inside his nostrils. The nurse instructed him to breathe deeply and cough for her. When he did so, she gave him a motherly pat on the head and said he'd been a good boy.

It was all Drake could do to keep from laughing, both because he was happy to see his friend breathing and because the nurse looked to be about half Casey's age.

Megan Casey stepped around the bed and kissed her husband on the cheek. "Hi, handsome. Bet you're glad I encouraged you to take Drake out for that Irish coffee."

Casey coughed again. "Well, that was fun," he said in a very scratchy voice. "How long have I been here?"

"Less than a day," she replied. "I'll bet you're hungry. I know you can't eat or drink with a breathing tube."

"Not sure I could swallow anything right now," Casey said. "Throat's sore." He looked at Drake. "You catch her?"

"No. I was kind of busy giving you CPR. But relax, buddy. It wasn't mouth-to-mouth."

Casey tried to laugh and grimaced. "That hurt, but thanks for telling me. I wouldn't want people talking about us. Seriously, you didn't catch her?"

"She was a pro, Mike. She kept her face hidden from the security video cameras. By the time the guy across the hall called security, she was gone. The video is being analyzed by the FBI. We'll find her."

Casey noticed his brother. "Phil, how come you're here?"

"You think I'd pass up the chance to see my big brother with a breathing tube stuck down his throat? Besides, I thought Megan might like some company on the plane."

This got a smile. "Thanks, Phil. Megan, how long do I have to stay here?"

"For the night, anyway. How are you feeling?

"I'm okay. My fingers and toes are sort of numb, though. Hope that goes away."

"It should. We need to get out of here for a bit and let the nurses decide if you still need the oxygen. I'll be right outside," she said as she turned to shoo the others out of the room.

"Adam," Casey said, "can you stay for a second?"

When it was just the two of them, he said, "She smelled like she'd just stepped out of the shower. She was probably staying at the Marriott. Bring me the video from the registration desk and I'll identify her. I know I've seen her face before."

THIRTY-SEVEN

Drake was watching the morning's news and drinking a cup of the hotel's room-service coffee when his phone rang.

"Buy me breakfast," said Liz Strobel, "and I'll tell you about all the changes at DHS." She laughed. "Your father-in-law said you might want to know."

"Where are you?"

"In the lobby."

"Weren't you in Washington when I called yesterday?"

"I was."

"Don't tell me you flew across the country to tell me about some changes at DHS."

"Okay, I won't." Strobel said. "Will you buy me breakfast, anyway, and tell me how Mike's doing?"

"Okay. Meet me in the Mission Grill on the second floor. I'll be down in a minute."

Drake thought about changing out of his jeans, a light-weight blue crew neck sweater, and tan moccasin loafers and even caught himself checking out his appearance in the mirror. What was he doing, he asked himself, worrying about how he looked for breakfast? He grabbed his black blazer and walked down the long hallway to the elevator.

When the elevator door opened on the second floor, his breakfast date had a smile on her face.

"Surprised to see me?" she asked.

"You could say that," he admitted. "You just happened to be in the neighborhood?" They entered the grill.

"Not really," she said over her shoulder as they followed the waitress to their table, "I took the red eye out here to tell you what we've discovered about the lady you weren't expecting the other night."

When the waitress had seated them and left their menus, Strobel leaned forward. "She's a Brazilian model by the name of Daniela Dekker. She was in London a month ago for a photo shoot, and the security cameras at Heathrow gave us video that we compared to the images of her at this hotel. She was here, Adam. She's your girl."

"Where is she now?"

"We're looking for her, but we're light years behind Britain. They have almost two million surveillance cameras, both private and public, a lot more than we have. We're going to have to find her the old fashioned way. Her agent is being questioned as we speak, and we're searching for credit card purchases, reservations, and such." She opened her menu. "It's just a matter of time."

"When we find her, who has jurisdiction to arrest her?

"Depends on where we find her," Strobel said. "If it's here in California, it'll be local law enforcement. If we have evidence terrorism is involved, then it moves to the federal level. And that's another reason I'm here. Senator Hazelton asked me to brief you on the intelligence we have concerning Iran."

As the waitress reappeared to take their orders, they both quickly scanned their menus. Strobel ordered almond granola with blue berries, skim milk, a bagel, and coffee. Drake ordered a bacon avocado omelet, toast, and coffee.

Before their food arrived, Strobel summarized what she knew.

"Iran is pouring a lot of money into cyber warfare with help from Russia. They deny it, but the evidence is clear that the cyber attacks on our biggest banks were Iranian-sponsored. The attacks on several of the Persian oil and gas companies last year were traced to hackers inside Iran. A source inside Iran is saying there's a rumor that the next attack will be made on our energy grid and that it will be blamed on someone else. But the only two players in this cyber war game with the sophistication to mount an attack like that are China and Russia. We don't think they're stupid enough to hit our energy grid, though, because it would mean war."

The waitress arrived with their plates. Drake immediately took a bite of his toast and sat back in his chair while the waitress refilled his coffee cup.

"So what does a rumor circulating in Iran have to do with Energy Integrated Solutions?" he asked after she'd left again.

Strobel picked up her fork. "When Bill Bradford was in Washington to finalize the DAARPA grant for his energy grid antivirus software, he met with your father-in-law. They had met before. At a conference about modernizing the energy grid, the Smart Grid project. Bradford said his company had been experiencing a somewhat clumsy phishing attack, something you might expect from a bunch of inexperienced hackers. The phishing continued, he said, and then started getting more sophisticated. This was about the time we learned that Russia was helping Iran with its cyber warfare unit. Senator Hazelton mentioned Bradford's concerns to Secretary Rallings, his old friend, as you know, and my boss. They thought it was something that might be related."

Drake nodded. "Bradford says that his systems haven't been penetrated, that none of the phishing was successful. I met with his security analyst. He said the same thing. But if nothing got through and nothing was stolen or infected with a virus from Iran, why send me to EIS?"

As I understand it," Strobel said as she worked on her granola, "Bradford called your father-in-law and asked if he was obligated to report the phishing attacks to the SEC when they weren't successful. Bradford's corporate counsel thought they should, but Bradford wanted another opinion. Secretary Rallings and Senator Hazelton thought they'd kill two birds with one stone by sending you in on the SEC question. You would also make sure cyber terrorism wasn't somehow involved. You sniffed out the assassination plot to kill the Secretary, so they both respect your ability to connect the dots."

Drake's cell phone vibrated in the pocket of his blazer, and when he took it out, he saw that he had a text message from Larry Green. Mike Casey wanted to see him.

"Would you like to come with me to the hospital and say hello to Mike?" he asked as he signaled to the waitress for their check. "He wants to see me. I know he'd like to see you."

"I'd love to see Mike," she said. "Since I invited myself to breakfast, will you allow me to pay for it."

"This one's mine, but thanks for offering."

"Well, then, will you let me buy you dinner? I've offered several times, you know, if you were going to be in Washington. Since you haven't taken me up on my offers, let me take you to dinner here."

Drake accepted the invitation. As they walked across the

room, he could see that she was being followed by every pair of male eyes in the place. He hadn't been to dinner with a woman since his wife died. Now he discovered that he was looking forward to the evening.

THIRTY-EIGHT

They found Casey sitting up in his bed intently staring at something on a laptop. An empty cafeteria food tray sat on the rolling over bed bedside table that Megan had pushed aside so she could pull her chair up close enough to see the laptop screen. Larry Green was looking at it, too, from the other side of the bed.

When Casey looked up and saw Liz Strobel, he smiled and introduced her to his wife. "Megan, Liz was with us in Oregon when Adam was injured.

If Phil Casey hadn't told Drake about the spat his brother and his wife had had over Mike's doing field work at his request the month before, Drake might not have noticed the slight squint of Megan Casey's eyes as she stood up and shook hands with Strobel. He'd have to be careful, he reminded himself, when Megan Casey was around and the topic of conversation turned to the adventures he'd been having lately with Mike at his side. Although the poisoning wasn't something that could be directly blamed on him, he had no doubt that that wasn't the way Megan Casey was seeing it.

Liz Strobel also noticed the somewhat chilly welcome she got from Megan Casey. She stayed at the foot of the bed as she asked Mike how he was feeling.

"I'm fine," he said, sounding less hoarse than he had the day before. "My throat's a little sore when I eat, and you know how I like to eat." He paused for the obligatory laughter. "But the food here will kill you quicker than a poison dart tipped with curare," he joked.

As soon as he saw the tight smile on his wife's face, he quickly added, "Larry brought over the security video from the front desk at the Marriott. I think I've found the woman who poisoned me. You only see her once briefly when she checks in, and you don't a great look at her face, but I'm pretty sure this is her." He turned the laptop around and pointed to a tall, beautiful woman standing at the counter. "Larry's called the Marriott," he added, "and asked them to identify the woman who checked in at this precise time two nights ago. We're waiting for the day manager to call us back."

Liz Strobel leaned down to get a closer look at the mystery woman. "I don't think you'll have to wait that long. That's the same woman our facial recognition program identified when we matched the images of her coming down the hallway from Adam's room with video of her walking through the Heathrow airport in London. Her name is Daniela Dekker."

"Who is Daniela Dekker?" Megan Casey asked.

"She is a Brazilian model who sidelines as an assassin," Strobel said. "When we told Interpol why we were asking for security camera video, and we matched our woman here with Daniela Dekker in London, they lined up her travel stops in Europe with several unsolved murders Interpol thinks she might be responsible for."

Before anyone could say anything, Larry Green's cell phone buzzed and he stepped out into the hall to take the call.

Megan Casey turned to Drake. "Adam, why was she trying to get into your room? Is this someone you know?"

Drake held up his hands to slow down her obvious train of thought. "I have no idea who she is or why she was trying to get into my room. That's what we're trying to find out. Look, I'm sorry Mike got hurt. I'll take all the blame for that."

"Megan," Casey croaked, "it's really not Adam's fault. I should have seen what she was up to before I got so close."

Larry Green came back into the room and interrupted the *mea culpas*. "The Marriott says the woman Mike recognized didn't register as Daniela Dekker. She checked in as Adriana Hermann."

Drake turned to Strobel and said, "Could you see if Interpol can connect Dekker and Hermann to the murders they think one or the other of these women committed? One of the names is obviously an alias, so we have to chase them both. Also, see if Dekker's agent knows whether Dekker is her modeling name. Models often use stage names, like actors, authors, and musicians do."

Strobel nodded and left the room to call her Interpol contact and pass along the information.

"Mike," Drake said, "did the doctor tell you how long she wanted to keep you here?"

Megan Casey answered as her husband groaned. "She wants him to stay until the numbness in his hands and feet goes away. She thinks it'll probably be next Monday or Tuesday."

"All right," Drake said. "I'll need to check in with Bill Bradford at EIS and let him know what's going on. Larry, can you stick around until Mike's discharged?"

"Got it covered. I promised Mike I'd bring him some real food when one of our guys from L.A. spells me for a while. Maybe by the time you get back from EIS we'll have a lead on

Daniela Dekker or Adriana Hermann, or whoever she is. I'm looking forward to meeting that lady."

THIRTY-NINE

Drake drove to the EIS offices in Hunter's Point and arrived in time to catch Bill Bradford before he left for lunch. When they were alone in Bradford's office, Drake brought him up to speed on the events of the last day and a half.

"When I asked a friend of mine at DHS to help me identify the woman who poisoned Mike, I learned that your SEC problem wasn't the only reason I was asked to come see you. Were you aware there's new intelligence about an Iranian attack on our energy grid?"

"I wasn't told about any new intelligence," Bradford said, "but that kind of attack is why we were given a grant to develop software to prevent just such a massive blackout. When our software is installed next week in all of the major utilities around the country, we'll be protected from anything Iran or anyone else can throw at us."

"Bill, the detective handling the investigation of your manger's death last week thinks his murder, the drive-by shooting I was involved with, and my friend's poisoning are all connected somehow. Do you have any idea how that could happen?"

Bradford thought for a moment, then shook his head. "The only connection I can see is you. Nick Kawasaki was killed before you arrived, but the other two events directly involved you. I certainly don't see any connection to me or my company."

"Frankly, "Drake said, "I don't either, and that's what bothers me. Maybe when we catch up with my friend's attacker, we'll find the connection. So your work on the DAARPA grant is finished. Congratulations."

"We'll still be involved in a support role with the utilities," Bradford said, "but, yes, we finished our testing of the software this week. The other teams are working on a variety of projects to make the energy grid more digital. And more efficient."

Drake stood up. "Well, I better get back to the hospital. I'm afraid I didn't help you with much, but it was a pleasure working with you."

Bradford stood and shook hands with Drake. "You allowed me to override my attorney and do what I wanted to do on the SEC reporting. Don't minimize that. Let me walk you out."

When they reached the reception area, Bradford asked, "How much longer do you think you'll be in San Francisco?"

"Mike should be released next Monday, so I'll head back to Oregon then."

"Keep driving the Audi until then if you want," Bradford told him. "Drop it off on your way to the airport when you leave, and good luck with your friend. I hope you find whoever's responsible for poisoning him."

"Thanks, Bill. We'll find her," Drake promised. As he headed to the elevator, he looked back and saw Bradford talking with the young man who had replaced the manager that had been murdered.

SALEEM CANAAN HAD OVERHEARD enough of the conversation between Bradford and Drake to know that Adriana Hermann had to be killed soon, before she was found in Los Angeles. He also knew that terminating his employment at EIS had to happen now.

"Mr. Bradford," he said, "could I have a word with you in your office?"

"Sure, Tony. I'm leaving for a luncheon engagement in a bit, but I have some time before then."

When they were both seated in Bradford's office, the CEO said "What's on your mind?"

"I appreciate the opportunity you gave me to work here," Canaan said, "but I'm going to go back to work for Ra Solar if they'll have me. You have a great company, but I miss working there. Solar power is the future, and that's where I want to make a contribution."

"I'm sorry to hear that, Tony. You've been a great addition to our team. But if your passion is solar power, then that's where you need to be. How soon do you plan on leaving?"

"Sir, my work on the electric utility software is finished. I thought I'd leave today, rather than start on a new project."

"So soon? Well, then, I'll let HR know to prepare your severance pay. If you need me to put in a good word for you at Ra Solar, let me know," Bradford said as he stood up to dismiss the young man. "Good luck. I hope you'll be happy there."

Saleem Canaan left to clean out his cubicle with a smile on his face. With the money he had earned at EIS and the money Rein Walkur was paying him, he now had a tidy sum to put away for a rainy day. On top of that, after he cleaned out his condo, there were three people he got to kill, starting with the woman Walkur thought he couldn't handle.

FORTY

When Drake stopped by the hospital to check on Casey, he found him finishing a double cheeseburger and chocolate shake Larry Green had smuggled in from the closest In-N-Out. Megan Casey was still giving off cool vibes to him and Larry Green said Liz Strobel had returned to her hotel, so Drake returned to his room at the Marriott. A few miles on a treadmill and some free weights in the hotel's fitness center, followed by a trip to the steam room would give him time to sift through everything that had happened since he arrived in San Francisco. He'd also have time to think about dinner with Ms. Strobel that evening.

After a quick change into a pair of gym shorts, T-shirt and running shoes, he took the elevator down to the fitness center. Settling into an easy six-minute mile pace to warm up, Drake let his mind drift while he watched ESPN on the personal TV monitor on his treadmill. Baseball season was over, college football was in its second full month of games, and the news channels had talking heads talking about how Congress was still unable to do its job and pass a budget. The president blamed the Congress and the Congress blamed him for his lack of leadership. And Iran continued to threaten Israel with annihilation if anyone messed with its *peaceful* nuclear energy program. He switched to a soft rock channel and vowed to get rid of his television when he got home and watch sports in a sports bar, where adult beverages could help him forget the problems of the world.

If Iran was planning a cyber attack on America's energy grid, what did it hope to gain? Several senators had already proclaimed that such an attack was an act of war and would be swiftly punished. The administration was less bellicose, trying to keep its Middle East peace initiative alive, but Iran couldn't be foolish enough to think it could get away with it. The intelligence about a forthcoming attack didn't make any sense.

Drake slowed his pace to a jog for five minutes after his run. He then moved to the free weights and started through his set of reps for the workout he used when he was traveling. After his workout, he grabbed one of the hotel's white terry cloth robes and walked to the empty steam room to relax.

Sitting on the upper bench, he let his thoughts return to the attack on Casey. Unless the woman had been so taken by his handsome looks and just wanted to slip in bed with him, she had been there to slip some curare into his blood stream and paralyze him. But why? Clearly the latter was the most likely scenario, but, again, why? His review of the EIS responsibility to report on the company's well-being on Form 10-K wasn't a threat to anyone. It went along with the CEO's position on the matter. No feathers were ruffled with his recommendation. The unsuccessful phishing attacks the company had experienced didn't amount to anything...if he believed what the company's security analyst told him, and he had no reason to doubt the man's word.

That left him with the possibility that *he* was the reason for the mayhem since his arrival. But it still didn't explain the murder of the EIS manager the day before he got there.

Starting to get a headache trying to figure out what was going on, Drake slipped down to the lower bench, rested his arms on the upper bench, stretched his legs out, and began thinking about his dinner date that night with Liz Strobel. Why did he think of it as a *date*, he wondered. They were professionals working together. Neither of them was

looking for romance. She had invited him twice to dinner in Washington, but these had been courtesy invitations so he could meet her staff. Why did he feel so uncomfortable, then, at the prospect of having dinner with her?

He closed his eyes. In his heart, he knew the reason, and it felt like he was betraying his dead wife. In the last week of her life, Kay had made him promise that he would move on and find someone else to love him. She had been insistent that he not live alone for the rest of his life, that he deserved to be happy. He hadn't agreed with her, because he didn't mind being alone, but he had in fact promised he would try to move on. Whatever that meant.

He also knew that he had been wrong. He had quickly found that he hated being alone. Without Kay's companionship, he had lost his focus, all but destroyed his law practice, and had been well on the way to becoming a certified drunk. Fortunately, his father-in-law had thrown him a lifeline. A constituent's secretary had been murdered and Drake had been asked to help the man deal with the murder investigation and the press. That referral, meant to steer a good client his way and help to drag him out of his depression, had involved him in an assassination plot and brought him back to the commitment he had made the day after 9/11, when he had enlisted in the army. He had vowed to fight an ignoble enemy who loved death beyond all reason and loved killing innocent people.

Shaking the sweat from his forehead before it dripped into the moisture that was building in his eyes, Drake knew that he was moving on. It made him sad. He had loved the life he had been building with Kay and wanted it back, but he knew that wasn't possible. He also knew that the path he was now on wasn't likely to allow anything approaching the happiness he had lost. Look at the way Casey's wife, Megan, was handling her husband's poisoning. What woman in her right mind would put up with a man willing to take the risks he'd been taking?

Not anyone he knew, he realized, so why worry about it? Enjoy the evening with a beautiful woman who knew who you really were, and then get back to the task at hand; finding Casey's attacker and connecting some of the dots.

FORTY-ONE

After dressing for dinner in a two-button, navy, pin-stripe suit, a white shirt, and a subtle black, gray, and red striped tie, Drake drove to the top of Nob Hill and the Big 4 restaurant in the Huntington Hotel, where he had been invited to meet Liz Strobel for dinner. She had apologized for asking him to meet her there, but explained that she had always wanted to stay at the Huntington and the Big 4 was supposed to be one of the best restaurants in the city.

While waiting for her to arrive, he took a seat at a small, glass-topped table across from the bar and nursed a glass of McCarthy's Oregon Single Malt whisky. The dark Janesero wood paneling, crystal chandeliers, Italian marble and the nearby cozy fireplace had been created to transport diners back to the era of the nineteenth century railroad tycoons the restaurant was named for—C.P. Huntington, Charles Crocker, Leland Stanford, and Mark Hopkins. Drake liked the way the place tipped its hat to the grand old days of the city's past.

Liz Strobel looked spectacular when she made her entrance and walked to his table. Wearing a black satin dress with a wide neckline that put on display her curves and a tasteful glimpse of cleavage, she not only offered her hand when he stood up but also leaned in and gave him a light kiss on his cheek.

"Adam, thank you for coming," she said. "I thought I'd better make good on my promise to buy you dinner while I was here." She smiled. "Since you don't get to Washington very often."

Drake pulled her chair out and waited for her to sit before he returned to his seat. "Washington reminds me too much of why I left the army. I try to leave politics to my father-in-law. Would you like a cocktail?"

"Yes, please. A martini with a lemon twist. How's Mike doing?" she asked as he waved to the bartender and ordered her drink.

"They're keeping him until Monday because the numbness in his hands and feet hasn't cleared up yet. Otherwise, I think he's okay. I haven't had a chance to talk with him much without Megan being there."

"I've only met Megan once," Strobel said, "but I couldn't help notice some tension between you two."

"She blames me for Mike being poisoned. She doesn't want him hanging with me and taking risks that might get him hurt."

Drake watched as the bartender put the martini on the table and waited until she had taken a sip and nodded her approval.

"Well, I don't blame her, Adam. I'm sure your wife would have felt the same way. Are you comfortable with the risks you've been taking?"

What he was uncomfortable with was her question. Was she asking him because *she* was worried about him? Or was she asking as his liaison with DHS and was she worried about asking him to check out the cyber attacks at EIS? Either way, he didn't need to carry around the weight of someone else's worry.

He'd seen what that did to married soldiers who became more cautious and careful with each worried letter from home. The hesitation caused by the weight of worry got some of them killed.

"Why do you ask, Liz? You took risks when you were with the FBI. Were you comfortable taking those risks?"

"That was different," she said quietly. "It was work. But this isn't something you're obligated to do. I guess I'm curious about why you're doing what you're doing."

Fortunately, he didn't have to answer the question because the waitress arrived to take them to their table in the main dining room. He was still thinking about how to explain himself when they were seated and were handed their menus.

"I already know what I'm having," she said, giving him a little more time to think about his answer, "I looked at the menu in my room. The seafood risotto looks wonderful."

Drake decided on the pan seared Angus steak and a Dungeness crab and avocado salad.

"I'll have the crab and avocado salad as well," Strobel said. "Would you like to order the wine for us?"

"Only if you'll let me pay for it."

When she agreed, he ordered a bottle of 2002 Chateau St. Jean Cinq Cepages, then sat back to finish the whiskey he'd brought with him from the cocktail lounge.

"You're still thinking about my question, aren't you?" she asked with a smile. "I didn't mean to make you uncomfortable."

Now it was Drake's turn to smile. "You're very perceptive. I'm still thinking about why I'm doing what I'm doing. I'm not sure I can explain it."

"Do you like being a lawyer?"

"I haven't been doing a lot of lawyering lately, as my secretary will quickly attest," he replied. "But, yes. I like the premise that we're a nation ruled by laws, that no man is above the law, and that justice prevails. But we both know that far too often, that premise doesn't prove to be true. Laws that should be enforced, aren't. Men and women of wealth and power put themselves above the law. And they get away with it. Equal justice for all has come to mean empowering groups and causes by creating rights the Constitution never intended. So I guess the short answer to your question is I liked being a prosecutor. And I'm trying to like being an attorney in private practice. But I'm not there yet."

"Did you like being a soldier?"

He looked into her hazel-green eyes and considered whether he wanted to allow her to continue interrogating him. She was seeking permission to enter the private domain of his thoughts that only one person had ever been allowed to enter. His wife.

"I'm still a soldier, Liz. The oath I took to protect and defend this country didn't expire when I left the army. That's one of the reasons I agreed to work with you and the Secretary. The other reason is we're still at war with an enemy that wants to destroy us, and all the drone strikes in the world aren't going to keep them from coming after us. The FBI can continue to round up stupid Islamists who are enticed into one made-up terror plot or another, but the guys I worry about are still waiting to strike. We're not going to win this war by hoping for change in the Middle East, regardless of what the President thinks."

The waitress arrived with their salads, and Drake apologized for preaching to the choir.

"You're right, of course," she said with a fork of crab paused midway to her mouth, "and that's something I need to talk to you about. I'm thinking of leaving Homeland Security."

"Why?"

"Secretary Rallings had a heart attack last month and

tendered his resignation to the President. He's okay and agreed to stay on until after the election next month. I'm not sure I want to work for the person I think is going to take his place."

"What are you planning on doing?"

"Senator Hazelton has offered me a position on his staff to oversee his work on the Senate Select Committee on Intelligence. Would you be comfortable with me working for your father-in-law?"

"Why wouldn't I be?" Drake asked.

"Because I like you, Adam, and I don't want to do anything that will ruin our relationship."

Before Drake had a chance to digest what she had said, the maître d' approached and said that Ms. Strobel had an urgent phone call and would she care to take it? He watched her follow the maître d' to an old-fashioned phone booth. What had she said about liking him? He knew he was attracted to her, and he felt guilty about it so soon after Kay had died. But he hadn't thought that Liz might be attracted to him.

When she stepped out of the phone booth and walked toward him, Drake realized he was staring at a very beautiful woman. He stood up to seat her and push in her chair.

"My assistant located the model's agent," she said. "She's finishing a photo shoot tomorrow morning on the *Queen Mary* in Long Beach. Shall we finish our dinner, or do we need to head to LA right away?"

FORTY-TWO

The final photo shoot on the *Queen Mary* for the Lebanese fashion designer, featuring his Gowns of Illusion collection, was scheduled for 7:01 Saturday morning to catch the natural glow of the sun's first rays. Drake and Liz Strobel watched from the Sun Deck, as the photographer's crew set up along the starboard railing on the Main Deck, two decks below.

The night before, after they had learned that Daniela Dekker, the assassin and fashion model who had poisoned Mike Casey was in LA, Larry Green had made his boss's Gulfstream G280 available and had flown with them from San Francisco to the Long Beach Airport. There they had met a hastily organized team from the Los Angeles office of Puget Sound Security and moved on to the Hilton hotel on Queen's Way Drive. Sitting in a small conference room with a view of the ocean, they had worked until midnight to put together a plan to confront Dekker.

Built in 1930, the *RMS Queen* Mary had sailed the Atlantic as the grandest ocean liner in the world from 1936 until the start of World War II, when the ship was transformed into a troopship. Painted in grey camouflage and dubbed the *Grey Ghost*, she'd been capable of transporting 16,000 troops across the Atlantic at thirty knots, an unheard of speed for so large a ship. After the war, she was retrofitted and resumed her regular passenger service until she was retired in 1965 and sold in 1967 to become a floating hotel and event venue in Long Beach, California.

Although tours of the *Queen Mary* wouldn't begin until after the photo shoot was finished, Green had arranged a pre-tour security sweep of the ship on behalf of Puget Sound Security and a fictitious VIP client with special security requirements. This sweep was to take place while the fashion designer was working. Two of Green's men were stationed at the bottoms of the two gang planks that were being used to make sure no unwelcome paparazzi intruded into the so-called VIP client's private tour of the ship. Green and another of his men, on the main deck to size up potential security risks, were standing outside the Garden Lounge, where the models were getting their last-minute touchups. Drake and Liz, who had been introduced as the advance staff for the so-called VIP, had paused on the Sun Deck to watch the photographer adjusting the portable light reflectors that surrounded his staging area along the starboard rail.

"When Larry signals that Daniela Dekker is coming out for her session," Drake said without taking his eyes off the scene below, "I'll move down to the main deck. When she heads back to the Garden Lounge to change for the next set, we'll escort her off the ship, where you can use your Homeland Security special agent authority to arrest her. Stay up here until then and report anything that looks out of place. All right?"

"I said I would," Strobel said. "But be careful, Adam. She's a killer. She won't go without a fight."

"That's why taking her now should work. She can't conceal a weapon during the wardrobe changes and three of us should be able to handle the hand-to-hand stuff." Drake checked in with his spotter below. "Larry, have you seen any security or personal bodyguards that might interfere with our plans?"

Green had provided each of them with small wireless earpieces that were invisible when inserted into their ears and were connected to modified cell phones that worked as transmitters. The units were similar to what the Secret Service uses and provided concealed communication capability for all members of the team.

"None that we've seen," Green replied. "Unless these hairdressers and makeup people are tougher than they look."

"How close are they to getting this thing started?"

Larry took a quick look at the door of the Garden Lounge, where a young woman assisting the photographer was impatiently checking her watch. "I'd say pretty close," he said. "It's 6:55. Sunrise is in six minutes."

Drake walked to the port side of the aft Sun Deck and looked down at the two gangplanks. There was no activity on the one that had been opened for the fashion shoot, and the other was being used by men pushing hand carts and unloading restaurant supplies from a Sysco truck.

To the east and above the skyline of Long Beach, a pink glow highlighted the horizon.

When he returned to stand next to Strobel, the first model walked out wearing an elegant, long, black lace gown. Then, at the direction of the photographer, she began working through a series of fashion poses.

"Drake," Green said, "they just let Dekker know she's next."

Drake moved quickly to the stairs at the rear of the Sun Deck viewing gallery and started down to the Main Deck.

When he arrived, he looked through the window in the stairwell door that opened next to the Garden Lounge and saw Daniela Dekker walking out to take the place of the first model.

She was wearing a long, black, "illusion gown" that appeared to be sheer above her waist. It had a thigh-high slit through which flashed a long, tanned leg when she placed one hand on the rail and turned back to look at the photographer. As she began to move through her choreographed poses, her eyes moved from face to face in a distant, but always vigilant, appraisal of her audience.

Liz was right, Drake thought. Despite her dazzling beauty, this one would not be taken without a fight. He recognized the cold wariness of a proficient killer even as she obeyed the voice of the photographer who was coaxing her to make him feel the warmth of her smile. Obviously a trained operative, she was storing the images of every face she scanned, searching for any sign of danger.

When her eyes flared and her head suddenly snapped to her left, Drake knew she had sensed danger somewhere nearby. He followed her eyes and saw a young man wearing a blue jacket with white lettering on it walking quickly toward her. His lips moved in the recital of a silent prayer and his eyes had the thousand-yard stare Drake had seen before.

"Larry, get down!" Drake shouted as he watched the martyr stop next to the photographer and shout *Allahu Akbar* as he raised his arms above his head. Drake dove to the floor in the stairwell as the explosion blew out the window in the door above him.

FORTY-THREE

Rising to his knees as he brushed the pebble-like pieces of glass off his head and shoulders, Drake jerked the dislodged stairwell door open and looked out. The martyr's bomb had blown a twenty foot gap in the starboard railing where Daniela Dekker had been standing. A bloody leg and bits of body and flesh were all that remained of the bomber... except for his head, which lay on the aft deck twenty feet away. The photographer and two of his assistants lay on their backs where they had fallen, and judging from the blood pooling beneath them, they were dead.

Larry Green was sitting on the deck to the right of the Garden Lounge, shaking his head. His eyes were glazed, and he was opening and closing his mouth as he tried to restore his hearing. He waved Drake away when he approached, indicating that he and the other PSS man next to him were all right. "Go help the others," he signaled.

The photographer's assistant who had been standing at the door of the lounge where the models were made up was now sitting slumped against the wall with her chin on her chest. She was breathing when he checked, but Drake thought she was unconscious. He was reluctant to move her. He could hear cries and sobbing Inside the Garden Lounge, where the fashion designer and other models had been watching the shoot.

Feeling a hand on his shoulder, Drake turned to see Strobel mouthing words he took to mean "Are you all right?"

"I'm fine," he said too loudly.

Queen Mary employees were beginning to gather on the Main Deck and staring at the carnage. As his hearing slowly returned and Strobel walked away, Drake could hear her instructing someone to keep everyone back, that this was a crime scene and that she was with Homeland Security and that help was on the way.

Surveying the destruction, Drake knew that the bomb the martyr had worn had been designed with a directional charge and that Daniela Dekker had clearly been the target. The gap in the railing was exactly where she had been standing. The bomber had, so to speak, pulled the trigger when he was standing directly in front of her. There might be some remains of her body in the water below, but there wouldn't be many. The photographer and his assistants who had been ten feet away from Dekker would have been killed by the concussive blast of the bomb that collapsed lungs, stopped hearts, and destroyed internal organs.

For whatever reason, someone had wanted to make sure that Daniela Dekker was killed. Otherwise, the bomber's vest would have been filled with all the usual ingredients—like shrapnel and nails and ball bearings dipped in rat poison—that would indiscriminately kill as many people as possible.

When Strobel returned and reached up to pluck small pieces of glass that remained in his hair, she said "When I said she wouldn't go without a fight, I was wrong. She never saw it coming."

"No," Drake said, shaking his head. "She saw it coming. She was aware that she was in danger. I could tell by the way she was looking at everyone. Someone wanted her silenced. It's as if someone knew we were closing in on her."

Strobel nodded. "I'll be right back," she said. "I've got to calm the models down and make sure none of them leave. They may be able to tell us something about the mysterious Daniela Dekker. Tell Larry's guys down on the gangplanks to keep everyone on the ship until the police arrive."

Drake walked to the port-side rail and yelled down to the two PSS men below to block off the gangplanks until the police and fire departments arrived. He saw that the huge parking lot beside the ship was already filled with onlookers, even before the wail of sirens now rushing down Queen's Way Drive had been heard. Hundreds of faces stared up at him, including one standing next to the blue Sysco truck that he vaguely recognized.

It would be a long day before anyone on board the grand old lady of Long Beach was allowed to leave, and an even longer time before the FBI and Homeland Security completed the investigation that would conclude that the Hezbollah martyr had acted alone. In the suicide video that was posted online later that day, he proudly proclaimed that his sacrifice was in protest of the way the West allowed women to flaunt themselves and wear shameless clothing. Daniela Dekker, aka Adriana Hermann, had been in the wrong place at the wrong time, and without additional evidence, she could not be positively identified as the assassin Interpol thought she might be.

No link was found between anyone onboard the *Queen Mary* that day and the suicide bomber, and no one identified a second man wearing the same blue jacket with the name of the restaurant food service company on it who had been unloading supplies.

No one ever learned that a second man had been standing fifty feet behind the bomber with a remote control to guarantee the success of the mission, or that he had been able to slip off the ship before the police arrived.

FORTY-FOUR

The flight back to San Francisco on Sunday morning in was a quiet one. After a full day of answering questions and giving recorded statements about why they had been on the *Queen Mary* and what they had witnessed, Drake, Strobel and Green had little to say beyond the occasional expletive Green couldn't contain. Daniela Dekker, or whatever her real name was, had been the one who had poisoned Mike Casey and now she was fish food in the waters below the *Queen Mary*.

Why she had been at Drake's door at the Marriott was still a mystery, and who had sent her was even more mysterious. There were no obvious connections to the four separate acts of violence that had occurred since Drake had arrived in San Francisco. No obvious connections, that is, except Drake himself and the company he'd visited on just two occasions.

A manager at Energy Integrated Solutions, Inc. had been killed before he flew in. The drive-by shooting that killed the mother in the parking lot at the foot of the Presidio might have been a random event, but only if you discounted Drake's presence there. As Megan Casey had been quick to point out, Mike

Casey had been shot with a poisoned dart right outside Drake's hotel room. But the execution of Daniela Dekker, if that's what it was, didn't make any sense to Drake. Unless, he was beginning to think, it was meant to erase a connection to someone who wanted him dead.

Drake was sitting with his head back and his eyes closed, trying to let his mind come up with something that made some sense, when he felt the Gulfstream begin its descent into San Francisco. There was something gently pulling on the shirttail of his mind, something that he knew was important, but it disappeared every time he looked down to see what it was.

When he opened his eyes, he saw that Liz Strobel had turned in her seat and was watching him intently.

"You had your eyes squeezed shut so tight I thought you were in pain," she told him as she shut her eyes the same way.

"Do that again with your eyes."

"Hey, I'm sorry, Adam, I didn't mean to make fun of you. I was just—"

"No, just do it again. It reminds me of something that I'm trying to remember."

Strobel squeezed her eyes shut and sat facing him for a long minute.

Then he remembered.

"That's it!" he said, slapping his leg. "When I went to the railing on the *Queen Mary* to tell the guys to keep the gangplanks closed, I was amazed at how many people were down there in the parking lot looking up at me. They all had that shocked look on their faces, like you see at a fire when onlookers know there are people inside the firemen will never reach. Except for one guy. He was standing next to a Sysco truck. He was squinting and he looked angry. I've seen him before! He works at EIS. He's the guy Bradford hired to replace his manager that was murdered."

"It's Saturday," Strobel said. "Maybe he was just there for a tour of the *Queen Mary*?"

"No, I don't think so. He was wearing the same blue jacket with white lettering as the bomber. Liz, he's involved in this... somehow. When Bill Bradford tells us where he lives, I'll need to have a talk with Mr. Squint Eyes."

He didn't wait until they had landed to call the CEO. "Bill, it's Adam Drake. Are you in your office?"

"No, I'm out sailing. Why?"

"Do you know where that new guy lives? The one you hired to replace your murdered manager?"

"Not off the top of my head, no. I think he had a condo somewhere in the city."

"Would someone in your office know?"

"HR would have it in his personnel file. But there's no one in HR on the weekend. Besides, he just quit. He said working for me wasn't his cup of tea.

"When did he quit?"

"Yesterday."

"Bill, that guy may be involved with my friend who got poisoned. And a lot more. I need to know where to find him. Can you meet me at your office?"

"I'll head there now. But it'll take me half an hour to get there."

"I'm just landing," Drake said, "so that's about how long it will take me. See you there."

Closing his phone, he told Strobel what Bradford had said, then repeated it again when Green moved to the seat in front of him.

"If this guy's involved in poisoning Mike and killing Daniela Dekker," Green said, "then there's something more going on at Bradford's company than those cyber attacks."

"And you seem to be right in the middle of it," Strobel added.

"Whatever it is," Drake said, "I think we need to get Mike out of town and back home in Seattle. If they, whoever *they* are, don't know we've positively identified Dekker as his attacker, they might want to make sure Mike never identifies her. Larry, can you make sure he gets home when he's released tomorrow?"

"Sure. But what are you planning on doing?"

"I'm going after Bradford's guy."

"And what will you do if you find him? If he's working with a bunch of crazy *jihadis*, you can't go after him by yourself. Are you even armed?

"No. I'm not licensed for concealed carry in California. I didn't think I needed to be when I came here.

Green got up and walked to the back of the Gulfstream. When he returned, he handed Drake a brushed aluminum briefcase.

"Mike had these outfitted for us when we're doing executive protection work. This case holds two of the new Colt Close Quarter Battle Pistols, two loaded .45 magazines for each one, a folding combat knife, and a tactical flashlight. Getting caught without a California concealed weapons license will be the least of your troubles if you find this guy and you're not armed."

"Do you have another one of those?" Strobel asked. "I didn't bring anything with me, but I am a Special Agent of Homeland Security. I got him into this. I'd better go with him."

FORTY-FIVE

Saleem Canaan, aka Anthony Capelli, former employee of Energy Integrated Solutions, Inc., returned to Ryan Walkur's mansion on Pacific Avenue Sunday morning to return the keys to Walkur's condo and the BMW M3 he'd been driving. He was escorted by the same bodyguard as before to the upper level of the three-story home, where Walkur was having coffee and croissants on the deck.

"Coffee, Mr. Canaan?" Walkur asked. "Or would you like some champagne to celebrate your success on the *Queen Mary*?"

Canaan sat down in a chair across the small glass-topped table and helped himself to a croissant. "I'm not in a mood to celebrate the needless sacrifice of a martyr," he said. "You should have let me kill her."

Walkur shook his head. "We've been over that. I'm rather pleased that the FBI is calling this a terrorist attack. You should be, too. No one's looking for us."

"That may not be true. That attorney from Oregon may have recognized me."

"Please explain."

"Not sure that I can," Canaan said. "I was standing on the dock next to the truck we used and Drake was looking down from the deck of the ship. He looked right at me."

"But he only knows you as an employee of Energy Integrated Solutions. He couldn't know about your work for me. Besides, your work here is almost finished. Now I need you to go to Lake Tahoe before this Thursday and take care of the two men who are about to be blamed for the blackout."

"Why Lake Tahoe and why before Thursday?"

"Because that's where the men are staying before they attend a trade show that starts in Reno on Thursday. David Klein has a large estate on the north shore of the lake. And Thursday is the day the virus you planted will activate and cause transformers all over the energy grid to fail." Walkur smiled. "I thought it was a nice touch to start the blackout on the same day the solar energy trade show opens."

Canaan laughed and said, "You really are a bastard. Have you planted the evidence the police will find that incriminates the two men?"

"The police will find a thumb drive in the safe in David Klein's office when they follow up on emails we've planted on his laptop from his co-conspirator Bobby Parker. The thumb drive has an exact copy of the blackout virus on the thumb drive I gave you."

"Well, that should do it," Canaan said, picking up his cup of coffee. "How do you want me to kill them?"

Walkur studied the young man seated across the table. It was easy to see why Hezbollah had selected him for special training and then given him a command position in its American contingent. He seemed eager to kill two men he knew nothing about, just as he had been eager to kill the Brazilian model. He had the skills of a warrior and the looks of a Latin movie star. His only weakness was his brazen arrogance, which Walkur feared would get him killed one day.

He explained some of the game plan to his assassin. "Mr. Klein and Mr. Parker must appear to have been remorseful and ashamed and to have decided that suicide was the only way to avoid being tried as terrorists. They're cowards for choosing the easy way out, so an overdose would seem to be appropriate. But I don't know enough about either man's drug use history. I think hanging would fit the picture we want to paint for the authorities, don't you?"

"I think that will work. Is there a suicide note you want me to leave?"

"It's on a thumb drive in my office. I'll get it for you on your way out. Just upload it onto Klein's laptop, or whatever he uses at home. When you're finished there, get away as quickly as you can. Come Thursday, transportation around the country will become difficult. Airports will be closed, trains won't run, and gas stations won't be able to pump gas."

Walkur stood up and led Canaan to his study, where he gave his young killer a map to the mansion on the north shore of Lake Tahoe and a small white thumb drive with an eloquent suicide note decrying America's dependence on oil.

FORTY-SIX

When they pulled into a guest parking space in front of the EIS building, they immediately spotted Bradford's white Audi A8 parked in the CEO's reserved space. Drake opened the door of the Audi Bradford had loaned him for Strobel and walked with her into the building. Bradford was waiting for them in his office.

The CEO sitting at his desk with Anthony Capelli's personnel file open on his desk and a look of obvious concern on his face.

"Bill," Drake said as they walked in, "I'd like you to meet Elizabeth Strobel, Secretary Rallings' administrative assistant. Liz, this is Bill Bradford."

"Ms. Strobel," Bradford rose and walked around his desk to meet her, "please have a seat. Adam, I retrieved our guy's personnel file. There is an address for him, but I tried the phone number he gave us. It's no longer in service."

"What do you know about him?" Drake asked.

"Not much, I'm afraid. In my haste to complete the energy grid software project, we didn't check him out as thoroughly as we normally do. He was referred to me by a CEO I know, and I relied on his recommendation."

"Who's the other CEO?"

"Robert Parker. He runs Ra Solar and is a member of a business leaders association I belong to. He said Capelli had done some consulting work for him and was looking for a permanent position here in San Francisco."

"Maybe Parker knows more about him," Drake said. "Give him a call, will you? Liz and I'll check out the address he gave you. If he's gone, maybe his neighbors will have a new address."

"What did he do for you, Mr. Bradford?" Strobel asked. "I'm familiar with the DAARPA grant you were working on."

"Anthony Capelli replaced Nick Kawasaki, the team manager who was murdered, on our internal testing team. The energy grid security software was back from our external beta testers, and we were fine tuning the final version of the product before its release last Friday."

"Was he qualified to do the work?"

"According to his resume, he was probably over-qualified. I did check with another CEO that he listed as a reference. I learned that he had worked on a project for him that was more technical than what he was doing here."

"If you will make a copy of his application for me," Strobel said, "I'll have DHS take a closer look at him."

Bradford made a copy of the four-page application as Drake said, "Liz, would you like to go with me to check out this address? Or do you need to stay and get this to your people?"

"I have an app on my phone that allows me to scan and send documents," she told him. "I'd like to go with you. If you don't mind."

"Great. Bill, call me if you learn anything from the guy who recommended Capelli. We'll check out his last known address. Meet you later for a drink?"

"Sure," Bradford said. "Just let me know where and when."

As they walked out of the EIS building into the warm fall sunshine, Strobel said, "I'm concerned about Capelli's quitting the same day the software he was working on was released."

Drake nodded. "There's a number of things concerning me right now, not the least of which is his work for EIS. I have a hunch this guy is involved in all the weird things that have happened since I got here."

When they were belted in Bradford's black Audi and Drake had entered the address from their quarry's personnel file into the navigation GPS, they drove to South Beach and found the luxury condos known as the Infinity Towers. There was parking garage next door.

"This all looks pretty upscale for a software consultant," Drake said a few minutes later as they stood on the street looking up at the forty-two floors of the round, glass-walled tower.

They went in and learned from the secretary in the on-site property manager's office that all 650 homes in the residential tower were sold and occupied. The only exception was the condo on the thirty-sixth floor that had been listed as the residence of Anthony Capelli. He had moved out of the condo that weekend, they were told after Strobel had shown the secretary her Special Agent DHS badge and asked to see him. If they wanted to speak with any of his neighbors, whose names she wasn't authorized to release, they would need to have the neighbors' permission in advance. The Infinity protected the privacy of its residents.

They left the building. "I'll have the ownership of the condo identified, along with the other information on his resume," Strobel said. "This just smells. The guy moves before the end of the month as soon as he quits his job." She shook her head. "It's what you'd expect when an operation is rolled up and everyone clears out of town."

Drake nodded. "Let's go back to the Marriott. I'll buy you a late lunch. Maybe Bradford's learned something that'll help us find this guy. Right now he's all we have. Whatever's going on, our guy's the key."

FORTY-SEVEN

Saleem Canaan decided to ride his Suzuki Hayabushi motorcycle to South Lake Tahoe and spend a night there before riding north to Crystal Bay to deal with the two fools who had gotten in bed with Ryan Walkur. Desperate men did stupid things, he knew, but thinking they could work with someone they barely knew to cause a blackout all across America was beyond stupid. If they had known the fascist Alliance fixer like he did, they would have known there was only one way their plan would end.

Muslim elders had long kept a watchful eye on the Nazi looters during and after World War II as they fled to South America and began to construct a new German empire, or *reich,* there. Hitler had made a lot of promises to his Arab collaborators in return for their assistance in building up the Third Reich. This thousand-year *reich* had not endured. Now, almost seventy years later, the Nazi progeny and their *Alliance* were making the same promises of mutual assistance and cooperation between a new Islamist *caliphate* and a new fascist *reich.*

Well, Canaan told himself, he didn't believe any of it for a minute. And he didn't trust Ryan Walkur or the Alliance, either.

As he rode through central California on I-80 East to Sacramento, and then on US-50 East through Placerville and the mountains of the El Dorado National Forest to South Lake Tahoe, Canaan daydreamed about his role in the world of the future. In his world, men would be men and he would be able to enjoy a woman without having her run to the police crying rape every time. In fact, it would be would be like tonight, with a woman skilled in her trade who would do as he wished.

Two and a half hours after leaving San Francisco, Canaan rode into South Lake Tahoe and took an "executive king" room at Harveys Lake Tahoe. After a shower and change of clothes, he took the elevator down to the casino and made his way through the slot machines and past the black jack tables to the roulette gaming area to begin his night of pleasure.

From past experience, he knew that it wouldn't be long before there were two or three beautiful women at his side, watching him and gauging both the size of his bankroll and his willingness to share some of it. And then after a dinner, during which he had pleasantly negotiated a respectful quid pro quo with one of them and adjourned to his room, he would begin the ritual he had developed. It would begin with escalating carnal pleasure that prepared him for the greatest pleasure of all, killing two men the next day.

FORTY-EIGHT

Drake treated Strobel to the grilled chicken chopped salad and a glass of chardonnay at the 4th Street Bar and Grill. It was the middle of the afternoon and there was only a scattering of customers eating or having drinks while they watched highlights of the previous weekend's NFL games.

When he playfully started to slap her hand when she reached for a fry on his plate, she said meekly, "Do you mind? They never come with a salad. It's so judgmental, thinking that because you like a salad you don't want french fries to go with it."

"You could have ordered fries," he said. "They're on the menu."

"Yes, but it's more fun to steal them from your plate."

He grinned. "Doesn't that negate the whole gender equality thing?"

"Adam, I never said I wanted to be your equal. Besides, women don't strive to be equal. We strive to be superior." She batted her eyes, fluffed her hair, and gave him a coy smile.

He laughed. "At least you're honest about it."

"Will you think less of me if I'm honest and say I'd like another glass of chardonnay?"

He laughed again and signaled the waitress for another round for both of them.

She assumed a more serious expression. "Adam, what do you think is really going on here?"

"Aside from enjoying a nice lunch and forgetting for the moment about people being killed and poisoned and blown up, well, I'm not sure."

She pushed her salad aside and sat with both of her hands wrapped around her new glass of wine. "Do you think this has anything to do with the Iranian threats to launch some serious cyber attacks at us? Should I get DHS involved and let them handle this?"

"That's your call," he said. "When we were looking for the nuke the terrorists smuggled in to blow up the dam in Oregon, you didn't want to get DHS involved without solid evidence that was what was going on. We don't have anything solid here either. What's different now?"

Strobel turned her head slightly and looked past him at one of the flat screen TV's on the wall for a moment before she answered. "I was going to tell you the other night at dinner," she began. "I have decided to accept your father-in-law's offer. I'm leaving DHS. I guess that's the difference."

"Care to explain?

"I love what I've been doing," she said, "but it's all changing. DHS now has more than 200,000 employees. We're into everything, and we're not doing anything well, in my opinion. Secretary Rallings has submitted his resignation, citing health reasons, which are valid after his heart attack. But it's more than that. The place has become a cesspool of political infighting. We have factions arguing over whether homegrown terrorists are more of a threat than al Qaeda, whether the borders are more or less secure, whether the TSA should use full-body scanners or adopt the Israeli system of profiling terrorists instead of searching everyone. We even debate whether climate change is more of a threat than transnational crime."

He gave her a slow smile. "It sounds a lot like why I left the army. The Pentagon's the same way. We don't fight wars to win them anymore."

Her smile was bitter. "We don't even call them wars. We call them 'man-caused disasters'!"

"What will you do for the Senator?"

"He wants me to serve as his special assistant for intelligence and national security. Which will include homeland security. It's pretty much what I've doing for Secretary Rallings at DHS."

"When do you join the Senator's staff?"

"I'll stay until Secretary Rallings leaves and his replacement has been confirmed."

Drake picked at his fries before saying, "I guess that ends my short career as consultant/troubleshooter for DHS." He offered her the plate of fries.

" At least with DHS." She ate a couple fries. "But your father-in-law and the Secretary jointly came up with the idea to use you. I think Senator Hazelton would like to continue to call on you in the same capacity. He's a member of the Senate Select Committee on Intelligence as well as the ranking minority member of the Committee on Homeland Security and Governmental Affairs, so he's well aware of the concerns of both committees."

Drake took a pull at his beer. "You said you were reluctant to accept the Senator's offer at first. You said it was because you didn't want to ruin our relationship. Liz, will you be honest and tell me what you meant by that?"

She smiled. "Fair enough, if you'll be honest with me as

well."

"Depends on what you want me to be honest about. There are some things that are better left unsaid."

She nodded. "Okay. I'll just come out and say it, although I think you already know what I'm going to say. I'm attracted to you. I'd like to be more than just a go-between for what you'll be doing for the Senator. I also think you're not ready for a relationship so soon after your wife died. I didn't want to appear to be chasing you."

Drake met her direct gaze with his own as he thought about what to say. "Before Kay died," he began, "she told me a number of times that she wanted me to be happy and hoped that I'd find someone to be happy with. I never told her I wouldn't. But I kept telling myself that would never happen because I'd found the love of my life and didn't need to look for another one. I felt like I'd be betraying her if I found someone else who made me happy." He ran one hand through his hair. "It's only been a little over a year since she died, and I guess I still feel that way. But I also know that when I'm around you, I feel guilty about being attracted to you. So...you may be right that I'm not ready for a *relationship*, but I think I would miss not being able to see you. Is that honest enough?"

Her smile told him that it probably was.

"Will you come and see me in Washington?" she asked.

"I will, if you'll come to Oregon and go skiing with me."

"I'd love to."

Drake's phone vibrated in his pocket. When he pulled it out, he saw that Bill Bradford was calling. "Liz, excuse me while I step outside and take this. It's Bill."

When he returned, he signaled for the check and sat down.

"Bill's invited us to join him for dinner at his home. He's found where the CEO who referred Anthony Capelli is staying."

FORTY-NINE

After a quick visit to their respective hotels to change clothes, they drove across the Golden Gate Bridge to Bradford's home for dinner. The sun was low in the western sky and the lights of San Francisco were just starting to come on across the Bay when they arrived.

Bradford met them at the front door of his contemporary Corinthian Island home. "Welcome," he said as he turned and led them down a short hallway to his spacious kitchen/dining/great room with its magnificent view. "I hope you like Chinese food."

In Bradford's gourmet kitchen Drake saw three large empty woks sitting on a professional range. On an eight-foot long butcher-block island with a small preparation sink in the middle were three heaps of food items. One was a platter of thin-sliced, seasoned beef, sesame seeds, oil, and soy sauce. The next was a selection of fresh vegetables. The third had cooked white rice, fresh bay shrimp, peas, scallions, and two eggs. In front of each selection stood a white five-by-seven inch card.

"I like to have my guests help cook their dinner," the CEO explained. "The cards have instructions for preparing and cooking the items in front of them in one of those three woks." He waved to the range. "You can select the dish you'll be cooking. While you make your selection, I'll pour us some wine."

Predictably, Strobel chose the stir-fry vegetables and Drake picked up the card for the Sesame Beef, leaving the Fried Rice for Bradford.

When they each had a glass of chilled riesling, the host proposed a short toast, "May the food be as good as the company," and suggested that they get to work. An hour and another bottle of wine later, they were seated at Bradford's dining table.

"I appreciate the way you two jumped in and helped with dinner," he told them. "Cooking Chinese food is sort of a hobby of mine, but I don't like to cook it alone. Mary, my wife, has been in Denver for the last three weeks with her mother. I had a craving for the Sesame Beef."

"It's delicious," Strobel said, "even though Adam cooked it. Bill, thanks for allowing me to see another side of him."

Drake looked up from his plate. "Hey! I'm a good cook! And I thought the Sesame Beef was excellent. The stir-fry vegetables, however, seem a little overcooked...."

Bradford laughed. "Sounds like it might be a good time to change the subject. Are you ready to talk business?"

"That's an excellent idea," Strobel said with a show of contrived anger, "before someone gets more than his feelings hurt."

"I called Robert Parker's office," Bradford told them, "and learned that he's in Nevada getting ready for a solar energy conference in Reno this Thursday. He didn't answer his phone when I called him, but I know where he's staying."

"Where?" Drake asked.

"In the house next to mine. He's staying with another solar CEO, who just happens to live next to me on the lake."

"Could we get there tomorrow while he's still there?" Strobel asked.

"Probably," Bradford said, "if you let me fly you there. "I have a plane and a pilot's license. If you drive, it'll take you three, three and a half hours. I can get you there in less than half that time. We can rent a car at the Lake Tahoe Airport, and I'll drive you to my place."

"What do you know about these two CEO's?" Drake asked.

"They're friends, they both have master's degrees from Stanford, I think they started their companies based on what they did their theses on. Parker's company sells home solar recharging stations for electric cars. My neighbor's company builds electric cars. You've probably heard of his Apollo Roadster. It's been featured in the all car magazines."

Drake nodded. "I have. It's supposed to be the next big thing. I've never seen one on the road, though."

"I don't think they're selling very well. The word at my business group is that both companies are losing money, despite the stimulus grants they received from the government."

"What did Anthony Capelli do for Parker's company?" Strobel asked. "What did he base his referral on?"

"Parker said he brought him in to work on a problem he was having with the quality control software for manufacturing the recharging stations. He seemed pretty high on Capelli, based on the work he'd done for him."

Drake pushed his empty plate away. "What do you say, Liz? Shall we take Bill up on his offer and fly to Lake Tahoe?"

"Sounds good to me. I won't get the information on his condo and his resume from my office until sometime tomorrow. Maybe we'll learn something that will help us locate Mr. Anthony Capelli before he disappears completely."

"Excellent!" Bradford said. "Drive across the Bay Bridge tomorrow morning to the old north field of the Oakland International Airport. That's where I keep my plane. Be there by eight. You'll see the Audi parked outside my hangar."

FIFTY

The next morning Drake and Strobel drove across the eastern span of the new, and controversial, San Francisco-Oakland Bay Bridge, which had been built in China, to Oakland's international airport. At 7:45, they parked next to Bradford's white Audi and found him performing a pre-flight inspection of a Cirrus SR22.

Taking a look at the sleek, single-engine plane, Strobel said, "Now I know why he said to have a light breakfast. I didn't think we'd be flying something this small."

"I heard that," Bradford said as he walked around the front of the plane toward them. "I suppose you think you'd be safer in an executive jet or something? Well, you'd be wrong. Come here, Liz."

Standing beside the open door of the plane, he pointed to a small pod on the ceiling above the pilot's seat. "That's where I activate the parachute for this plane. Unlike a commercial jet or the executive jet you were hoping to be flying, my Cirrus SR22 has a one thousand square foot parachute that's rocket propelled. If something goes wrong, we just float down safely. I recommended a light breakfast because I thought you might like to fly the plane and I didn't know how strong a stomach Drake has."

She turned to see Drake smiling as well. "Don't look at me," he said. "You're the one who dissed his plane."

Drake climbed in and sat behind Strobel, who sat to Bradford's right in the well-appointed cabin. From his leather-covered rear seat, he had a clear view of the digital instruments in the cockpit. Bradford plugged their destination into the GPS/Auto system, then listened to ATIS (the Automatic Terminal Information Service) on the radio to get the current wind, weather, barometric pressure, plus runway information.

Next he contacted Oakland ground control and requested Flight Following to Lake Tahoe/Minden Field. Aside from the easy-to-read display panels and the luxurious appointments that he hadn't expected, Drake was most surprised to see that the plane didn't have the usual two-handed yoke to control the plane. Instead, it had a single-handgrip that looked like a joystick. Bradford rested his left arm against the window glass and steered the plane with his left hand as they taxied toward runway 27 Right, to which they'd been assigned.

Bradford proved to be an excellent pilot and tour guide as they flew east to South Lake Tahoe, calling out the names of towns like Antioch and Lodi and Elk Grove in the two-way headsets they wore. The flat valley of central California soon gave way to the green hills of the El Dorado National Forest and then the rocky peaks to the southwest of Lake Tahoe. They began their descent to the Tahoe/Minden airport.

On land again, while Bradford tied down his plane with the help of his new co-pilot, Drake called for a taxi to take them to the car rental agency nearby, where Bradford had reserved a new Jeep Grand Cherokee for the drive to Crystal Bay and his summer home. By ten o'clock, as they drove past the four large casinos at the south end of Lake Tahoe, they caught glimpses of the pure blue water of the largest alpine lake in North America. Minutes later, they crossed the state line into Nevada and turned north toward the far end of the lake.

"We have a forty-five-minute drive ahead of us," Bradford said. "Any one need coffee before we leave town?"

"Not for me, thanks," Drake said. "Liz, do you want something?"

"I'm fine. I can't get over how beautiful this place is. I've skied here, but I've never been here in the fall. I think it's even more beautiful without the snow."

"You'll enjoy the aspens up north then," Bradford promised.

"How well do you know your neighbor on the lake?" Drake asked.

"Not very well. David Klein III isn't the kind of neighbor you invite over for a drink. When he's here in Tahoe, he throws lavish parties at his estate or on his sixty-five-foot, solar-powered catamaran. You can hear them all over the lake. He gives the *nouveau riche* a worse reputation than even they sometimes deserve."

"So he probably won't let me take his electric roadster for a spin around the lake, is that what you're saying?"

Bradford laughed. "If he's been drinking, he might not even invite you in his mansion. Klein's a bully who enjoys intimidating people. It'll be interesting to see how you two get along."

"That's where Liz comes in. She'll either charm him or flash her special agent badge and make him wish he'd been nice to me."

"Or," Strobel said, "I could just let boys be boys and watch the fun from the sideline."

"I doubt it'll be much fun if I find out the guy Klein's friend referred to Bill had anything to do with Mike being poisoned. I tend to forget my manners with people who hurt my friends."

FIFTY-ONE

Thirty one miles away, at the north end of Lake Tahoe, David Klein III was indeed drinking in his mansion. He was celebrating the brilliance of the plan he and his friend, Bobby Parker, had set in motion the week before.

"The beauty of it all," he told Parker, "is that when the power grid goes down, and gas pumps can't pump gas, then everyone will wish they had an electric car and one of your solar charging stations. I'd give anything to see my old man's face when it sinks in that his Cadillac dealership is going to take it in the shorts when my electric cars start outselling his gas guzzlers."

"I'll settle for surging sales of my charging stations so I can keep my company afloat," Parker said.

Klein got up out of his blood red leather arm chair and brought the half-empty bottle of vintage vodka back to the cocktail table that sat between his chair and a matching chair. Both chairs faced the floor-to-ceiling window that provided a panoramic view of the lake and Klein's catamaran docked below.

"Did the Congressman's fixer, Walkur, give you a date for the blackout?" Parker asked. "I want to be sure I'm not flying somewhere when the power goes out at all the airports around the country."

"Bobby, you were too drunk to remember what he told us. The man said the less we knew about his plans, the better off we'd be. If we're ever questioned."

"Why would we ever be questioned? There won't be anything that links us to what he's doing. Will there?"

"Don't be naïve. Congressman Sanchez knows we met Walkur. If they ever put the squeeze on that little prick, he'd give us up in a minute."

"But Sanchez only knows we met with Walkur. Walkur wouldn't share his plans with Sanchez if he wouldn't share them with us."

"Relax, Bobby. No one's ever going to think that two upstanding and successful solar CEO's would get involved in domestic terrorism. They'll blame it on Muslim extremists or the Tea Party before they'd ever think of us."

"Hope you're right. I don't think I'd do jail well."

"Did you worry about going to jail when you were doing your eco terrorism thing?"

"Not much. I was pretty much obsessed with stopping the logging of old growth forests. And I was young. I didn't have a lot to lose. Now I do."

"Tell me about it. I think I'd rather commit suicide than be poor and have my dad laughing at me."

SALEEM CANAAN STOOD SILENTLY at the other end of the great room listening to the two men. He had walked his motorcycle down the long driveway to make it look like he was out of gas, and then he had simply let himself in the unlocked front door. For men involved in such a devious plot, he thought, they were amazingly careless.

And hearing the men talk so casually about their chances of getting caught made him want to shoot them both in the back of their heads and be done with it. Their wealth and success must have blinded them to reality. The country they were willing to cripple would never stop looking for them, just as it had not stopped looking for bin Laden. The trail from EIS Inc. would inevitably lead back to them, with or without the evidence that Ryan Walkur had planted for the government to find.

Canaan almost wished that there was a way the two could be left alone to suffer through the humiliation of a trial and imprisonment leading to their execution, for surely the death penalty would be sought for their crime of treason. Instead, here he was, about to give them an easy way out; he'd decided a quick bullet to the brain would be easier than a hanging and would still look like the cowardly choice of two men remorseful about the destruction they had caused.

But as much as he wanted to continue eavesdropping on these two sacrificial lambs, it was time to put an end to the charade.

Canaan walked across the great room without making a sound and touched the silencer on his FN FiveSeven pistol to the back of David Klein's head.

"Stay seated, both of you," he said in a pleasant voice, "or Mr. Klein will get his wish to die rather than become poor."

FIFTY-TWO

Bradford beckoned Drake and Strobel out to the deck and pointed to a prominence that jutted out into the lake to the west of his property. "That's David Klein's estate."

From where they stood, it looked like a lakeshore hotel. A lawn the size of a football field bordered by a stone fence lay below the main house. A private pier reached fifty yards out into the lake, and they could see the futuristic, flat-roofed yacht with solar panels moored beside it.

"It's beautiful," Strobel said. "In a sort of over-the-top sort of way. Does he live there year round? That's a lot more than just a lake shore getaway."

"Not full time," Bradford told her. "Klein comes up here a couple times a year for parties on his yacht. And a little skiing during the winter. There's a guest house on the other side where his caretaker lives, but the main house is empty most of the time."

"The yacht's impressive," Drake said.

Bradford nodded. "He had it built in Europe. He claims it can cruise around the lake for up to six hours at ten knots using only electric propulsion. He uses it to demonstrate the efficiency of solar power, of course. I'll give him credit, though. The thing cruises by, and the only thing you hear are his guests laughing. No noisy motors. It doesn't disturb the tranquility of this end of the lake at all."

"Do you want to call and let him know we're coming over?" Drake asked.

"I think we should just walk over. The exercise will do me good. And he'll be less likely to come up with a reason why he can't be bothered today."

Bradford led them back through the house, then they walked to the road that led to the estate next door. The late morning sun had taken the chill out of the alpine air and the calls of blue jays in the pines overhead followed them along the way.

The long driveway that meandered down to Klein's house passed a waterfall flowing over a massive rock formation and into a pond surrounded by golden aspens. Fifty yards ahead were the courtyard and the covered entry that led to the mansion's front door. To the right, the driveway curved away from a four-car garage to the small guest house set back in the pine trees.

Drake had stopped to look down at the red and white koi swimming in the pond when he heard a motorcycle roar to life around the side of the garage. When it came speeding into view and raced up the driveway toward them, the rider leaning low behind the windscreen, he grabbed Strobel's arm and pulled her off the driveway. At the same time, Bradford jumped to the other side. As they spun around to watch, the rider accelerated up the long driveway. When he reached the road, he dropped his left knee and made a tight racing turn to the left and sped away.

Drake shook his head. "You were right Bill," he said. "Your neighbor isn't very friendly."

"That wasn't Klein! He's six-seven or eight and heavy. And it wasn't Robert Parker, either. I don't know who that was."

"Whoever it was," Strobel said, rubbing her arm where Drake had grabbed her, "he certainly didn't seem too concerned about our safety. I hope your neighbor's a better host."

Drake took the lead and started toward Klein's house. "Let's find out."

Bradford pressed the button beside the massive front door. They heard the chimes inside and stood patiently, waiting to introduce themselves and ask if either Klein or Robert Parker had time to speak with them. After several minutes, he tried again. Still no one came to the door.

"Let's walk around back," Bradford said. "If he's out on the rear terrace or out on his yacht, he might not hear us."

A brick walkway took them around to the rear of the house and an empty flagstone rear terrace. There wasn't anyone out on the pier, either. Bradford looked around and shook his head.

"He could be out on his yacht. Want me to go check?" Drake offered.

"Yeah" Bradford said. "And let me go peek in the windows. He has a game room back here, with an antique pool table he loves. He could be playing pool with Parker."

Drake stood beside Strobel on the terrace as she looked out on the vast blue waters of the lake. "This is simply stunning," she murmured. "It's so quiet. You can hear the wind in the top of the pine trees."

Bradford's booming voice changed her peaceful mood. "Drake, come see this!"

FIFTY-THREE

Looking in the window, they saw two men sitting in two blood-red leather arm chairs. Blood was trailing down their faces. Each man had a round hole in his right temple. On the hardwood floor beside their chairs lay two snub-nosed revolvers.

Drake tried the door that opened onto the terrace. It was unlocked. Stepping inside, he motioned for Bradford and Strobel to wait as he listened for the sound of anyone else in the house.

"Liz," he said half a minute later, "help me clear the house. Bill, looks like suicides, so search for a note. It might tell us what's going on here."

It took them ten minutes to complete a cursory search of the four large suites upstairs, the gourmet kitchen and dining area, the pool room and library, the utility room and the four-car garage. When they returned to the great room, they found Bradford studying an open laptop sitting on a coffee table in front of the fireplace.

When he looked up, the color drained from his well-tanned face. "According to this," he nodded at the screen on the laptop, "they were remorseful over a plan to crash the energy grid and cause a nation-wide blackout. They wanted to show the country the importance of using more solar energy."

"You mean they killed themselves over something they were planning?" Strobel asked.

"This suggests that it's more than just a plan," Bradford said as took a screenshot of the suicide note with his iPhone. "It's something that's about to happen."

"What exactly does it say?" Drake said.

Bradford read the suicide note aloud.

WE SHOULD NEVER HAVE LET *it go this far and for that we are supremely sorry. When the lights go out all over the country, we just wanted people to know they could have avoided the misery by using free energy from the sun. But we never meant for anyone to die. It's out of our hands now, but it's not too late to prove how sorry we are. Please forgive us.*

STROBEL SHOOK her head and walked close enough to read it for herself. "This can't be real," she said.

"It's apparently real enough for them to kill themselves," Drake said. "Bill, could they really pull this off? Cause a nation-wide blackout?"

"It's possible," Bradford said. "They were smart guys. But they didn't have access to the grid. To cause a blackout all over the country, they would need to attack a number of strategic utilities that have sophisticated anti-virus systems. Some of the smaller utilities aren't up to speed yet, but if they went dark, it wouldn't bring down the whole grid."

"You said they didn't have access to the grid," Drake said. "Who does?"

Bradford thought for a minute. "Well, the new 'smart grid' will link most of the country's power grid to the Internet, so a cyber attack that penetrated the IT security program of a major utility would provide system-wide access. That's what we've been working on with our software—a way to prevent such an attack via the Internet. Also, anyone who supplied key components like transformers would have access. But that supplier would have to sabotage all the transformers in the country so they'd malfunction at the same time for that to work."

"And these guys didn't supply components to utilities. Right?"

"I would know about it if they did."

"Then we're missing something." Drake looked around the room again. "Aside from this suicide note saying they wanted to bring down the country's electric power supply, the closest they were to having access to the grid was Klein being your neighbor."

"And," Strobel cut in, "referring the guy who just left your employment. The one we came here to ask Parker about."

Drake turned to stare at her for a long moment. "Yeah. It fits. Bill's manager is murdered and replaced. Anthony Capelli referred to EIS by Parker." He pointed to the dead man. "Capelli gains access to the power grid by working on the software Bill's developing. Capelli plants a virus the infected software is installed throughout the grid. And then the lights go out when the virus is activated."

"No way!" Bradford almost yelled. "We tested and retested that software. We would know if it carried a virus."

Drake shook his head. "Wasn't Capelli on the team that did the testing?"

"He was, yes. But he wasn't alone on the team."

"Could he have planted malware in the software after you finished your tests?"

"He wouldn't have had time. We finished testing and he quit the next morning."

"Just the same, I think you should have your IT security analyst take another look."

When Bradford walked out onto the terrace to call his analyst, Drake turned to Strobel. "Who do you want to call first about Klein and Parker?"

"Local law enforcement can handle the investigation for now," she said. "They'll want to know why we're here. And what the suicide note's about. I can truthfully say I don't know. All I know is that Bill just flew here to see if Klein or Parker knew where he could find Capelli and we tagged along. I don't want to cause a panic just yet. Let's not have any speculating about a blackout until Bill confirms that there really is a problem."

"If there is," Drake said, "I'm going after Capelli. Five people have died since I arrived in San Francisco a week ago. Mike was poisoned. And now this. If Capelli's the guy who just rode out of here on his motorcycle, then this is bigger than just Klein and Parker's crazy plan."

FIFTY-FOUR

By the time the detectives from the Washoe County Sheriff's Office responded to the call about two dead bodies at the Klein estate on Crystal Bay, Saleem Canaan, aka Anthony Capelli, was back in his room at Harveys Lake Tahoe.

He'd parked his motorcycle in the parking garage adjacent to the casino and, in case they came looking for it, covered it with a stretch-fit motorcycle cover. Seeing the attorney with his former employer at the mansion as he was leaving, he knew they would find the bodies of the two CEO's. That meant Walkur's plan to paint a picture of a remorseful double-suicide would probably fail. The immediate decision he had to make was whether to tell Walkur that he'd been seen.

As far as he knew, Walkur was the only one who knew his real name, but there was no reason to think that Walkur would give him up and risk having his relationship with Hezbollah discovered. Walkur liked being the puppet master who made things go smoothly for the cartels and his clients in the Middle East. Being recognized as such would paint a big red bullseye on the Alliance and its financial empire.

But as he had discovered when Walkur had betrayed the mastermind behind the plan to blow up a dam in Oregon the month before, the leader of the Alliance was not to be trusted. He would easily play one client against another if it suited his purpose and, in this matter, the sacrifice of one young Hezbollah commander to keep from being named America's most wanted terrorist was not hard to imagine.

Standing at the window of his suite and gazing out over the lake without really seeing it, Canaan decided there was no reason to alarm Walkur that his plan would fail when there was a chance it wouldn't. The authorities might conclude it actually was a double suicide, especially if Walkur had planted the evidence in their offices as he had promised.

Killing them had been easier than he'd expected. He had given them the chance to end their own lives at the moment of their own choosing. That way, he had not been forced to make it look like they had killed each other. They had accepted the bargain. All he'd had to do then was taunt them about being remembered as men who didn't have the guts to kill themselves before their horrific crime was discovered.

Klein had broken first. What he'd said was that the thought of his father believing he'd been a coward and a failure was more than he could stand. The other man hadn't said a word when Klein pulled the trigger. He had just watched, looking like a man standing on the gallows as the black hood was pulled down over his head. And then he had lifted his own gun.

Canaan had, of course, worn surgical gloves inside the mansion, so there was no trace of him anywhere, not on the two guns or the laptop where he'd left the suicide note. The only evidence that he'd been there was those three people walking down the driveway. Canaan laughed out loud. They might suspect that he'd been involved in the murders, but when all the forensic evidence established that each man had held his own gun, there would be no way to prove it. The problem, however, was the damn attorney.

Canaan turned away from the window. Walkur would be waiting for his report, but Canaan put some ice in his tumbler and refilled it with two fingers of good Scotch whiskey before he called. He waited for Walkur's bodyguard to answer the phone, then asked to speak with his boss.

"Mr. Canaan, how's the weather at the lake?"

"It's fine here, Mr. Walkur. But I can see some dark clouds at the other end."

"How unfortunate for those living there, I suppose. Will you be returning here?"

"I hadn't planned to. Why?"

"I'm having a guest for dinner I'd like you to meet. He's the one our two friends called on to solicit my help."

"Do you think it's a good idea for me to meet him?"

"I think it would benefit us both if you did. He's been seen with our two friends too many times. Dinner is at eight. Come early and you can tell me about your trip."

Canaan returned to look out the window again. He knew who had referred Klein and Parker to Walkur in exchange for a healthy campaign contribution. He was a U.S. Congressman his cartel connection was fond of saying was "in the bag." Now Walkur apparently wanted him to disappear.

Walkur was tying up loose ends, just as he had with the two solar CEO's. This meant that he, Canaan, would be the only person left who knew what Walkur had done. He would have to very careful that he wasn't the one blamed for killing the cartel's favorite politician. If he was, he wouldn't have to worry about Walkur tying up the last loose end. The cartel would do it for him.

FIFTY-FIVE

After giving their statements to the Sheriff's detectives at the Klein estate and making a quick drive back to the South Lake Tahoe airport, Bill Bradford received the bad news. The 'smart grid' security software EIS had just shipped out was infected with a sophisticated virus.

Drake listened to the call on the cabin headphones they were all wearing in the Cirrus SR22. "How bad is it?" he asked.

"If this is what we think it is, it's as bad as it gets. Some of the code Lewiston mentioned is from the Flame virus that was used against Iran's nuclear program. That virus is huge. Some 70,000 lines of code. And it's very sophisticated. We're still studying it, and we're not even sure we understand everything it's capable of doing." He sighed. "The good news is that a removal tool for the Flame exists. If we can get the word out soon enough, we can prevent this thing from being installed and infecting our clients' IT systems. If not, we'll have to send the removal tool out and hope it's effective against this variant of the virus."

"Bill," Liz said, "could the Industrial Control Systems

Cyber Emergency Response Team at DHS help if there's a virus?"

"Not really," he said. "The emergency response team is more interested in preserving forensic data after the fact. They would insist that no antivirus software be used and tell us to avoid making any changes because it would overwrite important information about the malware. I don't think we have that much time. This is what we're good at. If anyone can fix it, we can."

For the next hour, the team maintained radio silence as they considered the destruction that would result from a widespread blackout in America. With no electricity, lights would go out. Air conditioning and heating units would shut down. There would be no running water. No fuel supply because fuel pumps wouldn't pump. No functioning garbage or sewage systems. Public transportation operators would lose control of subways and trains and not be able to prevent crashes. Air traffic controllers wouldn't be able to clear planes for landings and airports would be the scenes of a thousand crashes. Electronic warning signs on freeways wouldn't function, nor would traffic lights on surface streets in any city or town across America. Electronic and telephonic communications and the Internet would cease. The economy would be in free-fall. Then would come the rioting as the inevitable panic spread. It would be a nation in chaos.

And it would remain a nation in chaos for months or even years because the mostly likely targets of such a cyber attack on the power grid would be the huge transformers, which are difficult to move and have a replacement time of months to years, as most of them are special-ordered and made overseas.

By the time they reached EIS in San Francisco, Bradford's rapid response team was in full war mode and working to identify the threat and what it was designed to do. John Lewiston, the IT security analyst, led Bradford, Drake, and Strobel into a small conference room near the area where the response team was huddled.

"We caught a break," he told them. "We found a file that had been added to our software and recognized it as the Wiper file that the Flame virus also has. I've got our customer support staff calling all our clients to see how many of them have already installed our software. We're ordering them to quarantine the infected computers so the threat doesn't spread over the grid. Detection and removal kits for this virus have been released by Symantec—also by the Iranian government after it was attacked. We're working on a patch we can send out."

Bradford slumped down in his chair at the head of the conference table. "John, how the hell did this happen?"

Lewiston managed an uneasy smile. "You know the *how* is the easy part. Slip a flash drive into a USB port of one our computers on the network, and the deed is done. *Who* is the harder question."

"And you think you know who it was. I can see it on your face."

"I've been here for nine years, Bill, and I know our people. I don't think it was any of them. There's only one person I didn't have time to get to know very well, and that's the new guy you hired just before we finished the DAARPA project. My money's on him."

Bradford nodded toward Drake. "He agrees with you. It's possible Capelli was involved. But why? What would he gain by sabotaging our work?"

Drake pushed himself away from the table and stood up. "You're focused on your software, Bill. You aren't the target. The electrical grid is. This isn't corporate espionage. It's the new form of terrorism. If Klein and Parker were the brains behind this, they tried to get into your system with the phishing attacks you were originally worried about. When that didn't work, they had to get someone inside."

"But to do that they had to kill my employee, Nick Kawasaki. I just don't see either Klein or Parker as a killer."

"They didn't have to be. They just had to find someone to do it for them." Drake leaned against the wall and looked at Liz Strobel, who was reading a text message she had just received. When she looked up at him, he continued, "And that reminds me of something I thought about when we were flying back here. Klein and Parker didn't have to create this virus. They just had to get their hands on a copy of it. Where would they do that, Liz?"

"A number of places, I suspect. Internet security firms like Symantec have copies of the virus to analyze. The Army Cyber Command has it. And may well have helped create it."

"So finding out where they got a copy of the virus isn't going to help me find Capelli. Is that what you're saying?"

"Well," she said, "it might lead us somewhere eventually. But the text message I just got might. Capelli isn't his real name. In fact nothing about him seems to check out. Not his parents, not his education and degrees, and not his work history."

"Who is he, then?"

"Someone with a very good set of faked credentials."

FIFTY-SIX

While the EIS rapid response team worked into the night to prevent a nationwide blackout, Ryan Walkur was preparing to wipe out any trace of a connection to the two dead solar CEO's and their plan, which he now knew would fail. The Army Cyber Command analyst he had blackmailed to obtain a copy of the Flame virus had called to say that DHS special agents were interviewing everyone who had access to the virus to determine if a copy of it had gone missing. The analyst had also said it was just a matter of time before they focused on him and that he was planning on leaving the country. Walkur knew that it wasn't a coincidence that the same day the bodies of Klein and Parker were discovered, a search began for the purloined copy of the Flame virus.

Walkur stood with his hands on his hips looking at the lights of the city. A soft twilight purple lingered after the fading sunset as he considered his options. Clearly, Congressman Sanchez had to be silenced. Once the financial records of Klein and Parker were studied, and the relationship they had established with Sanchez as they fought for the stimulus grants for their solar companies was discovered, said congressman would be questioned about his two contributors. If anyone looked closely at Sanchez's financial records and learned about the soft money he received from the cartels, Sanchez himself would be investigated. A threat of indictment, an offer of leniency in exchange for cooperation, and the oily politician would sing like the proverbial canary. Well, Walkur said to himself, Saleem Canaan would solve that problem tonight after dinner.

The remaining, and bigger, problem involved the attorney from Oregon who now had interfered three times in matters in which he and the Alliance had been involved. The last two matters had ended in failure, but not due to anything he was responsible for.

The current matter was different. *He* had been the one who proposed the cyber attack on the American power grid after Klein and Parker had clumsily approached him with their idea to make solar power more popular. *He* had been the one who had assured his partners in the Middle East that it was feasible to strike a blow that would bring the Great Satan to its knees and have the attack blamed on two homegrown terrorists. The current administration liked to promote the fears of the far right by using the words "homegrown terrorists," so why not offer up two scapegoat homegrown terrorists on a platter? The beauty of the whole thing was that the tool *he* had proposed was the very same virus the Jews and the Americans had developed and used on Iran. As *he* had pointed out, the irony was perfect. Yes, Walkur realized, *he* was deeply involved.

But the real irony was that while the organization he led, the Alliance, always operated behind the scenes and was never blamed for the violence created by the others. This time, he and the Alliance would be blamed for all of it.

The only way he saw to minimize the blow they were about to take was to get out of the country. Which he planned on doing tonight. There remained, however, the problem of the attorney who kept interfering with his plans. Perhaps Canaan would have some ideas on that. He seemed to have a particular dislike for the man.

Walkur left his study and took the winding stairs down to the kitchen on the first floor, where his personal chef was preparing Congressman Sanchez's elaborate last meal. When he was satisfied that it was well under way, he called his bodyguard into the library.

"Karl, we leave tonight. Pack our bags and make sure the Learjet is fueled and ready to leave at midnight. The house staff will remain here, but have security and communications pack things up to join us. I want to be home by tomorrow."

"Yes, sir. Will anyone else be coming?"

"Only Maxwell, my bank manager. I don't want him available to answer questions. He'll make an unscheduled inspection of our banks in Europe for a month or two. He'll meet us at the airport."

"Very good, sir."

Walkur filled a tumbler with twenty-five-year-old Chivas Regal and sat down in the leather wing chair next to the fireplace. It was time to consider how to best serve up the meddlesome attorney's head on a silver platter.

FIFTY-SEVEN

While the EIS rapid response team continuing working on the virus, Drake motioned for Strobel to join him in the hall outside the conference room.

"I know it's late back east," he said, "but do you have someone who can dig up some information about this guy posing as Anthony Capelli? He's our only lead right now."

"Intelligence and Analysis is always staffed," she replied. "What do you want them to look for?"

"Anything that'll lead us to his real identity. Is there anything in any of the data bases that will identify him? Who made his fake credentials? Someone went to a lot of trouble to plant him here. And see if there's any more intelligence about an Iranian plot to bring down our energy grid."

"His personnel file has a photo of him, I'll send that to them. What are you thinking about?"

"I thought I might give Mike a call and see if his hacker, Kevin McRoberts, would be willing to help us."

"What can he do that my people can't?"

"Something that you can't do without a warrant. Don't worry, Liz. This is on me."

She pursed her lips and hesitated for a moment, then nodded and took out her cell phone to call DHS.

Drake watched her walk back into the conference room to retrieve Capelli's personnel file. He appreciated her tacit approval of his intention to step outside the law to get the information they needed. He hoped Casey was as willing to work with him after being poisoned last week.

When Casey answered his call, Drake walked down the hall to the reception area so their conversation would be private. "Mike, how are you doing?"

"Megan's not letting me go into work until my doctor gives me a full release. And I haven't been able to convince him that the slight numbness in my fingers is no big deal. How are you doing? I haven't heard a word from you since I returned to Seattle."

"Well, I didn't want to give your wife another reason to hate me for getting you involved. But there's a bad moon rising here in San Francisco."

Casey knew enough from working with Drake in the past that they would be speaking in generalities from that point on. "That's too bad," he said in a neutral voice. "Anything I can do to help?

"I'm having a problem getting some information I need."

"Would you like me to have the technician who helped you last week give you a call?"

"That would be great. If you don't mind him helping me as he did before."

"In for a penny, in for a pound."

"Thanks, Mike. Hey—get better. I'll come see you as soon as I can wrap things up here."

When he returned the conference room where Bradford

was overseeing his team, Strobel told him that pizza was on the way for the team and that they planned to keep working for as long as it took.

"Would you mind taking me back to the hotel?" she asked. "I don't think I can do pizza and energy drinks tonight. But a nice bath and a change of clothes sure would be nice."

"I'll just let Bradford know we're leaving. We're just getting in the way, anyway. And something other than pizza sounds good."

Drake gave Bradford a business card with his cell phone number jotted on the back and walked Strobel out of the building to his borrowed Audi TTS. It was almost six o'clock and the sun was low in the west, but it was a warm fall night with a clear sky that promised another nice day.

"This is a great city," Strobel said as they pulled out of the parking lot to drive to her hotel. Lights were beginning to twinkle across the Bay. "I've always enjoyed coming here," she added.

"I hope you still feel that way when you leave."

"I will. Bradford's going to take care of the virus and we'll find the people behind it. Sooner or later. I've had a nice dinner, been flown to Lake Tahoe, and got to see you again."

Drake didn't say anything as she rested her hand on his right arm. He wasn't uncomfortable with her touch, but he wasn't sure he was ready to respond to it quite yet. The thought of intimacy with another woman still felt wrong, but Liz had said she was willing to wait for him

"When you're finished at your hotel," he said casually, "why don't you catch a cab and meet me in the View on the 39th floor of my hotel and I'll treat you to dinner. I'm waiting for Mike's guy to call. That'll give us both time to shower and change."

"I'll check in with DHS," she said, "and see if we've come

with anything. But I'll only accept your invitation for dinner on one condition. I get to select and buy the wine. Time you came to understand that California still makes the best wine."

Drake laughed. "You can select it, and I'll even let you pay for it, but don't expect me to agree with you. For me to betray Oregon wine would be like a Democrat voting for a balanced budget."

Strobel slapped him playfully on the shoulder. "I withdraw my invitation for you to visit me in Washington. Being seen with you would guarantee my name would be on the President's enemies list."

FIFTY-EIGHT

Rein Walkur waited for Congressman Sanchez in the living room of his mansion with a second tumbler of Chivas Regal. When the congressman was ushered in, he waved him to the coffee table and the drinks tray.

"Arturo, help yourself to a glass of your favorite, Johnny Walker Black. I had some on reserve just for you," Walkur said. There was no need to waste the more expensive twenty-five-year-old Chivas Regal on a man who didn't have long to live.

"Thank you for remembering," Sanchez said. "I didn't know you were in the country."

Walkur smiled at the lie. Sanchez had known the minute he had arrived in San Francisco because he had been picked up in the bank's limo. Sanchez's nephew was the limo driver, a favor extended to Sanchez when he had agreed to serve on the bank's board of directors when he was being prepared to seek public office. Sanchez wouldn't know when he left, however, because he'd been using a leased limo since then.

"I'm only here for a short time," he replied. "I'm on my way to Singapore. But I'm here because you asked me to see a couple of your constituents."

"Yes. Mr. Klein and Mr. Parker. Were you able to help them?"

"Unfortunately, no. They were seeking far more than I was prepared to invest on their behalf. Did they discuss their plan with you?"

Sanchez leaned forward to refill his Scotch and answered without looking at Walkur. "I assumed they needed money to bail out their companies and couldn't find a more, shall we say, traditional lender."

"Yes, they did hint at that. They seemed quite sure that I could help them since they had paid you such a handsome finder's fee."

"That's the way things work, no? Besides, the money was paid to the 501(c)(4) nonprofit I set up years ago to help the agricultural workers in California when I was a labor leader. It can't be traced to me."

It would be, Walkur knew, when the financial records of Klein and Parker were closely examined. Another reason for the congressman to retire from life, both public and personal.

"Have there been other contributions made directly to you for your campaigns?" he inquired. "I know you were instrumental in the stimulus money they received for their solar companies."

"Not nearly enough, I can tell you. For nearly a billion dollars in grant money, you would think those two *cabrones* could come up with more than a measly couple hundred thousand dollars."

"Arturo, what can you expect of men with no honor? From men who show no respect to a man in your position? Come, let us eat. The dinner I have had my chef prepare for you will show you that you are respected here."

Walkur led his guest to the dining room across the hall, with its curved wall of twelve foot tall windows that looked out onto a courtyard bordered with large pots of flowering purple bougainvillea. The long, formal dining room table had been replaced with a smaller oval table that allowed the men to enjoy the view of the courtyard. A footman wearing a white shirt with a black vest, trousers, and bow tie stood beside the marble-topped ebony buffet on which stood a decanter of pink wine, a bottle of white wine in an earthenware wine chiller, and a bottle of champagne in an ice bucket. Special glasses for each variety of wine waited on a silver tray for each course of the dinner.

When they were seated, another footman entered and placed a plate for each of them on the chargers on the table.

"I hope you enjoy the meal," Walkur said as the footman spread the creamy cloth napkin on his lap. "I asked my chef to specially prepare this for you, Arturo. I paired these veal sweet-breads with a Rosé de Richeys. He nodded to the wine server to go ahead and pour them each a glass.

"That will be followed by seared scallops and sautéed asparagus, with a watercress salad and a Sauvignon Blanc from the Santa Ynez Valley here in your California. For dessert we'll have a nice Riesling poached pear tart with a bottle of blanc de noirs Champagne. I don't get to see you often enough and may not see you again for awhile, so let me propose a toast to a long life and our mutual prosperity."

"To prosperity," Congressman Sanchez said and raised his glass of rosé and took a healthy drink.

When he put his glass down and reached for a fork to try the tender sweetbreads, another footman took his place behind his chair. As Sanchez leaned forward to take his first bite, a fine wire was looped over his head.

As Walkur scooted his chair back to watch, Canaan kept

his right leg against the back of the chair and pulled hard on the two wooden handles of the garrote. The congressman struggled and tried in vain to keep the sharp wire from cutting deeply into his neck. As his trachea was severely constricted and the supply of oxygenated blood to his brain was cut off, Congressman Sanchez stopped struggling and died in less than a minute.

Canaan continued pulling on the handles of the garrote until Walkur finally said, "He's dead, Saleem. Don't decapitate him. I don't need a mess in here."

As Canaan obediently removed the wire from around the dead man's neck and stepped back, Walkur snapped his fingers and two of his security staff entered the dining room and picked up the body.

"Saleem," Walkur said, "the congressman unfortunately didn't have time to enjoy his dinner, so please sit and enjoy it for him."

Canaan pulled another chair to the table and picked up a clean napkin to clean his garrote. "This has become one of my favorite tools," he said. "The wire is actually a very strong fiber that cannot be detected by a metal detector. With the handles detached, the screeners at airports have no idea what it is. What arrangements have you made to dispose of the body?"

"My men will take care of it. He will be buried at sea, and we will avoid the possibility that he would involve us when his relationship to Klein and Parker is investigated." Walkur took another bite of the sweetbreads.

Canaan smiled. "You've thought of everything, haven't you? Just like you did in Oregon when you tied up all the loose ends and had your own man blown out of the sky. Am I next?"

"Do I need to worry about you, Mr. Canaan? I rather thought your willingness to die for Allah was all the reason I didn't need to worry."

"Oh, I'm prepared to die a martyr's death, if necessary. What I'm not willing to do is sacrifice myself for you or your Alliance. You use our *jihad* to make money, just like the cartels do, but that doesn't mean we share a common goal."

"I'm afraid that strategic decisions are made at a much higher level than the one at which you operate, Mr. Canaan. Come. Join me and at least have the good manners your leaders expected of you when they assigned you to work with me. If you expect me to give you high marks for your service, you'll do as I say until I no longer need you. Then you can return to Mexico and continue your war with the West."

Speaking to Canaan as if he were a petulant young boy told to eat his broccoli, Walkur suddenly realized, as Canaan joined him at the table, that there might have to be a change in his plans where the young *jihadi* was concerned.

FIFTY-NINE

Fresh from showering and changing into more casual clothes, Drake took the elevator from his room to the 39th floor, where he found Liz sitting at a small cocktail table next to a window looking out over the Bay.

Like him, she had dressed casually, and with her hair swept back over her ears, she looked like a well-bred woman from an aristocratic family who didn't have to work at being beautiful or looking rich because it just came naturally.

Drake took a seat across from her. "You look like a million bucks, Liz. Rose is a good color for you."

"Thank you. It's one of my favorite colors. Are you ready for a glass of really good wine?"

"I am. What are we drinking?"

"I think you'll like it. But while we're waiting for it, I need to tell you what I've learned. We're still trying to identify our mysterious Mr. Capelli. We're sending investigators to the university where he said he received his master's degree, the University of California, San Diego, to see if anyone there recognizes him. There's no evidence that Anthony Capelli was ever enrolled there, though he might have enrolled under another name.

"We're making some progress with his finances, though. He was receiving $10,000 a month from a bank account in Singapore. The account belongs to a financial holding company in London that we think is somehow allied with Pacific First Security Bank of California. We should know more tomorrow."

While the wine server poured her a taste of the wine she had ordered and she approved it with a nod of her head, Drake wondered why a major California bank was possibly paying an IT saboteur $10,000 a month. When his wine had been poured, he took a drink.

"Tell me what you think," Strobel said.

"Sleek and understated," he said, and she laughed. "Okay. Seriously, it's very good. There's smoky oak, dried berry, sage and maybe anise. What is it?"

"A 2009 Acacia Russian River pinot. You're good."

"It's a hobby," he said with a casual shrug. "I hope someday I'll have my old vineyard replanted and make some wine myself. Would you allow me to order some food?"

"Order away. I've famished."

Drake studied the menu, then signaled their waiter. He was ordering a selection of hummus and pita bread, green salad, and pepper prawns for each of them when his cell phone vibrated.

He looked at it. "I need to take this, he told her. "Be right back."

He walked out to the reception area. "Hello, Kevin," he said. "What did you find?"

"I took a peek at the entity you were interested in, Mr. Drake. The assets you mentioned, the condo and car, are on the books there. There's no record they were being purchased by anyone."

"Were those assets signed out to anyone?"

"It lists the president of the bank as the last person to use either of them."

"When was that?"

"Ten days ago," McRoberts said.

"Did you find a home address for him?" Drake asked to borrow a pen and paper at the front desk and jotted down the name and address of the bank president. "Thanks, Kevin. I appreciate you getting on this so quickly."

"Mr. Casey told me to make it a top priority."

"Tell Mike thanks, too. And send a bill for your time to my office."

When he returned, he saw that their food had arrived and his guest was helping herself to the hummus.

"Anything interesting?" she asked.

"Let's enjoy our dinner," he said, pocketing his phone. "Then maybe we'll have a chance later to talk with that bank president we couldn't find."

SIXTY

Drake's car was waiting for them at the valet stand. He entered the address the hacker had given him into the Audi's GPS and started driving toward Pacific Avenue.

"What are you planning on doing when we get there?" Strobel asked.

"I'm going to politely ask to see Mr. Walkur. And then I'm going to find out why his bank is letting a murderer use its swanky condo and a BMW."

"And if he doesn't tell you why?"

"Then I'll suggest that paying said murderer $10,000 a month makes him an accessory, and will he please remain in his residence until the police arrive."

"What do I get to do?"

"Distract him with your good looks. Beautiful women make some men nervous."

"Thank you for the compliment," she said, "but you're starting to make me nervous. What if Walkur isn't just one of your run-of-the-mill crooked bank presidents? What if he's actually involved in planting the virus at EIS?"

"That's when you get to call in the troops and really scare the hell out of him. Don't worry. I don't expect this to be anything dangerous. We just need a few questions answered."

Drake turned west off of Pine onto Pacific Avenue and entered the exclusive residential area of Pacific Heights. They drove in silence down the tree-lined street until the GPS told them, *Your destination is ahead, one hundred feet on the right.*

"If that's his house," Strobel said as she stared at the three-story mansion, "my daddy chose the wrong line of work. That has to be worth six or seven million dollars."

"Closer to eight, according to Mike's hacker." Drake slowed to pull into an open parking space less than a block from the mansion. As he turned the car off, they saw a man walking down the stairs from the mansion's front door and put on the motorcycle helmet he was carrying. It was too far away to see his face clearly, but there was something familiar about him and the helmet.

Drake and Strobel had taken just one step when they heard a motorcycle roar to life up ahead on their side of the street. It made a U-turn and came toward them, and when it passed them Drake recognized the Suzuki Hayabusa he'd seen Anthony Capelli riding at David Klein's Lake Tahoe estate.

"Get in the car!" he shouted. "That's Capelli!"

Before Strobel's door was shut, Drake started the Audi. When she was in, he made a quick Y-turn and gave chase, burning rubber down the quiet street.

"You sure that's him?" she asked as she fastened her seatbelt.

"That's the same Suzuki we saw in Tahoe. See if you can get his license when I get close enough."

"Good luck with that. He must have recognized you. He's flying."

"He'll slow at the next busy cross street. Get out your

phone and take a picture. There might be enough light so we can blow it up and call it in."

Drake used the quick acceleration of the Audi to pull within twenty yards of the motorcycle as it raced through the intersection of Pacific Avenue and Gough Street. As he slowed to avoid a minivan entering the intersection, he glanced over and saw that Strobel was studying the picture she had just taken.

"I think I got it," she said. "I should be able to upload this on my laptop and blow it up."

"Good, because there's no way I can keep up with this guy."

Which proved to be true as they watched the motorcycle sweep left onto Franklin Street at the next intersection and speed away.

"You really think that was Capelli? He never looked back to see if we were following him?"

"It was him," Drake said. "Do you want to stop at an Internet café or go back to your hotel to blow up the picture you took?"

"My hotel will be faster, I think."

Drake headed to the Huntington Hotel and was a block away when his cell phone vibrated in its console mount.

"Adam, we have a problem," Bill Bradford said. "Can you come back to Hunter's Point?"

"What kind of problem?"

"The virus activates a command when a detection and removal kit is used. If we try to remove the virus, it accelerates the execution command on its own."

"When is it set to execute if the detection kit isn't used?"

"It's programmed to execute at noon tomorrow."

"We'll be there in ten minutes."

"Is Ms. Strobel with you?"

"She is. Why?"

We might need to get Washington involved after all."

Drake drove on past the Huntington. "That was Bradford," he said. "He wants us back at EIS. They've run into a problem and may need your help."

SIXTY-ONE

Bradford was waiting for them in his office. The possibility of failure was evident in the dejected look on his face.

"The virus has been modified," he said as they sat down in front of his desk, "to not only attack and destroy our energy grid, it's also been designed to execute on its own if anyone tries to remove or patch it." He shook his head. "Whoever worked on this thing is very, very good."

"Did you find out how many of your clients have already installed your software?" Strobel asked.

"Seventeen of the larger utilities are far enough along that the damage is already done."

"If we don't find a way to fix this, is that enough to bring down the grid?"

"We don't know Liz. The cascading effect of a large utility's failure on other utilities down the line is hard to predict. It's possible."

Drake leaned forward. "Bill, you said that whoever worked on this virus to target electric utilities is good. Does that shorten the list of people we should be looking for?"

"It might. This virus is identical to the Flame virus that attacked Iran's nuclear program, with a few tweaks so it's effective against electric utilities. It targets large transformers, making them fail. I really can't see Iran behind this, despite the rumor, because it constitutes an act of war. I don't think they're that stupid. They want their nukes. If Israel developed the Flame, with or without our help, they have people who could do this. But then, so do we, assuming we were in on the development of the virus."

"If our two dead solar guys were behind this, do you think they had the contacts to reach out to Iran and gain access to this virus?"

Bradford could only shake his head again. "Adam, I thought I knew these guys, so I'm probably the wrong guy to ask. But from what I know, they weren't marketing overseas. And I never saw them with anyone from that part of the world. The Mid-East."

"Well," said Drake, "the Israelis would never attack us. Unless we keep fooling around, trying to appease their enemies. So our best bet might be to focus on people here in the States who have access and enough talent to do this. Right?"

"We're already doing that, Adam," Strobel said. "I have DHS special agents interviewing everyone who worked on analyzing or, I will concede, may have helped develop, the virus.

"If we only have until noon on Thursday," Bradford said, "they better speed it up. Do you know how far along they are?"

"Let me call and find out." She reached into her purse for her phone. "Bill, Adam, do you want me to call in someone from Washington?"

"I don't know what Washington could do that we aren't already doing," Bradford said. "I've called Symantec, and they're sending a rapid response team from Santa Monica to assist us. They'll be here by morning."

Drake turned to her. "Liz, why don't you check in with your people and find out how the interviews are going. Maybe speed them up, given our new deadline. When you're finished, let's see if we can make out the license plate on that motorcycle we saw."

As Strobel left Bradford's office to call DHS, Drake told the CEO about their drive to question the bank president and how they'd seen Capelli on the motorcycle.

"Let me have her phone when she gets back," Bradford said, "and I'll have the license for you in seconds. What do you think he was doing at the bank president's place?"

"I think they're both involved. I just can't figure out how. Judging by his mansion on Pacific Avenue, though, I can't see the bank president and Capelli running in the same circle."

Strobel returned and Drake asked her to let Bradford have her phone. After connecting her iPhone to his PC, Bradford hit a couple of keys and wrote the license number on a Post-it note.

"California plate 2STZ012," he said.

Drake took the Post-it note and called Detective Cabrillo of the San Francisco Police Department.

"Mr. Drake," Cabrillo said, "What is so important that you had to call me at home?"

"Sorry, Detective. They didn't tell me you were at home."

"They weren't supposed to."

Drake smiled. "I think I might know who killed Nick Kawasaki," he said. "And a few other people. Are you still handling the case?"

"Until it's closed, yes, I am. Tell me what you have."

Drake told the detective about seeing Capelli at the *Queen Mary*, then about the murders at Lake Tahoe and the motorcycle rider's employment and probable involvement in the sabotage of an important project at EIS.

"I saw him tonight," he finished. "On the same motorcycle he was riding in Nevada. I think you need to pick him up so we can talk to him."

"I appreciate your help, Mr. Drake, but unless you have more than that, I can't pick him up. Is there a warrant for his arrest in Nevada?"

"You'd have to check on that. This is important, Detective. I can't explain it all now, but we don't have a lot of time to find this guy."

Cabrillo was starting to apologize for not being able to do what Drake was asking when Strobel reached for the phone.

"Let me talk to him," she said to Drake. He handed her the phone. "Detective Cabrillo," she said, "my name is Elizabeth Strobel. I am the executive assistant to the Secretary of Homeland Security. I am also a special agent at DHS and have arrest authority by virtue of that. It would be *very helpful* if you would put out a BOLO for this motorcycle, as Mr. Drake was asking you to do. If you need to verify my authority, call DHS in Washington."

Cabrillo's tone of voice changed immediately. "Give me the information you have, Miss Strobel, and I'll see what I can do."

"The California license plate on the motorcycle is 2STZ012. Just a second. Mr. Drake has the description of the motorcycle."

Drake took the phone back. "It's a Suzuki Hayabusa, pearl and gray, late model," he said.

"Is that enough, Detective?" Strobel asked.

"It should be, Miss Strobel. I'll be in touch."

As she disconnected, she smiled. "I believe there will be a BOLO out for Capelli and his motorcycle shortly," she said. "Maybe we'll get lucky."

SIXTY-TWO

Ryan Walkur was feeling very satisfied with himself and his work. In a couple of hours, he would be out of the country and beyond the reach of the FBI and any other agency that might be looking for him. With the two solar CEO's and the congressman dead, there was no one left who could tie him to the attack on America's electrical grid. When he was safely home in Paraguay, of course, he would have to reevaluate his working relationship with the Brotherhood. It was becoming more and more risky for him to be involved in their plots, even if this last one was his own idea. Experienced *jihadis* survived because they stayed off the radar, unlike the younger men who were so eager to sacrifice themselves for their religion.

He didn't understand it and knew he never would. Why did they keep sacrificing themselves for their Allah. He didn't believe in god, any god. It was much simpler to live that way.

He returned to his computer, where he had been making sure there were no messages he needed to respond to. Suddenly the phone started flashing to announce an incoming call.

"I thought you might like to know," a voice said without a

greeting, "there's a "be on the lookout" alarm out on your young *jihadi*."

Walkur recognized the voice of his cartel contact, the man who had arranged the drive-by attempt by MS-13 on the interfering attorney from Oregon.

"When was it issued?" he asked. "And by whom?"

"Our source within the San Francisco Police Department said it went out fifteen minutes ago. It's for a 2012 Suzuki Hayabusa registered to a Saleem Canaan."

"Do you know where he is now?"

"Why would we know? We work with Hezbollah from time to time, but we don't keep track of their men. They attract too much attention."

"Thank you for this courtesy," Walkur said. "It helps to make amends for your choice of MS-13 last week."

He smiled to himself when he heard the man end the call without another word. He did appreciate the information, but it wasn't time yet to let the cartel off the hook for the botched assassination and the money it had cost him to arrange it.

The man was right, though. Although Hezbollah was a well-trained and well-funded terrorist organization, with the recent publicity about them being more dangerous than al-Qaeda and setting up camp right across the border in Tijuana, they were attracting more attention than he liked.

Perhaps it was time to eliminate the last person who could tie him to the virus they had planted at EIS.

He took out his encrypted cell phone and called Saleem Canaan.

"Saleem," he said, "there's been a change of plans. I don't want to wait until tomorrow to dispose of Congressman Sanchez. It needs to be done right now. Tonight. Return here and take the body to his yacht at the San Francisco Yacht Club.

Take it out into the bay and set it on fire. There's a dingy you can use to get back to shore."

"Why can't one of your men do it?"

"I have them doing other things. I gave you the pleasure of killing him. Now I want you take care of getting rid of the evidence. I'll expect you within the hour. He's in the back of a van in my garage."

Walkur ended the call before Canaan had time to argue with him.

He took out a phone directory and looked up the number for the San Francisco Police Department. As soon as the dispatcher answered, he said, "I hear that you're looking for someone on a motorcycle by the name of Saleem Canaan. You'll find him later tonight at the slip of Congressman Sanchez at the San Francisco Yacht Club."

Walkur closed the burner phone he'd used. Let the police honor the promise the young *jihadi* had made not to be taken alive.

SIXTY-THREE

Standing well out of the way, Drake and Strobel were watching the EIS rapid response team at work. Bradford's four analysts were seated around a cluttered table with four open laptops on it, feverishly studying lines of code on the screens. Energy drinks and half-eaten slices of pizza lay abandoned as they focused on finding a hole in the virus that they could exploit.

"Bradford's not sounding very hopeful," Liz whispered to Drake.

"I know," he whispered back. "And I can't think of anything we can do to help."

"Well," she said, "I'm going to have to notify the Secretary and let him decide how to proceed. This is going to be a disaster, even if everyone knows it's coming. The FAA can make sure the airports know they'll lose power, but grounding all flights for who knows how long will ruin the airlines. Canceling Amtrak and every subway or light rail in the country will keep people from getting to work and even if they got there, they couldn't work without electricity." She shook her head. "I can't even imagine the financial cost of a blackout."

"And think about the loss of life," he said. "Most people aren't prepared to go without food and water for more than a couple of days, even if they've stocked up a little. We sneer at the so-called preppers, but we'll all wish we'd followed their lead if we don't prevent this." He stepped away. "I'm going to get some coffee in the break room. You want something?"

"No, I'm fine. Thanks."

Drake left the work floor and walked down the hall to find the hot coffee Bradford had promised would be there if they didn't want any of the abundant supply of Red Bull he provided for his employees. After filling his Styrofoam cup with real coffee, he sat down at one of the round tables to think. It was clear in his mind that someone had cleverly planned to attack the energy grid. Going after individual utilities, even if you used the Internet to launch a phishing expedition to gain access to them, would require a massive effort involving a host of hackers. China could pull that off, he knew, but why would they? It would be much easier to infect the software that was being provided to all the utilities on a government-sponsored grant by a company like EIS.

It wasn't a question of *why*, he thought as he took another sip, not *why* all the *jihadi* groups around the world would love to cripple the Great Satan. It was a question of *who*. Who had the means and the opportunity to slip a plant into EIS and supply that person with a powerful variant of the Flame virus? Whoever they were, he had to admit, they were proving to be a worthy adversary.

When he finished his coffee, he started back to find Strobel and ask her if DHS had made any progress with the interviews of government employees who had access to the Flame virus. As he came to the door, his cell phone vibrated in his pocket.

"We just got an anonymous tip that your man will be at the San Francisco Yacht Club later tonight," Detective Cabrillo said. "You know what he looks like. Wanna ride along?"

"You mean someone just called and said this is where he'll be?" Drake couldn't help sounding skeptical. "How did this someone even know we were looking for him?"

"You were a prosecutor," Cabrillo answered. "You've worked with law enforcement. What do you think?"

"I think Mr. Anonymous has a source in your department. The question is why he wants us to catch Capelli."

"His name isn't Capelli. The bike's registered to one Saleem Canaan from San Diego."

"The name Saleem sounds Muslim," Drake said. "Detective, this is getting more interesting by the minute. I'll meet you at the yacht club. I'm driving a black Audi TTS. Flash the lights in the car you're in a couple of times and I'll join you."

He found Strobel standing with her smart phone to her ear, listening and watching the rapid response team at the same time. She signaled for him to give her a minute. Then, when Bradford walked over, he told him about the anonymous tip that had been called in on Anthony Capelli, aka Saleem Canaan.

"So who the hell is this guy?" Bradford asked.

"We think he's someone we've been hearing about in San Diego," Strobel said as she joined them. "He was a student at UC San Diego and has a master's in computer science. But the rumor on the street is that he's Hezbollah operating out of Tijuana. His father is Lebanese, mother, Mexican, and he belonged to a radical mosque in San Diego that we've been watching."

"And Hezbollah is Iran's pawn," Drake said, "so the intel about an Iranian attack on our power grid is true."

"We don't know that for sure yet," she responded, "but it's

possible. One of the analysts at Fort Meade who worked on the Flame project our investigators wanted to interview is missing. He could have stolen a copy of the virus. Or it could have been re-gifted, if you will, from Iran. We don't know how big this is or who's responsible, but we're getting closer."

"Maybe I can help," Drake told them. "Detective Cabrillo called while I was in the break room and asked me to join him on a stakeout for Canaan. Someone called in an anonymous tip that he would be at the San Francisco Yacht Club later tonight. I'm headed there now. If we catch him, we might find out who he's been working for."

"I'll go with you," Strobel said.

"No, Liz. You stay here and coordinate what Bill's team is doing with your people in Washington. Cabrillo can handle it. I'm just going along to identify Canaan. If he shows up."

Strobel put a hand on his forearm as he turned to go. "Be careful, Adam. If Canaan is Hezbollah, he's dangerous."

"So am I, when necessary."

SIXTY-FOUR

Drake set the Audi's GPS for the San Francisco Yacht Club and drove north from Hunter's Point on El Camino Real through the city and onto the Golden Gate Bridge. The San Francisco Yacht Club, the oldest yacht club west of the Mississippi, was located across the Bay on Belvedere Cove near Tiburon. It was not far from Bill Bradford's home on Corinthian Island, where he'd had dinner a little over a week ago.

A lot had happened in that week. Bradford's young manager, Nick Kawasaki, had been murdered, and it now appeared he had been killed so that he could be replaced by Saleem Canaan, a Hezbollah terrorist, so he could plant one of the most destructive cyber weapons that had ever been developed.

Then he (Drake) had been standing next to the young Latina mother who had been gunned down in a drive-by shooting. That near miss still didn't make any sense, and he had learned to be suspicious of coincidences. While he didn't see a connection, he knew there probably was one.

And then there were those two dead solar CEO's in Lake Tahoe, plus what he thought now was probably a phony suicide note that said they were responsible for the cyber attack on the power grid. If he hadn't seen Canaan, or whatever his name turned out to be, racing away on his motorcycle, he might have believed the note.

But not now. Now there too much happening that suggested this was bigger than just two rich boys who might have been trying to demonstrate that solar power was the future of America. What was going on now smacked of terrorism. And if Hezbollah was involved in any way, Drake was sure of it.

The thought of terrorist involvement made him acutely aware that he was unarmed and headed for a possible encounter with a terrorist. California's strict gun laws and its refusal to honor Oregon's concealed carry permit meant that he had traveled to San Francisco without a weapon. He was trained in unarmed combat, but it was always nice to have a little firepower when the opposition favored AK-47's and Uzis.

At least, he knew, the police would be armed. He'd just have to make sure he stayed out of their line of fire if the situation went from green to red.

Past Marin City, Drake turned onto Tiburon Boulevard and drove south to Belvedere Cove. The GPS screen showed the yacht club on the east side of the Tiburon peninsula on Beach Road. He drove slowly as he approached the yacht club. The clubhouse was well-lit, but the parking lot near it was empty. Beyond the clubhouse a long parking lot ran to the south along the club's docks. There were a dozen or more cars scattered down the length of the lot, but he didn't see anyone in any of them, or anyone standing around, either. There were lights on a few of the yachts, but most of the berths had unoccupied sailboats with rigging gently slapping against their masts.

He pulled into a parking space near the north end of the lot and turned off the Audi's lights. The designated parking spaces ran down the center of the long lot and adjacent to the three docks marked Dock 100, Dock 200, and Dock 300. Halfway down on the west side of the lot, a single black Chevy Tahoe was parked next to a row of palm trees that were silhouetted against the lights of San Francisco across the Bay. When its headlights flashed once, Drake started the Audi again and drove slowly toward it. He pulled behind the Tahoe, stopped the Audi, and quietly got out and joined Detective Cabrillo.

"Evening, Counselor. Glad you could join us."

"Wouldn't miss it for the world."

Cabrillo gave him a narrow smile. "Our tipster said Canaan would be at Congressman Sanchez's yacht sometime later tonight. Sanchez's yacht is near the end of Dock 200 on the south side. There's another pair of night vision binoculars in the back seat, if you want them. I have six men at locations around Dock 200. Four in unmarked cars and two out of sight on the other two docks. I have another four men in unmarked patrol cars out on Beach Road for backup. So far, there's been no sign of Canaan or his motorcycle."

"What's the connection with the congressman?" Drake asked as he reached over the seat to pick up the night vision binoculars. He saw there were two sets of night vision goggles on the seat, too.

"As far as I know," Cabrillo was saying, "his yacht is just some place Canaan will be. My guess is our good congressman is involved somehow. We haven't been able to pin anything on Sanchez, but we've sure tried. He was a union organizer for our farm workers before he got into state politics. He still has strong ties to the workers that we think extends to the Mexican cartels as well."

"Any reason to believe he would get in bed with terrorists?"

"Take a look at his yacht. Before he got into politics, he was just another union organizer. Now he's one of our wealthier citizens. I think he'd get in bed with just about anyone if the price was right."

"And I thought I was the cynical one."

"Don't get me started, Counselor. I've had to work with and around enough dirty politicians to last a lifetime. Sanchez is just the latest." Cabrillo raised his binoculars to watch a dark-colored Ford commercial van enter the north end of the parking lot.

Drake also focused his binoculars on the van and watched the familiar night-vision green scene develop a hundred yards away. The van pulled into a space half-way between Dock 200 and Dock 300. The interior lights in the van went on for a second when the driver's door opened, but when the driver got out he walked north toward Dock 200. He was facing away from Cabrillo's Tahoe, so all Drake could see was the back of a short, slender man wearing a dark hoodie and carrying what appeared to be a small mechanic's tool box.

"Could that be Canaan?" Cabrillo asked.

"He's the right size," Drake said, "but I can't see enough of him to tell. Looks like he might be here to work on someone's boat."

"Let's see if it's Congressman Sanchez's boat."

The man walked to Dock 200 and stopped for a moment at the security gate. He seemed to have trouble finding the right key, but then he opened the gate and started down the long dock.

"Stay alert, everyone," Cabrillo said into the speaker of the tactical bone conduction headset he was using. "Wait for my command to move in. Let's see if he goes to the Congressman's yacht."

The man took his time walking down the dock, stopping to check the slip numbers of several large yachts. When he neared the end of the dock, he stepped to his right and prepared to board a yacht two slips away from Congressman Sanchez's yacht.

"Not our guy," Cabrillo told his team. "Looks like we're here for a little longer."

Drake glanced at his watch and saw that it was ten-thirty. "When was Canaan supposed to be here?"

"The tip was that he would be here sometime later tonight. Relax. The night is young."

SIXTY-FIVE

But Drake couldn't relax. There was something about the mechanic that just wasn't right, and when he focused his night vision binoculars on the yacht the man had boarded, he didn't see him. There were no lights showing anywhere on the yacht.

"Cabrillo, can any of your men see where that mechanic is?"

"Do we have eyes on that mechanic," Cabrillo asked his men.

Drake heard a small outboard motor start somewhere near the end of Dock 200. He swung his binoculars in that direction and saw a small dinghy pull away from the rear of the congressman's yacht and move along the breakwater that protected the marina.

The man sitting in the dinghy with his hand on the tiller handle of a small outboard motor was wearing a dark hoodie.

"That's gotta be him," Drake said. "The guy in the dinghy. He's heading out into the bay. He must have jumped onto the congressman's yacht when we weren't looking. He's gonna get away unless you do something."

"The only thing we could do is shoot him," Cabrillo said, "and I can't do that. It will take too long to a chopper here to follow him. I'm sorry."

Drake opened his door and started to get out. "Have your men keep an eye on him for as long as you can. I know where there's a boat nearby I can use and that dinghy can't be that fast. Lend me a pair of those night vision goggles and call me on my cell phone and tell me where he's headed."

"Here," Cabrillo said as he reached down and took his backup gun out of its ankle holster. "Take my Glock in case you catch him. Ten rounds in the mag."

Drake reached for the gun, then jumped into the Audi and tore out of the parking lot. Bill Bradford's place was on the other side of Belvedere Cove. He had seen a Zodiac Bayrunner tied up next to the racing yacht when he'd been there for dinner.

Racing along Beach Road, he slapped his smart phone in the mount on the center console and hit the speed dial for Bradford's number.

"Bill, I need to borrow your Zodiac. Canaan got away from the yacht club in a dinghy. I think I can catch him."

"Hit the garage door opener and pull straight into the garage," Bradford said. "The door into the house isn't locked. Just inside on the wall is a key rack. The Zodiac's keys are on a blue Yamaha floating key chain. It's a 70-horsepower outboard, so you'll have plenty of speed."

"Thanks, Bill."

When he reached the intersection of Main Street and Beach Road, he slowed the Audi to a slightly safer speed through the residential neighborhood. At Bradford's waterfront home, he hit the door opener before he turned into the driveway. The garage door was barely up enough to allow the Audi in when he locked up the brakes and slid to a stop a foot short of the storage lockers on the far wall.

Then he grabbed the Zodiac's keys off the key rack just inside the door into the house and ran out to the door at the back of the garage. The steps led down to the dock and the bobbing white inflatable. As he ran down the steps, he searched the water to the southwest, hoping to see dinghy Canaan had escaped in.

Bradford's home was directly across Belvedere Cove from the yacht club, but Drake thought it unlikely that Canaan would try to put ashore anywhere along Beach Road, which was lined with palatial waterfront homes built closely together. To the south, at the tip of Corinthian Island, was the Corinthian Yacht Club, and beyond the Tiburon Ferry Terminal to the east was Shoreline Park. At night, he figured, the park would provide the best place for a fugitive to land and disappear into the night. If Canaan was headed there, there was a chance the Zodiac could catch him.

Drake cast off the lines, jumped into the boat, and put the key in the center console's ignition. When the outboard roared to life, he shifted into reverse and gave it so much gas that it rocketed backwards and he was almost thrown over the steering wheel to the boat's front well.

Slow down cowboy, he told himself. *You won't catch him if you find yourself swimming beside the Zodiac instead of standing in it.*

After he shifted into forward and brought the inflatable up to a planing speed, he slipped on the night vision goggles and scanned the open waters ahead. The brightest lights on the water came from a ferry heading north from San Francisco. He didn't see anything coming from the San Francisco Yacht Club across Belvedere Cove to his right. When pulled even with the southern tip of Corinthian Island, however, he saw the green-hued wake of the dinghy three hundred yards ahead. Canaan was headed straight for the open space of Shoreline Park.

SIXTY-SIX

Drake closed to within a hundred yards of the dinghy before it reached the rocky embankment that ran the length of the park. Canaan turned and stared at his pursuer for a second, then jumped out and scrambled up to the path at the top of the embankment. He stood up and looked again at the speeding Zodiac, then took off running toward an old, two-story, white building at the southern end of the park where two cars were parked.

Drake veered right to follow, looking for a place to land and tie up. He wasn't prepared to leave Bradford's Zodiac adrift in the bay. As he got closer to the old house, he saw that the shoreline path that bordered the embankment had white cement posts every twenty feet or so with a safety cable strung between them. He turned in and cut his speed, letting the wake behind carry the Zodiac forward until it bumped against the rocks.

With a quick look, Drake saw that Canaan was trying to break into one of the cars parked next to the old building. He jumped out with the forward tie down line in his hand, climbed to the top of the embankment and threw a quick bowline hitch around the post.

Canaan was now trying to break into the other car. Drake ran along the shoreline path and pulled his cell phone out of his pocket. If Canaan made it out of the parking lot before he got there, Detective Cabrillo would have to cut off his escape with roadblocks around the Tiburon peninsula.

"Cabrillo, Canaan's at Shoreline Park in Tiburon. He's trying to break into a car. If he gets it hotwired and gets away, we'll never see him again."

"I know the park. We're on our way. Get the license number of the car."

Drake shoved the cell phone back in his pocket and pulled Cabrillo's Glock out of the waistband of his pants as he ran. Canaan was still trying to break the driver's side window of the second car, an older Ford Taurus. When he saw that Drake would reach him before he had time to hotwire the car and escape, the terrorist ran to the old building and kicked in a door and ran into the dark building.

Drake wasn't far behind. As his eyes adjusted, he saw the sign on the outer wall next to the door announcing it as the Tiburon Railroad & Ferry Museum. He ran to the side of the building and stopped to listen. He heard Canaan knock something to the floor inside. He edged closer to the door with the Glock held high near his shoulder.

"Canaan," he shouted, "there's no place to go. The police are on the way. Come on out."

When he heard glass breaking, Drake stepped inside and flattened himself against the wall beside the door. The night vision goggles showed him the large model train display of the original railroad and ferry terminal was directly in front of him. On the other side, Canaan was kneeling on a counter and breaking out the glass of a small window. He turned and spotted Drake's shadow and fired a shot at the open door.

Drake fired once. Canaan fell off the counter and behind the model train display.

"You shoot like a woman, lawyer. We should have killed you in Oregon. But here is just as good."

Drake suddenly knew who he was facing. "You were with Barak and his men when they tried to blow the dam. Too bad you failed." He started to move slowly around the model train display so he could get a shot at Canaan.

"He failed, I didn't," Canaan said, "and they weren't his men, they were mine."

Drake could see clearly through his night vision goggles. He picked up a miniature telephone pole from the model train display and threw it to the other side of the room.

Canaan reached up and fired toward the far wall where the telephone pole had landed.

The only way to get a clear shot at Canaan, he saw, was to step around the train display, but there Canaan would also have a clear shot at him. Drake moved back toward the door and stopped behind the museum's small ticket counter. He assumed a strong isosceles stance with the Glock as he waited for Canaan to make a mistake.

"Would you like to know how we knew you'd be at the yacht club?" he asked.

"I figured that out," Canaan said. "It was the banker, Walkur. He said he was tying up loose ends when he had me kill the congressman. That meant I might be next."

"You work for him?"

Canaan laughed. "He thinks we do. We cooperate with them when it serves our purpose."

"What purpose and who are *them*?

The approaching sounds of police sirens silenced their conversation.

Drake recognized the words of a Muslim prayer being said on the other side of the room.

When the words stopped, Canaan suddenly stood up and fired wildly as he dashed around the train display, then walked toward the door.

Drake fired twice, hitting Canaan's center mass both times.

SIXTY-SEVEN

What else was there to do? After making sure Canaan was dead, Drake walked outside and waited for Detective Cabrillo to arrive. It was all starting to make some sense. Canaan had been involved in the failed attempt to use a nuclear demolition device to blow up a dam in the Cascade Range. The death toll that would have resulted from the inundation in the valley below had been estimated at over one hundred thousand people; men, women, and children. The man behind the plot had been a Muslim terrorist by the name of David Barak. If Canaan had worked with him in Oregon, the chances were good they had learned who he, Drake, was.

When he had been introduced to Canaan as Anthony Capelli at EIS, Canaan had recognized him. The next day, he had almost been killed in a drive-by shooting, and then Mike had been poisoned outside his hotel room. Canaan was right. They should have killed him in Oregon. He kept turning up like a bad penny, spoiling their plans.

What he didn't know was how the banker figured into it. But he intended to find out.

Detective Cabrillo's black Tahoe stopped six feet from Drake. The detective opened his door.

"Gun shots just reported. Was that you?"

"Yep. Canaan's inside. He heard you coming, said a prayer, and came out shooting."

As Cabrillo gestured to his men in one of the two police cruisers that had pulled in behind him to check it out, Drake dropped the magazine out of the Glock, racked it twice to make sure it wasn't loaded, and handed it to Cabrillo, butt first.

"Canaan said he killed the congressman," Drake said.

Cabrillo nodded as he got out of the car. "We found his body in the back of that Ford van at the yacht club. There were ligature marks on his neck from a wire. It would be nice to prove it was Canaan, because if it's not wrapped up quickly, this will be one messy murder investigation once the press gets on it."

"Were you able to trace the call from the anonymous tipster?"

"Not before I left for the yacht club. Why?"

"DHS says Canaan is rumored to be Hezbollah operating out of Tijuana. We need to know who he was working for. If we don't prevent the blackout, someone will have to pay. If it is Hezbollah acting on orders from Iran, the President needs to know it."

"I'll check on the trace. Do you need to get back to EIS?"

Drake nodded. "If you don't need me here, there's something I need to check out."

"Go ahead. I'll get a statement from you tomorrow."

A crowd was starting to gather on the other side of Paradise Drive as more patrol cars arrived and the investigation of the shooting in the old Railroad & Ferry Museum got under way.

Avoiding the crowd, Drake walked along the shoreline path to Bradford's Zodiac, untied it, and picked his way back down the embankment. When he pushed off and got underway, he forced himself to slow his breathing and relax. The temperature was in the low sixties and the sky was clear, although the stars were faint overhead due to the light pollution from across the Bay. He stayed close to shore and let his mind spin to neutral for the remainder of the ride.

When the Zodiac was secured at Bradford's dock, he checked in with Strobel to see if the EIS rapid response team had made any progress.

"Not yet," she told him, "but they arrested the Fort Mead analyst at the Baltimore-Washington International Airport. He'd driven the extra thirty-two miles from D.C. because he knew we were looking for him. They're putting him on a plane tonight, and we'll have him here tomorrow, hopefully to cooperate with us and work out a way to prevent the blackout. Did Canaan show up?"

"He did. And we almost missed him."

"Is he talking?"

"Not anymore. He's dead."

"What happened?"

"He slipped out in a little dinghy and I followed him in Bradford's Zodiac. He chose to die a martyr's death."

"Did you find out how he was involved in all this?"

"He said that the 'banker' had set him up after having him kill Congressman Sanchez."

"The banker we were going to see?"

"That's my guess. I'm going back to his house in Pacific Heights to see if he's there. I'll come back to EIS after that."

"If the banker is the man behind the curtain, you shouldn't go alone."

"We don't have time to call in the cavalry. I'll be fine."

Backing the Audi out of Bradford's garage, he knew she

was right. If the banker had the pull to get Hezbollah to do his dirty work, he was no ordinary banker.

SIXTY-EIGHT

Drake drove back into the Pacific Heights neighborhood, where the banker's house was located. He drove past painted Victorians and a row of mansions, some of which he suspected housed the consulates of the six or seven foreign countries he knew were somewhere in the Heights.

Ryan Walkur's house looked like it could have been one of the consulates. It sat in the middle of a row of six mansions. Red brick steps led up from the sidewalk to a formal entry on the second floor of the three story structure. The mansions on either side had similar brick steps leading to their main entrances, and there was no wasted space between them. If the three period homes were connected, they would look something like the restored brownstones on the street in Georgetown where his in-laws lived.

There were no lights on that he could see as he walked up the twenty-one steps to the front door. He pulled the chain for the door chimes. Sandwiched between Walkur's mansion and the one next to it, the landing in front of the main entrance could not be seen from the street.

After a minute, he pulled the chain again and listened to the door chimes inside. When another minute passed without someone coming to the door, he pulled the chain one more time and considered his options.

If no one was home, he could find a way in, but a place like this was sure to have a sophisticated security system. By the time he'd had a quick look around, the security service or the police would be there, and he didn't have time to deal with that.

Detective Cabrillo could probably get a search warrant tomorrow, based on Canaan's statement that the banker had had him kill Congressman Sanchez, but the blackout was scheduled for the day after tomorrow. They were running out of time.

Drake took out his cell phone and called Strobel.

"Liz, I need your help. How soon can you get here?"

"Are you okay?"

"Yeah, but please hurry, I'm at the banker's house and I think evidence is about to be destroyed inside."

He didn't like deceiving her, but she needed to be able to say that she'd been told that exigent circumstances existed and that entry without a warrant was justified. When she arrived, he would apologize for the deception and hope that she trusted him enough to back him up when the police arrived.

Twenty minutes later, she pulled up to the curb in Bradford's white Audi. When she jumped out and ran up the steps, the scowl on her face told him she didn't like what he was thinking about doing.

"Let me guess," she said. "No lights on inside, no one's answering the door, so you want in?"

"Short answer, yes. We have twenty-four hours, plus or minus, before everyone's lights go out. This is the only lead we have."

"And what am I supposed to do? Help you break in?"

"I'll do that," he assured her, "but when I do, I'll probably set off an alarm somewhere. When the police get here, I want you to hold them off with your special agent badge so I can look around."

"And I tell them what?"

"That I told you I said I heard someone inside, that the lights went out, and that I thought evidence was being destroyed . Exigent circumstances. So you sent me in."

"No judge would believe that."

"Liz, who cares? This isn't about evidence to convict someone. This is about saving thousands of lives that will be lost in a nationwide blackout. I have to go in!"

"Okay, five minutes. Here, take these." She handed him a lock pick tool set in a small leather case. "I was afraid this was what you had in mind."

Drake took out a half-diamond pick and a tension wrench out of the case. As a Delta Force operator, he'd received extensive training in covert methods of entry. But it was a skill he hadn't used in years.

Relax, he told himself, and focus on the skills he'd learned and not on just opening the antique brass Schlage deadbolt lock. Just as sweat and frustration were about to break out on his upper lip, he felt the pins click into place. He opened the door.

"Stay here," he said to Strobel. "If I'm not back in five minutes, call me."

"And if you don't answer?"

"Come find me. I'm probably in trouble."

SIXTY-NINE

Drake stepped inside. As his eyes adjusted to the dark, he took out his tactical flashlight. Developed by Pelican for the L.A.P.D., it had a momentary mode that shot a quick 130-lumen beam for a split second to avoid detection. Not knowing if anyone was home, he intended to make a quick, quiet sweep of the house without disturbing anyone inside or outside the house.

From the street level, the house had four floors. Directly ahead of his position in the vestibule on the second floor, a quick flash of light from his Pelican 7060 showed him the stairs to the two upper floors. He moved quickly to them and kept going until he reached the top.

The top floor consisted of just three rooms, an open area that might have been a family room, a bathroom, and a study. He checked to make sure the bathroom wasn't occupied, then moved into the study. The elegant antique desk had a small brass lamp on one corner and a pewter mug with a couple of sharpened pencils in it on the other corner. The three drawers on the right side of the desk were empty, and all the center drawer held were a legal pad and a small container of paper clips. The three drawers on the left were locked, but there wasn't time right now to force them open.

Drake returned to the stairs and moved down to the floor below. Two doors closest to the stairs opened into empty bedrooms. Moving down a long hallway, he passed a large bathroom and then came to the door of a master bedroom suite that was also empty. Both the master bedroom closest and the antique wardrobe were also empty. He was beginning to think the mansion, large as it was, wasn't really anyone's home on a full-time basis. It looked more like the presidential suite of an elegant European hotel; elegantly appointed and functional, but not lived in. He went down another flight of stairs.

The floor below was obviously for entertaining. He checked out a long, formal, carpeted living room, a dining room with french doors leading out to a patio and garden, and a small bar. Down the hall were the kitchen area, a sitting room, and another study with a fireplace. It looked like the study on the top floor, and the antique desk was just as bare. Its drawers, which were not locked, were empty.

Drake checked his watch. He had another minute before Strobel would be calling, so he returned to the stairs for a quick look down at the first floor where he knew the garage was located at street level. At the bottom of the stairs, a metal fire door opened onto the small, empty garage. A quick beam from his flashlight located a wall of cabinets at the rear of the garage on either side of another metal fire door.

As he moved toward the door at the rear of the garage, he could hear a muffled conversation on the other side. He couldn't make out what was being said, but he distinguished two voices, both male.

His time was up, and he knew Strobel would be calling. Putting his phone on mute, he knew he could continue his search or get out without being discovered, but without what he was looking for. *That's a no-brainer*, he thought, as he moved forward.

The overheard conversation ended, and he heard a door close in the next room. It sounded like the door of a bank vault being secured. Whatever secrets the old mansion was hiding, he was willing to bet they were on the other side of the door in front of him. The trick was going to be gaining access without an invitation.

He slowed his breathing and settled into a familiar place where he visualized what he was about to do. If one man opened the door when he knocked, he would use the flashlight to momentarily blind him and quickly move to put him down. If both men were in the next room, he would deal with the first man and then engage the second.

If the second man were armed, he would have to improvise.

He took a deep breath and ran his hand down the left side of the door. The right hand fire door had three exposed hinges, which meant that the door would open toward him. Drake put the flashlight in his left hand and raised it level with his eyes. With his right hand, he knocked hard on the door twice and took a hold of the door handle.

When the door opened a crack, Drake pulled hard and aimed the flashlight up into the eyes of the man being pulled toward him. The man's hold on the door handle caused him to take a step forward, and Drake hit him hard with a right cross to the jaw. Fortunately the man, who was a big as an NFL lineman, had a glass jaw and crumpled to the floor on his back. Out for the count.

Drake stepped over him and shot a quick beam around the room. On the left were a large commercial standby generator, stacked cases of bottled water and boxes of military Meals Ready-To-Eat. To the right he saw six deployment-hard cases for M4 carbines and twenty of so dark green ammo boxes labeled 5.56mm NATO, the ammunition for the M4's. Either the old mansion was the headquarters for some paramilitary group or someone was preparing for a disaster of some sort. Like a prolonged blackout, for instance.

In the back wall was another steel door, a steel vault door with a biometric, fingerprint-keypad lock, the kind you might find protecting a safe room in a very security-conscious residence. Knocking on that door wasn't an option this time.

He looked back at the unconscious man on the floor. At an earlier time and place, he wouldn't have hesitated to cut off the man's thumb to see if its fingerprint would open the vault door. But here at home, he knew, the rules of engagement were different. The enemy might be the same, but you had fewer options.

Drake turned on his flashlight and swept it around the room, then across the ceiling. Two overhead fire sprinklers had been installed in a line down the middle with a smoke alarm between them. The owner of the mansion was making sure his survival cache of arms and ammunition were protected, even if the sprinkler system wouldn't do much to save the cardboard boxes of MRE's.

He returned to the man on the floor and searched for a lighter or matches. In the left front pocket of his shirt, he found a pack of long cigarettes or something. A quick beam from his flashlight showed him they were Cuban Cohiba cigarillos. But there were no matches in either shirt front pockets.

A man who smoked mini cigars should have a lighter. He started to roll the man on his side to search the pockets of his cargo pants when he grunted and tried to rise. Drake spun around behind him, locked his legs around the man's waist, and applied a sleeper hold. Before he made another sound, the man was again unconscious again.

In the left pocket of his cargo pants, Drake found a well-used Zippo lighter like the ones most of the men in his old unit in the sand box had carried. The lighters were wind-proof, but they also produced an excellent flame for lighting cigars.

Back in the middle of the room, he flipped the lighter open and used his flashlight to find the smoke detector. A spin of the striker and he had a flame an inch long going directly under it. When the smoke detector began its loud beeping, he ran to the right side of the vault door and waited.

"Raul, what the hell, man, you can't smoke out there!" a man shouted as the vault door swung open.

Drake moved from behind the door, grabbed the second man's right wrist with his left hand and stepped in to deliver a horizontal elbow strike that impacted just in front of the man's left ear. As the man fell forward, Drake entered the vault before the door closed.

SEVENTY

The man sitting at the gray metal desk staring at him over the top of an ultra-wide flat screen monitor didn't move as Drake surveyed the room.

The back wall displayed a large, global conflict map with colored balloon icons marking the world's armed conflicts. A flashing satellite track moved across it from left to right. To the right of the conflict map, a mini-supercomputer that looked like a high-end stereo sat in a three-foot-high, black-framed case. A work bench ran along the right wall with a couple of Iridium satellite phones like he had used in Afghanistan hung in wall mounts above it. Along the left wall was a single, neatly-made, metal, military bed.

"Who are you?" the man said as he stood with a subcompact Sig Sauer pistol pointed at Drake in his left hand.

"I'm more interested in who you are and what you're doing in this bunker."

The pistol's steady aim told Drake the man wasn't afraid. He looked to be in his forties, fit, with light brown or blond hair, wearing round wire-framed glasses, and a Bluetooth headset in his left ear.

"I said, who are you?"

"I came here to see Mr.Walkur. Who I am isn't important. But I should know your name before the police arrive. Are you Walkur?"

"I'm not Mr. Walkur, he's not here. But, *we* have done nothing wrong! It is you who broke into our house. I could shoot you in self defense."

"You could," Drake replied, "but then, when the police investigate my death, you'd have to explain why you were working with Walkur to cause a blackout all across the country. They know I'm here."

The man's eyes squinted ever so slightly. "If you know that much," he said calmly, "then you know you're already too late. The blackout can't be stopped."

"Don't be so sure. The cyber analyst you stole the virus from is being flown here, even as we speak."

The man laughed and started around the desk toward Drake. "I added a suicide function to it. If you try to uninstall the malware, it triggers a detonate command immediately. So you see, you lose, we win."

Drake still hadn't moved. "Who are *we*? You don't look like an Islamist."

"I'm not," the man said. "We just use them to advance our cause. But enough with the questions. Let's go upstairs and find a place where you will, unfortunately, be shot as an intruder." Staying a safe distance from Drake, the man motioned toward the vault door with his pistol.

Drake turned around slowly and, as he did, put his thumb over the on button at the end of his flashlight. When he reached to push the vault door open with his left hand, he brought his right hand up under his left bicep and aimed toward the man's face.

The rapid pulsing of the 130 lumen beam caused a momentary blindness in the man's eyes. Drake spun around and lunged back. A roundhouse strike with the flashlight knocked the pistol to the floor. Then a straight, left-hand, punch to the man's nose knocked him off his feet and sent him crashing across the metal desk and through the ultra-wide monitor.

Drake picked up the Sig Sauer and peered over the desk. The man was on the floor, on top of the ruins of his monitor. Blood was gushing from his nose, making a bubbly sound. He would live long enough to be interrogated. That was all that mattered at the moment.

Within seconds, Drake heard people running from the other end of the ground floor and stampeding down the staircase into the garage.

"Drake," Liz Strobel shouted, "where are you? Adam!"

He opened the vault door. "Back here."

Detective Cabrillo followed Strobel into the storage room to the man that looked like an NFL line man and checked for a pulse. "This one's alive," he said. "Friend or foe?"

"Definitely a foe," Drake said. "And you better restrain him. He's big, and he might be a little angry when he wakes up."

Strobel continued to the second man, who was lying on the floor in front of the vault door, and knelt down to check on him. "This one's alive, too," she said. "Restrain him, too?"

"Sure," Drake said. "We wouldn't want him to think we gave his friend special treatment."

She stood up and looked beyond Drake into the vault room. "What is this place?"

"Come take a look. I think this is their operation center.

The guy on the other side of the desk back there told me he worked on the virus. He said he added a suicide function to it that would activate the malware if we tried to uninstall it."

"I'll better call Bradford and let him that," she said and walked out of the vault room to use her phone as Detective Cabrillo entered and took her place. He stared at the global conflict map on the back wall and then moved to get a closer look at the computer.

"I think it's one of the desktop supercomputers I've read about," Drake told him. "A FASTRA or something. Whoever these guys are, they're working with some expensive tools. There are two sat phones on the wall. And I'll bet that blinking light on the map is the orbit of a communications satellite."

"Who's the guy groaning on the floor?"

"He's the one we need to talk to. Said he worked on the blackout virus."

The detective frowned. "Drake, I can't let you interrogate him. I don't even have a reason to arrest him. You, however, could be arrested for breaking and entering. Your lady friend wasn't very convincing with your 'exigent circumstances' story."

"Then let Liz handle this, Detective. She's a federal agent, and she knows what's going on. This is cyber terrorism. He can be detained for as long as we need him. The FBI or DHS can do the interrogating, but we're running out of time."

Strobel came back into the vault. "I called the FBI. They'll take custody of these three. I'll question the one behind the desk. Bradford's sending someone over from EIS. Maybe there's a clue here that will help us deactivate the virus."

SEVENTY-ONE

Strobel walked around the gray metal desk to see if the man on the floor was alert enough to talk. As she reached down to tap his shoulder, however, a gurgling growl initiated sudden spasms of his neck muscles that arched his head back and jerked his chin toward the ceiling.

"My God," she said, "he's having a seizure."

Drake and Detective Cabrillo rushed to help, but the first thing Drake did was to grab her shoulder and pull her away.

"Stay back, Liz. He's poisoned himself."

The man's skin was turning blue and his pupils were now fixed and dilated. A slight but distinctive odor of bitter almond lingered over him.

Drake leaned down for a closer look. "He must've had a poison capsule or a fake tooth. I sure didn't see that coming."

"Who is this guy?" Detective Cabrillo asked. "I've arrested a lot of tough criminals, but none of them committed suicide to keep from going to jail."

The man was now flat and unmoving.

"Do you want me to search him?" the detective asked.

"Let the paramedics do it when they get here," Drake said. "Liz, the other two men might have the same poison on them. You might want to make sure they don't wake up before you have a chance to remove it. Don't let them know this guy's dead just yet."

As Strobel led Detective Cabrillo out of the vault room to deal with the two unconscious men in the next room, Drake began searching for anything that might help Bradford with the virus. The metal desk had two large drawers filled with hanging files. He took out the first file. It contained twenty or thirty pages of programmer's code. He set it aside. Bradford would have to sort through it. The rest of the files, numbered 1 to 25, were similar, with page after page of programmer's code. The bottom drawer held files numbered 26 to 50.

In the center drawer, he found five white USB flash drives neatly lined up on a programmer's mouse pad, which was red. In its center was a black Greek meander motif inside a laurel wreath, the symbol of Greece's Golden Dawn Party. The symbol looked a lot like a Nazi Party banner.

What have we here, he wondered. A neo-fascist symbol on a mouse pad tucked away in a secret vault in a mansion in San Francisco, and a dead programmer using cyanide. Strobel was going to shake up some people in Washington when she turned in her report on this. A well-known San Francisco bank president found to have ties to a Hezbollah commander involved in a plot to crash America's electrical grid, and possibly to a neo-fascist political party in Greece.

Drake gathered up the five flash drives and dropped them in his pocket. Then he took out his phone. Bradford needed to know about the suicide function imbedded in the virus. He also needed to get someone over here on the double to check out those fifty files of programmer's code and the mini-supercomputer in the vault room. Drake would also make sure the flash drives made it safely back to EIS before they were bagged as evidence.

After a quick conversation with Bill Bradford, who promised to have someone there in fifteen minutes, he found Strobel upstairs in the vestibule talking with two FBI agents. She started to introduce him, but he pulled her aside before she could give them his name.

"Liz," he whispered, "you're going to have to handle this end. Bradford's sending someone over to look through the stuff down in the vault, but you need to take a look first. Look in the center drawer of the desk. Then decide how much of what we've found you want to share with everyone. There might be an international connection here that could be explosive. I'm going back to EIS to talk with Bradford."

"What kind of international connection?"

"The Golden Dawn in Greece. It's just a mouse pad, but you don't buy one of those at Target."

She shook her head. "I'd better call the Director. This is moving too fast and in a direction I don't care for."

"And not fast enough in another direction," Drake said. "The blackout's set for noon today. That gives us a little less than twelve hours."

RYAN WALKUR SAT LOOKING DOWN at the lights of San Diego from an altitude of 35,000 feet in his Learjet 75. He was thinking about the best way to distance himself from the operations of the Brotherhood while still maintaining the Alliance's role as facilitator for the drug cartels and the *jihadis*. The last several operations the Brotherhood had undertaken had all been failures.

When he was home in Paraguay, he would have to find a way to make things right. He would begin—

"Excuse me, sir." The copilot pulled back the cockpit curtain. "Sir, you have a text message on your sat phone."

Walkur took the Iridium satellite phone from the panel compartment next to the executive table he was working at and read the message from his cartel contact in San Francisco.

C4: *My SFPD source reports your residence on Pacific Avenue is being searched by DHS, FBI and SFPD. Two men in custody, one dead. Suggest no stops where extradition treaties exist.*

SHAKING HIS HEAD IN DISBELIEF, Walkur read it again. That couldn't be possible! With Canaan dead, no one knew he was involved in the blackout plan. His bank manager had reported that a man and a woman had asked for him at the bank, but they didn't have access to any of the bank's records, and the bank manager was on the plane with him as a precaution.

And yet, he had left the house staff behind. Two security men and his IT expert. He typed in a reply:

RW: *Urgent that I know why and what they know. I will reward you and your source generously. Flight plan will be revised. Thank you.*

WALKUR INSTRUCTED his pilot to cancel their planned stop in Mexico City and continue on to Cuba.

SEVENTY-TWO

When Drake arrived at the EIS offices, he found that a serious case of panic had developed. The EIS team and the rapid response team from Symantec couldn't agree on how to proceed with the suicide function set to activate if they tried to override the coded commands. The amount of code they needed to study was so voluminous they would never get through it before noon.

Bradford waved to Drake to follow him to his office.

"The cyber analyst DHS is flying here won't arrive for another hour," he said as he slumped down in his chair, "and we're running out of time. Did the guy in the vault say anything else?"

Drake shook his head. "All he said was if you try to uninstall the malware, it activates a detonate command."

"That's a suicide function. That doesn't get us anywhere."

"Maybe these will," Drake said as he took the five flash drives out of his pocket and laid them on Bradford's desk.

"What are these?"

"They were in the top drawer of the programmer's desk. I

don't know what's on them. And there are two drawers of files of programmer's code at Walkur's residence your man can study, along with that mini supercomputer I described. We'll find a way to beat this thing, Bill."

"If we don't," Bradford replied, "I'm ruined. All these years, and I let my guard down just once and rely on someone I thought was a friend. Then *this* happens. It's my fault, all of it. I should have vetted Canaan—Capelli—more thoroughly and not rushed to meet our deadline when Nick Kawasaki was killed. The very thing my security software was designed to protect against is about to be the Trojan horse that brings down the entire energy grid."

Drake tried to sound optimistic. "It might be the fourth quarter, but the game's not over yet. Why don't you take these flash drives and get your team started on them. I need to call Liz and find out if she's learned anything from the two guys she's questioning."

On his way to the break room for a much needed cup of coffee, he called Strobel. "Liz, have you learned anything helpful from our two captives?"

"They're not very talkative. They may both have concussions, but they're alert enough to demand that the consulate of Paraguay be notified that they're being detained. They claim they're citizens of Paraguay."

"Did they say who they're working for?"

"They claim to work for our Mr. Walkur. Members of his house staff. But they look like bodyguards to me."

"That's what I thought, too. Sounds like both of them need some enhanced interrogation."

"Don't think it hasn't crossed my mind."

"Want me to come back and assist you?"

"I'll have another go at it first. I was polite initially, but they need to understand that as co-conspirators of a plot to destroy or damage the electrical grid where a death results, they're facing the death penalty. Paraguay can't help them. Neither can their boss."

"What did Director Rallings say when you called him?"

"He's asking the CIA to send him what they have on the Greek Golden Dawn. He told me to focus on preventing a blackout. And he told me to tell you he had no idea that Bradford's cyber attacks would lead to something like this, but he's glad he asked you to check things out."

"We're lucky he did." Drake admitted. "Is the FBI cooperating?"

"They are for now. The two agents are watching me closely, but I think they've been told to stay out of my way."

"The Cyber Command analyst should be here at EIS within the hour. If you learn anything, or if Bradford's man finds something in those files or on the computer in the vault, let me know immediately."

"You do the same. Good luck."

SEVENTY-THREE

Four DHS special agents arrived at the EIS offices at 2:00 a.m. with the Cyber Command analyst, now wearing an orange jump suit, handcuffs, and shackles. The young man's hair was disheveled and his eyes were bloodshot. He was clearly frightened of the men who had flown him across the country.

Drake introduced himself to the lead agent and explained that Ms. Strobel was questioning two other men, and would join them soon. He directed them to take their prisoner to the conference room.

When they had shuffled him down the hall and seated him on the other side of the big conference table, Drake asked them to leave so that he could talk with the analyst alone.

"I'll have some coffee brought in," he said in his good cop voice. "You look like you could use some. Did they treat you all right?"

The analyst raised his eyes. "They think I'm a traitor. How do you think they treated me?"

"You *are* a traitor," Drake said, "but I still hope you were treated fairly.

"They were rough, yes, but they didn't beat me, if that's what you want to know. Who are you? Their boss?"

"Who I am isn't important," Drake said with a shrug of his shoulders. "Right now, I'm the person standing between you and a trip to Guantanamo. You are a co-conspirator in a terrorist plot to hurt a lot of people in this country. If you tell me what I want to know, you might get to stand trial here instead of being detained indefinitely on an island in the Caribbean."

"I'm not a traitor. And I'm sure as hell not a terrorist."

"You gave a copy of deadly computer virus to a terrorist who's using it to crash the U.S. power grid. What would you call yourself?"

"Listen," the analyst leaned forward, "first, the Flame virus I worked on is available all over the place. Iran made it public once they discovered it. If someone's using it for some terrorist thing, I don't know anything about that. Second, the Flame virus is designed to carry out cyber espionage, not shut down an energy grid. Theoretically, the virus is smart enough to do what you say, but you'd have to modify it a lot do it that."

Drake got up and walked the long way around the conference table. He stopped behind the analyst and leaned down and spoke directly into his right ear. "You haven't denied that you gave the virus to someone. Why is that? I think it's because you did and that's why you were trying to flee the country. Am I right?"

The analyst stared straight ahead and remained silent.

Drake stepped back and waited through a full minute of silence. Then he reached around and slammed the table with his right hand and shouted in the analyst's ear, "Am I right?"

The analyst jumped an inch off his chair and began

shaking.

When he was back in his seat on the other side of the conference table, Drake calmly said, "This is going to end badly for you if you don't start cooperating. So let's make this easy for both of us, or at least for me. I killed a man tonight. A Hezbollah terrorist. I raided another man's home, the man I believe you gave the virus to. One of his men committed suicide rather than talk to me. Is that what you're prepared to do? Are you going to bite down on a poison fake tooth and kill yourself? 'Cause if you are, go ahead and do it. I'm tired and would like to go to bed."

The analyst began rocking back and forth in his chair. When he stopped rocking a minute or so later, he said quietly, "I had a big online gambling debt I couldn't pay. I was told that if I provided him a copy of the Flame virus, he would wipe my debt off the books. If I didn't, he would reveal my gambling to my employer. I didn't have a choice."

"Did you modify the virus to attack the energy grid?

"I would never do that. I stole a copy of it, but I didn't do anything that would hurt my country."

"Do you know the man who was blackmailing you?"

"No. He was just a voice on the phone. But he knew me! He knew my unlisted cell phone number, everything about my gambling. Things no one else could know. At first, I thought it was a counter-espionage test the Cyber Command was running. Until he killed my Golden Lab as a warning."

"Do you think you can help us find a way to keep this virus from activating at noon today?"

"I can try." By now the analyst looked almost pathetically eager. "I can't promise anything, though."

"That's all we can ask right now. I'll have some coffee and a sandwich brought in. The agents who brought you here are right outside, so it's best if you don't try and leave."

SEVENTY-FOUR

Stepping out of the elevator into the EIS reception area, Strobel waved to Drake down the hall, where he was talking with two DHS agents she knew.

He waved back and walked to meet her.

"How'd it go?" he asked her.

She grinned and brushed her hair behind her ears. "We have two soldiers of something called 'the Alliance' detained now. They gave me their names and little else. But I was able to learn that Asuncion, Paraguay, is where they call home and that Mr. Ryan Walkur, their employer, is apparently also the leader of this Alliance."

"Did they admit to the Alliance being behind the virus?"

"Not so much. But both of them seemed to be proud that we'd think so. I think they know the Alliance is involved but aren't willing to admit it. We'll find out, though it might take some time. So how are you doing here?"

"The analyst from the Cyber Command is here," Drake said, "but he denies modifying the virus. He says he was blackmailed into stealing a copy of the Flame virus."

"Has Bradford made any progress?"

"Let's go find out. I brought some flash drives back that might help.

They found Bradford looking over the shoulder of John Lewiston, his cyber security expert, who was studying lines of programmer's code on a monitor.

"We may have found the key on one of the flash drives you gave me," Bradford said without looking up. "John thinks this is the exact code for the suicide function. Now we can get to work building a repair kit to counter it."

"Will you have enough time?" Strobel asked.

"It'll be close. But we have all our utility clients on standby right now. As soon as we have the kit completed, they'll have it in seconds."

"Good luck, Bill," Drake said. He stepped back as two members of Symantec's rapid response team moved in to see what Bradford was talking about.

Hearing her cell phone beep in her purse, Strobel walked to the back of the work area and took out her phone to read a message she had just received. After texting a quick response, she returned to Drake's side.

"Your father-in-law just landed and will be here shortly," she told him. "He wanted to come and let Bradford know he'd have his support when all this gets investigated."

"Did you know he was coming?"

"He let me know when he left D.C., and, yes, I knew he was thinking about coming. He asked me to keep him informed.

She watched Drake's reaction on hearing that she'd been communicating with his father-in-law. When she had told him at dinner the week before that the senator had offered her a position on his staff if she left DHS, a phone call she'd received had kept her from hearing if he would be comfortable with her working for his father-in-law. Later, he had told her it he didn't think it would bother him. But she knew in her heart that if accepting the offer harmed her relationship with Drake, it wouldn't be worth it. For that reason, she was willing to be patient. At the same time, she had no intention of giving up on her hope of securing his love some day.

Drake was watching her think. "Have you decided to join his staff, then?"

"I haven't informed DHS yet, but yes."

"Good, I think you'll be a great addition to his team. When Secretary Rallings leaves DHS, I won't be his troubleshooter any longer. I might have to visit my in-laws more often in D.C., though," he said with a quick smile.

She returned his smile and prayed that the color rushing to her cheeks wasn't too obvious. "Well, I'd better check on the cyber analyst in the conference room," she said to avoid an awkward moment. "And make arrangements for his return to D.C. if he's not going to help us here.

When she turned away, she firmly resisted the urge to celebrate with a quick fist pump.

SEVENTY-FIVE

Drake was still watching as Bradford huddled with his team. They had worked through the night, and despite the endless cups of coffee and cans of Red Bull, they were tired and clearly worried. It was half past eight in the morning, and they hadn't finished putting together a repair kit that they were confident would keep the virus from destroying power transformers across the United States.

After a week and a half of seemingly random violent events, they were now facing a threat at high noon that would cripple the country. At any given time of the day, there were 5,000 commercial airliners in the air that would have to land without the benefit of air traffic controllers guiding them down. There were at least 125,000,000 cars on the road each day that would have to make it safely home without the aid of traffic signals. The Internet would be lost for commercial transactions and cash would suddenly be king when people couldn't use ATMS or their credit cards or do online banking. Water and food supplies would be exhausted in days.

How did we let ourselves become so vulnerable? Drake

shook his head at this apparently unanswerable question. A government's first responsibility was to protect its citizens, and what was more basic than keeping the country's lights on? But he knew that in this new age of warfare—cyber warfare—there were very few crucial infrastructures that were really safe. Bradford had shared with him that the tiny country of Israel alone fought off a thousand cyber-attack hits *a minute*! It wasn't hard to imagine that ten times that many cyber-attacks were aimed at the U.S. each minute.

As Drake stood there, watching a new breed of warriors working to defeat an unseen enemy and trying to get his head wrapped around the scope of the vast threat facing the country, he didn't notice his father-in-law enter the room until the senator walked up behind him.

"Is Bill going to figure this out in time?" Senator Hazelton asked quietly as he rested a hand on Drake's shoulder in greeting.

Drake turned and they exchanged a warm one-handed man hug. "It might be close," he murmured, "but I think he will."

"Liz tells me you've had quite a time here the last week."

"That's an understatement. Five dead, and it looks like the man behind it has safely left the country."

"Liz mentioned the banker. Is that who you mean?"

"Oh, he's more than just a banker," Drake said, trying to keep his voice low. "He used a Hezbollah terrorist to take out an international assassin on the *Queen Mary*, two solar CEO's who were somehow involved in this cyber attack, and a California Member of Congress."

The senator shook his head. "Where is he now?"

"I don't think we know. Liz has interrogated two of his men. They say they're citizens of Paraguay. So he might be in South America."

"So this isn't domestic terrorism. The President won't like hearing he has another foreign policy problem."

"I doubt that he'll label it 'foreign' right away," Drake said. "There was a faked suicide note left near the two dead solar CEO's. The FBI will investigate that...while the press does his bidding and demonizes a few more patriot groups."

Senator Hazelton chuckled. "And here I thought you were apolitical!"

Drake avoided telling the senator, whom he respected as a man and as a politician, what he really thought about the president and politics in America by turning back to look at Bill Bradford, who was slapping his cyber security expert on the back and waving the Symantec team over to the monitor.

Both men watched the excitement growing in Bradford's group of security experts. Now they were waiting for an indication that a breakthrough had been made.

Liz Strobel came into the room and stood beside Drake. "Have they done it?" she asked.

"We're waiting to hear."

"Liz," Senator Hazelton said, "if they have, we need celebrate. If you and Drake can find someone to cater lunch for everyone, I'll pick up the tab. Order some champagne, too. The country will never know how close we came to disaster, but that doesn't mean we can't recognize these heroes."

Bradford left his team and walked over.

"Senator, you brought us good luck. We've got a repair kit that works. The utilities will have it within the hour, which gives them enough time to use it before noon."

"Good work, Bill. The country owes you."

"Actually, it owes you and Secretary Rallings. If you hadn't suggested that Drake pay us a visit, we would have blacked out."

SEVENTY-SIX

While Strobel used her iPhone to search for a local caterer and order lunch, Drake slipped out and took the elevator down to the building's entrance. He needed both some fresh air and a moment alone. His felt his life was changing. Some decisions had to be made.

The last ten days had convinced him that he could honor the commitment he had made the day after 9/11 to take the fight to the enemy without being in uniform. The anger had burned so hot that day that he had walked away from a job at one of the best law firms in Oregon and headed straight to the local army recruiting office. That anger, aimed then at an enemy that delighted in killing innocents, was more controlled now. But he could still feel it just as strongly when he thought about the banker and the men behind the attempt to crash America's electric power grid.

He walked to Bradford's car in the parking lot, stopped beside it, and looked north at the San Francisco-Oakland Bay Bridge. Cars were still streaming into the city for another day of work, work that was possible because there was still electricity to keep the lights on and run computers and elevators and air conditioners.

One decision he knew he had to make was how he wanted to keep fighting the fight. Did he want to continue his law practice and occasionally answer the call when someone like the Secretary of DHS or his father-in-law requested his service? Or did he want something more?

The other decision he knew he should make was closer to his heart: What did he want to do about the feelings he had for Liz Strobel? He didn't want to feel guilty about the way he felt when he was with her, but he also didn't want to betray the love he would always have for Kay. He'd told Liz he wasn't ready to pursue a relationship, but he also didn't want her pursuing a relationship with someone else.

Both decisions, he realized, would have to be made fairly soon. With Secretary Rallings retiring from DHS and Liz joining his father-in-law's senate staff, he needed to decide what he wanted to do with his law practice and how he was going to handle seeing the woman he was attracted to working side-by-side with the senator.

He inhaled deeply, stretched his arms high over his head, and turned to go back inside the EIS building. That's when he noticed the three young men watching him from the other side of the parking lot.

Their heads were shaved, and they were all wearing black T-shirts, jeans and combat boots with red laces. He couldn't make out the tattoos on their arms, but he would bet money they showed the Nazi and rebel flags somewhere on their bodies. He had prosecuted young men like these for hate crimes while in the District Attorney's office. He knew a skinhead when he saw one.

He returned their stares, and was giving them a mock salute when he saw the tallest of the three raise his cell phone and take his picture. Whoever they were, they were there observing him.

Drake walked back inside, and from the vestibule near the elevators watched through the glass doors as the skinheads turned and left the parking lot. It was no coincidence, he knew, that they had shown up so soon after he had left Walkur's mansion, where he had found the neo-Nazi mouse pad with the flag of the Golden Dawn of Greece.

He found Senator Hazelton where he'd left him, watching Bradford instruct him team on the distribution of the virus repair kit.

"Senator," he said in a quiet voice, "when you return to Washington, I think we'll want to look into the connection between the banker and American skinheads. Three of them were outside just now, watching me. It's possible he's working with the neo-Nazis as well as the Islamists."

SEVENTY-SEVEN

At noon, Pacific Time, precisely when the blackout had been scheduled to roll across the land, four catering chefs wheeled trolleys into the EIS conference room and set up serving tables. In minutes, a big pot of steaming clam chowder, hot loaves of sourdough bread, beer-battered prawns, a heaping platter of In-And-Out burgers, and an ice bucket full of bottles of beer were ready for the weary cyber warriors and their guests.

Bill Bradford stood next to Drake at the end of the long conference table and watched his employees and the Symantec team move down the serving line. The banter and laughter reminded Drake of a locker room after a winning game.

Bradford took a folded check from his shirt pocket and handed it to him. "I thought I'd save you the trouble of sending me a bill."

"We never discussed my fee, Bill." He unfolded the check and let out a whistle. "And this is a lot more than I would have charged you."

"You earned every penny of it, buddy. Without those flash

drives you found and everything you did before, the blackout would have ruined us."

Drake nodded. "We were lucky this time. It's still hard to comprehend how destructive a cyber attack like this could have been."

"And unfortunately, way too easy to pull off. You mind if I ask you a personal question?"

"Depends on the question," Drake said with a smile.

Bradford looked across the room to where Liz Strobel was talking with Senator Hazelton. Drake was prepared to deflect a question about his interest in the beautiful woman standing next to his father-in-law, when Bradford threw him a curve.

"I reached out to your father-in-law because I knew him personally," the CEO said. "I didn't want to risk a government investigation of the cyber phishing being leaked to the press. I imagine there a lot of situations like mine that require a more *delicate touch*. Would you be willing to help others like you helped me? Or is this a one-time favor for the senator?"

Without taking his eyes off the senator and his soon-to-be staffer, Drake said, "I don't know the answer to that right now. There are some things I have to sort out first."

Handling things with a *delicate touch* wasn't exactly how he would have described the events of the last week and a half, but he understood what Bradford was saying. Being a lawyer with a unique skill set would indeed allow him to help out in a number of situations similar to Bradford's. What he needed to decide was whether that was the role he wanted to be playing.

Senator Hazelton tapped a glass of champagne with a knife and proposed a toast. "In the days to come," he said to the exhausted experts, "there will be a few more people who will learn about what you did here today but, for the most part, your countrymen will never call you heroes. On behalf of your government, therefore, I will do it for them. Thank you for keeping the lights on. You all deserve a medal."

When he lowered the glass, the senator waved Drake and Bradford over.

"I wanted both of you to know that I've been approached by a couple of freshman congressman asking about their recently departed colleague, Congressman Sanchez. One of them is another California congressman and one is from my state. They had asked that Sanchez be investigated by the Attorney General for campaign contributions they believe he received from the drug cartels. Since he appears also to have been involved with our missing banker, I'm interested in looking into the allegation for a number of reasons. The Attorney General probably won't, since Sanchez is dead and was member of his party. So if you've come across anything that you think might be helpful, let me know." Then he smiled again. "Also, Liz has just informed me that she's accepting my offer to join my staff as my liaison with the Senate Intelligence Committee. Anything you care to share, share it with her."

Drake acknowledged her decision with a nod and a smile. "Congratulations, Liz. Senator, you mentioned there were a number of reasons you were willing to investigate Sanchez. May I ask what some of the others are?"

"There are some members of Congress who vote consistently for measures that favor our Islamist enemies. Sanchez was one of them. I'm interested in knowing if others are taking money in exchange for their votes."

SEVENTY-EIGHT

When the lunch gathering started to break up, Liz Strobel asked Adam Drake if he would give her a ride back to her hotel. Senator Hazelton was returning to Washington later that afternoon and had asked her to join him on the flight to discuss her new role in his office.

The conversation during the drive to the Huntington on top of Nob Hill was subdued and unusually shallow, as neither of them was willing to bring up the one subject on both of their minds: their future relationship. They talked instead about how kind Bradford had been to let him use the Audi, how they enjoyed the flight to Lake Tahoe, and how beautiful his summer home on Crystal Bay was.

When they arrived and had entrusted the car to the doorman, Strobel slipped her arm through his and walked him through the lobby. "Come see my room while I pack," she said. "I splurged and booked a suite. It has one of the best views of San Francisco you'll ever see."

Drake followed her into the ornate old elevator, with its red floral paneling and brass molding. It was a grand reminder of an elegant past, and also a clue to the romantic nature of the woman beside him. His taste ran more to the modern luxury of the Marriott Marquis, but he could appreciate the choice she had made.

"My mom and dad used to stay here whenever they were in San Francisco," she was saying. "They always left me home."

"Is that why you wanted to stay here?" he asked.

"That's one reason," she said as she led him out of the elevator and down the hall. "The other is you're staying at the Marriott. I didn't want you to think I was chasing you."

When she stopped in front her room, she opened the door with a flourish. "Come enjoy the view."

Drake started to say that he was already enjoying the view, but thought better of it. The last thing he wanted to do was to appear to be flirting with her while they were alone in her hotel room.

She was right. The room had a great view of the city. As she began putting clothing in her suitcase, he kept his back to her, standing at the window to allow her some privacy.

He heard the suitcase locks snap closed and felt a change of energy as she walked toward him.

"Is the offer to take me skiing in Oregon this winter still open?"

"Would you like it to be?"

She stepped around in front of him and put her hands around the back of his neck. "What do you think?" she said, and pulled him down and kissed him.

Her kiss lingered and then she looked up for his answer.

Drake leaned down and returned her kiss.

"I'll take that as a yes," she said.

The End

NEXT IN THE ADAM DRAKE SERIES

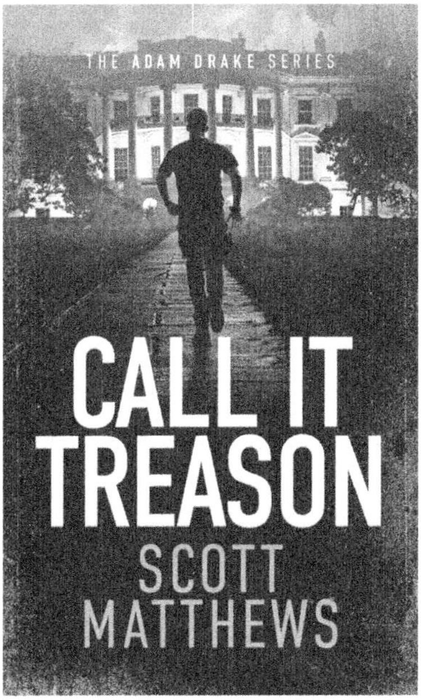

vinci-books.com/treason

Airliners are falling out of the sky. The United States is on lockdown. The President is about to punish the country behind the atrocities.

But Adam Drake knows they have the wrong people.

Printed in Great Britain
by Amazon

46418356R00169